QUESTLAND

Carrie Vaughn

A John Joseph Adams Book   *Mariner Books*   *Houghton Mifflin Harcourt*

BOSTON   NEW YORK

2021

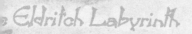

For information about permission to reproduce selections
from this book, write to trade.permissions@hmhco.com or to
Permissions, Houghton Mifflin Harcourt Publishing Company,
3 Park Avenue, 19th Floor, New York, New York 10016.

hmhbooks.com

Library of Congress Cataloging-in-Publication Data
Names: Vaughn, Carrie, author.
Title: Questland / Carrie Vaughn.
Description: Boston : Mariner Books/Houghton Mifflin Harcourt,
2021. | "A John Joseph Adams book."
Identifiers: LCCN 2020034169 (print) | LCCN 2020034170 (ebook) |
ISBN 9780358346289 (trade paperback) | ISBN 9780358346500 (ebook) |
ISBN 9780358540120 | ISBN 9780358540199
Subjects: GSAFD: Science fiction. | Fantasy fiction. |
Adventure fiction.
Classification: LCC PS3622.A9475 Q47 2021 (print) |
LCC PS3622.A9475 (ebook) | DDC 813/.6 — dc23
LC record available at https://lccn.loc.gov/2020034169
LC ebook record available at https://lccn.loc.gov/2020034170

Book design by Margaret Rosewitz
Map by Rhys Davies

Printed in the United States of America
1 2021
4500825796

Praise for

QUESTLAND

"A fantasy lover's thrill ride. Between the geektastic
protagonist and the snappy yet elegant prose, Vaughn will
bring you straight to Mirabilis and may even keep you
there for good."

—Michael Witwer, *New York Times* best-selling coauthor
of *Dungeons & Dragons Art & Arcana*

Praise for

BANNERLESS,

winner of the Philip K. Dick Award

"Amazing and compelling, Vaughn brings her deft char-
acterization and humanity to bear on a post-apocalyptic
world that is all too real."

—Tobias S. Buckell, best-selling author of *Arctic Rising*

"A deft portrait of a society departed so completely from
the complexities of the now-destroyed civilization (except
for some technological scraps) that survivors don't even
understand what it is they've lost . . . Well-crafted
and heartfelt."

—*Kirkus Reviews*

"A compelling, deft post-apocalyptic tale."

—*Library Journal*

QUESTLAND

1

The End of All Things

"Okay, Professor Cox, so yeah, what I want to do is show that *Moby Dick* and Pokémon are both symbolic of rampant capitalism by portraying the inherently destructive nature of the relentless pursuit of abstract consumerism." The kid took a gasping breath and seemed relieved to have gotten all that out at once.

I had been so pleased when a student showed up in person for office hours. I had been so ready to be helpful, a wise mentor ushering this wide-eyed undergraduate through the sometimes-harrowing expectations of academia, fanning the spark of learning and critical thought. He would go on to change the world and remember fondly the words of wisdom, the kindly advice I had given him. This meeting would remind me that my work really was worthwhile.

Someday, a student meeting would actually remind me that my work in academia was worthwhile.

Rodney was a white kid with unbrushed, uncut hair stuffed under a ball cap. He'd grown into his full height but was still gangly as anything, all elbows and knees. A baggy T-shirt and cargo shorts, ratty sneakers, hollow black gauges the size of a quarter in both ears. A sophomore, so around nineteen.

The thing was, he had the core of a good idea in there. I just wasn't sure he understood half the words coming out of his mouth. He'd been in college long enough to learn the vocabulary but not quite how to wield it.

I studied him from the chair at my desk, which I had pushed against the wall so I could face my students with nothing between us. It was supposed to be more welcoming, inviting them to open up. Not that many of them actually ever came to my office. They usually left messages begging for extensions. But Rodney must have thought he had a better chance of talking me into his ambitious theme in person. His expression pleaded with me.

"Tell me the truth," I said finally. "Are you just wanting to play a bunch of Pokémon Go and somehow call it working on your midterm paper?"

He deflated right in front of me, all those knobby limbs drooping.

"Have you at least *read Moby Dick*?" I asked. When I had come up with the class, Pop Culture as Literature, I had failed to anticipate how many students would sign up thinking it meant they'd be able to spend the semester playing video games for credit.

"I watched *The Wrath of Khan* instead," he said. "You said you wanted us to compare one modern thing and one classic thing. *Wrath of Khan* counts as classic, right?"

I spoke carefully. Encourage, encourage. I'm a mentor, I'm a mentor . . . "I think tackling the entirety of rampant capitalism is too big a topic for a fifteen-page midterm paper. Maybe you can talk about *Moby Dick* and Pokémon together—assuming you actually read *Moby Dick*—but bring the focus in a little tighter. Talk about whales and Pokémon as metaphors. How they change over the course of the story, how they affect the narrative. Why people always seem to want to chase metaphorical fantasy creatures."

"So, like, how my, uh—I mean someone's—obsession with finding a Zapdos in the middle of the quad might be like Ahab and the whale." He did have a bit of a crazed look in his eye. Like he'd seen things. Virtual things on his phone, mocking him.

"Something like that. Yes."

"But what about rampant capitalism?"

What about it, indeed. "That's your job, to tell me what it means, hmm?" He looked daunted, not inspired. I had failed to mentor him. "Look, don't worry so much about it. You've obviously found a topic you're passionate about. Just . . . explain it to me." I was going to have twenty of these essays to grade. I had made a terrible mistake.

He squared his shoulders and gave a determined nod. "Right. I won't fail you, Professor." His intensity took me aback, but he shrugged his way to the door before I could suggest he calm down a little.

When he started to close the door, I half jumped out of my chair. "Leave that open, please. Thank you."

He glanced back at my anxious tone, confused, but left the door wide open and sauntered down the hallway.

With the door open, I could hear everything that went on in this half of the building. Everyone coming and going. I needed to hear that. My office was safe, the shelves filled with books, from the big literature survey textbooks we still used to piles of pulp paperbacks with lurid covers that always made my students go a little wide-eyed. A few obscure movie posters on the wall, *Legend* and *Hard Boiled*, because I was the *cool* professor. A couple of spider plants tucked in the high windowsill making a go of it. Sticky notes all over the wall, because however many apps I had trying to run my life and manage my students, sometimes nothing replaced pen and paper.

I turned on the electric kettle for another cup of tea and got back to the stack of first-year composition essays on the desk. These kids tried so hard and yet had such a tenuous grasp of the basic rules of grammar. Practice, I reminded myself. They just needed practice.

A class period ended. Voices filled the hallway. Sounds echoed. This was an old building, with linoleum floors and wooden doors, smelling of cozy dilapidation. A loud bang from the other end of the hall rattled doors all the way down. My body clenched, my heart jumped to my ears, and I splashed tea out of my mug. A door. It was just someone slamming a door. There was laughter. No one was shooting anyone. I held on to the arms of my chair and breathed slowly.

Funny thing, some days I could hear a car backfire and not even blink. Fourth of July? I knew to get out of town and stay someplace where no one would be launching a single bottle rocket. Most days, I had it under control. And then a door slammed, and my body reacted before my brain had time to catch up. Breathe slow. Put both feet on the floor, sit straight so my lungs had space to fill. Count to ten or twenty, and let the adrenaline drain away. Fine, everything was fine.

My computer beeped an incoming message request and I jumped again. "Shit!" I said it loud enough to carry and glanced guiltily out in the hall. God, I was so finished with today.

I clicked *accept* without really looking, assuming another student wanted to discuss their dubious relationship with deadlines. But a video chat window opened on the screen, and the face that appeared wasn't a wide-eyed panicking undergrad, but a prim, very serious, pale woman in a high-collared suit and short haircut. She wasn't university—a suit like that cost money.

"You're not a student," I blurted.

She raised a perfectly shaped brow. "No, Professor Cox."

I was about to ask if she'd messaged the wrong person. But she'd said my name. "Can I help you?" I asked, confused.

"I think you can. I represent Lang Analytics, and we have a project we think you'd be interested in. We'd like to meet with you to discuss the parameters and requirements."

Lang Analytics was a conglomerate of personal electronics companies and online services, both mass market and high end. They made the messaging app that let my students beg for extensions without looking me in the face, which meant this woman had snuck her video chat into my office under false pretenses. Which was basically Lang Analytics' entire business model. Its founder, Harris Lang, was one of these eccentric tech-guru icons. I tried to avoid knowing anything about it.

I wasn't able to hide my skepticism. "Exactly what kind of project could you possibly need someone like me for?" I was an assistant professor of comparative literature. The exact opposite of cutting-edge tech.

"We'd like to discuss that in person, Professor Cox." Her expression hardly changed. Was she some kind of secretary AI?

"I'm sorry, I'm right in the middle of office hours—"

"I have a car waiting outside the building for you."

I was starting to get angry. "I'd really rather do this on a conference call—"

She glanced down, as if checking her phone, and tapped a couple of keys. "If you look at your email, you'll find a preliminary receipt for a donation made by Lang Analytics to your department, a grant of twenty thousand dollars. All you have to do to receive the grant is come meet with us."

I checked my email, and there it was. On Lang Analytics letterhead, a receipt for a $20,000 grant made out to the English Department. That much money would fund a couple of research assistants for a semester, conference travel, scholarships. English departments never got corporate grants. This was . . . odd.

I returned to the chat window with the icily competent Lang Analytics representative. "Is this a bribe?"

That got the tiniest bit of smile from her. "You're the language expert, Professor."

"I don't even know your name."

"The car is waiting for you." The chat window went blank.

2

Wisdom Save

Outside the humanities building on a narrow lane that was meant for university maintenance carts, a shining black town car was parked. The severely prim woman from the video chat stepped out of the passenger side. Not an AI, then.

I should have held out for another ten grand.

Maybe I should have been bothered that I had such a predictable price. But it wasn't for me. It was for the department. I could go to a stupid meeting.

I put on a bright smile. "Hi, I'm Addie Cox. It's nice to meet you."

"Thank you for agreeing to this meeting, Professor. Please." She opened the car's back door and gestured inside, which seemed dark and cavernous. She still hadn't told me her name. I climbed in, and the door closed behind me with a soft click, like an air lock sealing. The driver was male, dressed in a formal dark suit, and didn't glance back at me. Maybe I should have insisted on meeting in public. This suddenly looked like the first chapter in a lurid horror scenario.

The woman leaned over the back seat and handed me a tablet. "I need you to read and sign this nondisclosure agreement. It's straightforward, requiring only that you not discuss anything you're about to learn in this meeting."

"What if I don't want to sign?"

"We'll pull over right now. But . . . there's the grant to think about, hmm?"

Did she think she could just buy me off? Well, yes, I suppose she did. She wasn't wrong, and she worked for a company that always got what it wanted. I just couldn't figure out why it wanted me.

The NDA was short, saying exactly what she'd explained: I wouldn't talk about what went on at the meeting, unless required to by a court of law. And wasn't that comforting? I signed, because ultimately, even apart from the grant money, I wanted to see what this was about.

"Can't you give me a hint?" I said, handing the tablet back to her.

"Everything will be explained soon." Which was exactly what I should have known she would say.

After twenty minutes we ended up in downtown Boulder, at the St. Julien, the city's nicest hotel. Formally, the prim woman opened the car door and guided me to the entrance. The doorman snapped to attention.

So, at least there were witnesses now.

After a ride in an elevator requiring the touch of a special chip card, we arrived at an expansive suite. As in, the elevator opened directly into the suite, a posh living room with clean white sofas, glass coffee tables, and vast windows looking out over the city. I'd only ever seen this kind of room in movies.

Two men waited. One of them was Silicon Valley tech guru Harris Lang himself, founder of Lang Analytics, inventor of a revolutionary telecom device that nobody understood, founder of a private company flinging satellites into orbit. Wasn't a month went by that he didn't have his picture on the cover of some magazine or didn't get interviewed on some news show about tech trends, with his steel-gray buzz cut and rectangular wire-rimmed glasses.

Technically I had seen him in person once before, from the back of an auditorium filled with a couple thousand people. He'd been a tiny shadow onstage, so I'd mostly watched his speech on one of the big screens, which was basically like watching him on TV. My boyfriend at the time had been awestruck with the man and dragged me to the presentation. Everyone loved the enigmatic Harris Lang. Brilliant Harris Lang, saving the world with carbon sequestration and space junk mitigation. For the kind of person who had big dreams and unshakable faith in technology, Lang was inspiring. Me . . . I would never trust that just one person could single-handedly save the world.

Close up, Lang seemed thin, the kind of thin from not eating enough rather than working out. His face was lined, and he seemed tired. Older than his fifty-some years. He wore his trademark gray turtleneck, dark jeans, and had an earbud in one ear. Sitting on the sofa, studying a tablet, he didn't even look up when we entered.

To the side of the sofa stood a man in his early forties, muscular and square jawed, with sun-browned skin. He studied me with dark eyes like he was peeling back layers. He wore slacks and a suit jacket over a T-shirt, but they looked like a costume on him.

He made me nervous. The bad kind of nervous, like when a door slammed or someone set off a firecracker. The kind of nervous that made me want to hide under a table. I was very out of place here, in my oversize cardigan, peasant skirt, and ballet flats. Usually I felt comfortable in my clothes, but here

I was an oddity. I self-consciously brushed at my hair, in short rumpled curls around my ears.

We waited until Harris Lang finally looked up, set aside his tablet, and rose. Should I bow? Look away? Introduce myself? I froze.

"Professor Adrienne Cox, it's very good of you to come. I'm Harris Lang."

How strange that he knew my name. In the real world, no one like him should ever notice someone like me. But here we were; he'd bribed me into his domain.

Lang had a New England drawl to his voice. Lang Analytics' headquarters—US headquarters, at least—was on the other side of the country. He hadn't flown here just to meet me, had he? That didn't seem right.

"Call me Addie," I said, and started to extend my hand for shaking. But his remained clasped in front of him, so no, there would be no hand shaking. "Nice to meet you." I glanced at the man who looked like he was standing guard and waited for an introduction. It didn't come.

"Please, have a seat. Tea? Coffee? Something stronger?" Lang smiled thinly, making a joke he knew was perfunctory. Now that I got a better look at him, the smile seemed strained. He had puffy eyes, like he'd been losing sleep. Nothing like how he looked on slick magazine covers.

"Um. Tea? Black, no sugar."

The prim woman marched off to the suite's bar. I glanced again at the other man. He loomed like he might put everyone here in a headlock any minute now.

Lang returned to the sofa. "This must seem strange, so I'll come straight to it. You're here because I need a consultant with exactly your expertise."

"Like, you're doing one of those cable documentaries and you need an expert interview or something?" That was the only thing I could think of, but surely Lang wouldn't arrange something like that personally. He had People for that. The military man—he had to be military—pressed his lips together, hiding a smile.

Lang didn't smile. "No, Professor. I'm afraid not. Let's see . . . this is turning out to be much harder to explain than I was expecting. The heart of it has been top secret for so long, I'm not used to saying it out loud."

The assistant brought over the cup of tea, complete with saucer, and I almost resented the distraction of having to take hold of it.

"Maybe you should just show her," the tough guy said, nodding at the tablet. He had a steady, commanding voice. Of course he did.

"Ah, yes," Lang said. "Professor, this is Captain Octavio Torres. He'll be leading your team. Assuming you say yes."

Team? What team? "Hi," I murmured at him.

Torres nodded. "Professor."

Lang held out the tablet so I could see the screen, which showed a picture of a unicorn. Not a drawing, but what looked like a photograph of an impossibly lovely white horse, slender, with delicate legs, a luxurious mane and tail. And a pearlescent horn spiraling from its forehead. It looked out at me with dark, liquid eyes. I wanted to hug it.

"This is a special effect," I said, uncertain. People had been retouching and altering photos of horses for years to get images like this.

"No, Professor," he said. "It isn't."

I didn't understand. "So this is, what? Some kind of surgical procedure? Where—"

"Insula Mirabilis," he said with breathless awe, so the name sounded like a prayer.

The Wonderful Island. And was that a tear at the corner of his eye? He blinked and it was gone. The self-possessed tech guru, in command of the entire world, returned.

"I had an idea. A vision. I hired the best people, set out my goals very clearly . . . I'm sure you're familiar with the expression 'Any sufficiently advanced technology is indistinguishable from magic'?"

"Of course, that was Arthur C. Clarke."

"Well, I set about proving it."

He swiped to the next picture, which showed a great gray castle, incongruous against the backdrop of a northwestern rain forest. Huge blocks of stone made up its thick walls, and a round tower reached to a great height. It was something out of a fairy tale.

The next photo showed a village of timber-frame cottages with thatched roofs. And the one after that featured what had to be a dragon. Not a big dragon but around the size of a Great Dane. A sinewy, snake-like lizard, rust red, with spindly legs, bat-like wings, and a mouth full of teeth. It crouched in a barred cage, reaching a claw out for a chunk of meat held by someone just out of frame.

"It's some kind of robot—"

"No," Lang said. "It eats. It bleeds." At this, he smiled. The sly, proud smile of a child who has caught his first lizard and built a particularly ornate terrarium for it.

This wasn't an amusement park with plaster buildings and animatronics. This didn't look like a Renaissance Faire or museum exhibit. It was . . . *real.* "Where is this place? What is it? What's it for? Why . . . how . . . ?" I ran out of words.

Lang took his tablet back and scrolled through more pictures, gazing fondly at the images. "I set out to build a fantasy world. It would be fully immersive: a game, a resort, and an extreme vacation all wrapped into one. And I did it. Wizard worlds? Sci-fi franchise theme parks? They'll look like cardboard dioramas compared to my park. There's nothing else like it."

He kept saying *I,* as if a project like this wouldn't take hundreds—thousands—of people to implement it, design it, build it, and keep it all running. Lang certainly hadn't laid any of the stonework on that castle himself. Then again . . . he'd had the idea, he'd fronted the money—why shouldn't it be his?

So why did he look so sad?

"But . . ." I prompted, because this was all leading to a "but."

Lang scowled and turned away; Torres answered instead. "Lang Analytics lost contact with the production team."

"What does that mean?"

"We've been cut off." Lang started pacing, hand on his head, pulling nervously at his short hair. "We haven't been able to get any aerial pictures of the island. They're blocking our communications. No one who wasn't already there has set foot on the island in . . . in months."

"How do you lose contact with a whole island? Can't you send a boat, or . . . or . . ."

Torres said, "A Coast Guard cutter was destroyed trying to get through. There's some kind of energy field—"

"A what—" I suddenly had a bad feeling about this. A worse feeling.

"—and the cutter crashed into it. All hands lost."

"How many is all hands?" I asked softly.

"Ten," Torres said.

Lang made a sharp, frustrated motion with his hand. "This is a mutiny. A rebellion. Someone on the production staff staged a coup. Maybe the entire production staff. I don't know who's involved, what's been happening—I'm cut out." His arms fell limp at his sides. This was a man not used to being cut out of anything. He had no plan.

Pieces started to fit together. Way too many pieces. I glanced at Torres. "You want someone to go in and take back the island. That's why you need a . . . a . . . what are you? Army? Marines?"

"Navy SEAL," he said. "Retired. I'm an independent contractor now."

An actual real-life mercenary, almost as fantastical as that unicorn. "Shouldn't you be calling the . . . the police, or the military, or something?"

Lang said evenly, "I need to secure my investment before other entities become involved."

If he could get there before any outside agency, he could keep the whole thing from being impounded. He could control the narrative. That seemed on-brand for him.

"That still doesn't explain why you need me. I'm just a literature professor—"

"We figured we might need a guide," Torres said. "Someone who can play the game."

Lang said, "We've been out of contact with the island for several months now. We have no idea what the design team has accomplished. Dragons may be the least of it. You'll be very well compensated, of course."

My stomach twisted in knots. As fantastic as this island must be, as curious as I was—I couldn't do it. I just couldn't.

"You're talking about an assault. With guns." Torres definitely looked like someone who knew his way around guns. I set aside the tea I hadn't even tasted. "I'm not the right person for this. I'm absolutely the wrong person. There are thousands of other scholars who can help you." I steadied myself so I could explain, but I couldn't get the words out. "Thank you very much for thinking of me, but I . . . I *can't*."

Lang and Torres exchanged a glance. There was more to this, a lot more, and they weren't telling me. Lang got that sly smile again. The one that said he knew he was in charge here. He wouldn't have it any other way.

"But, Professor—I need *you.*"

He didn't. He couldn't. "If you did any kind of background check on me—and I know you did—you know why I can't do this. I'm the worst person for this." I squeezed my eyes shut. I could *not* start crying.

Lang said, inexorably and without remorse, "Yes. You were a student at West Lake High School during the shooting there fifteen years ago. Eight students were killed, ten injured. You watched two of your friends die. I'm sorry if I've upset you by bringing up those memories." I didn't believe he was sorry at all.

I was very calm when I said, "It's taken a lot of therapy to get me to a point where I can even talk about this. But I can't be part of your assault. I can't." I looked at Torres and thought I saw pity there. Some level of understanding that Lang and his prim assistant weren't capable of. I started toward the elevator door, stepping around the assistant.

Then Lang said, "Professor Cox, I'm surprised you haven't yet asked me about Dominic Brand."

And there it was. The thing we'd been talking around, the real reason I was here, and the two words that could keep me from walking out. Dom was the boyfriend who had dragged me to that Harris Lang talk years ago. Lang had sponsored a prize —one of these XPRIZE innovation deals, looking for not just technological revolutions but cultural revolutions. Dom had been part of a team working on portable medical containment units for use in disease outbreaks. Their idea had been to use an energy field, so it could be set up anywhere with the flip of a switch, and be impermeable to bacteria and viruses.

The team hadn't won the prize, but Dom had gone to work for Lang Analytics. This was right after we broke up, and I hadn't heard from him since.

That sinking feeling in the pit of my stomach this whole

conversation came from realizing this situation had Dom's fingerprints all over it. He'd kept working on that energy field, on a grand scale, apparently.

"So, what about Dominic?" I murmured, turning.

Lang said, "Dominic is the head designer on the Mirabilis project. You're right, Professor—a thousand other scholars could serve the team as a consultant and guide. Perhaps I ought to be talking to someone with military experience, rather than someone like you—"

"Someone like me?" I said, my tone bitter.

Torres interceded, putting up a calming hand and cutting Lang off. The billionaire didn't even look offended. "You have the knowledge we need about what we might find on the island. But you're also the one person Brand will talk to."

Oh, I wouldn't bet on that.

Lang opened his hands. "You see, Professor, you are the perfect person for this job."

Torres said, "I need to ask: Do you think Brand is capable of murder?"

I squeezed my hands into fists, so they wouldn't shake. "I—I wouldn't have thought so. He was passionate about his work, maybe even a little crazy. He did some martial arts, but archaic stuff like fencing and archery. We did Ren Faires together. It was a game."

"Whoever is behind the mutiny on the island—a Coast Guard crew is dead because of them. When we catch them, they'll be charged with murder."

Dominic, what the hell are you doing? I realized . . . I was going to say yes. Not for the money, but to find out what had happened to Dom.

And maybe to see a unicorn.

"I'm not sure I can do this."

"I'm not sure, either," Torres said frankly. "But if seeing you makes Brand hesitate in pulling whatever trigger he might be holding—well, we'll bring you along."

If I didn't know better, I'd say it was destiny.

3

Where the Shadows Lie

The rolling of the Coast Guard cutter on Pacific waves a hundred miles or so off the coast of Washington State wasn't what was making me nauseated. It was the cold. The damp. I was bundled up in fatigues and a waterproof coat, but they didn't seem to help. The pitch-black nighttime water, the smell of diesel, and an otherworldly purple glow on the horizon all seemed ominous and illness-inducing. Torres had given me a seasickness patch, like he'd expected this. If I wasn't wearing it, maybe I would feel even worse.

I didn't belong here. I shouldn't have come. I was going to throw up, and we hadn't even gotten to the island yet.

"Professor?" Torres said from the motorized raft lashed to the side of the cutter. "It's time."

I touched my hip, felt the hard shape of my lucky d20 in my pocket. Roll-saving throw against nausea . . .

Two members of the cutter crew helped me over the side and onto the raft. Almonte, one of the three other members of Torres's team, caught me as I nearly tumbled on top of her. She skillfully gripped my arm and settled me to the side, out of the way with the rest of the gear.

Torres exchanged a hand signal with the cutter crew. Wendell, Torres's tech guy, threw off the line. The fourth soldier in the party, Rucker, revved the raft's motor, and just like that we were gone, racing into darkness.

While steering, Rucker also held a rifle braced across his knees. I'd had ten days to get used to the idea of being in close quarters with four people who all had guns.

It wasn't enough time.

Surprisingly, I was the one who suggested desensitization therapy at the indoor shooting range during our preparations for the trip. Torres watched me carefully. Waiting for me to collapse, to lose my shit, whatever.

"You decide you want to fire off a few rounds of your own, let me know. I could train you on one of these." He showed me a handgun locked in its brown leather holster. The gun was matte black, plastic and metal. It lurked.

"No," I said. "I really don't." He stood over me, huddled on a bench at the back of the range, my arms tightly crossed.

He nodded curtly. "That's fine."

I was afraid he'd push, that he'd insist I go armed like the rest of the squad. But he didn't. "Really?"

"I don't want you running around with a loaded gun unless you're comfortable with it. That's how people get hurt."

"Yeah, I know," I said.

His lips pressed in a sympathetic almost-smile. "Don't worry, Professor. We'll look out for you."

Famous last words.

The three handpicked members of Torres's squad fired off a truly ridiculous number of shots. Ear protection that entirely covered my ears and pinched my head muffled the sound but didn't erase it. The lights seemed to flicker with the noise of it, and even with the fans going, the air was thick with the biting smell of spent gunpowder.

I knew that smell. My gut and heart knew that smell. It was part of why I didn't go to big fireworks displays. Everyone understood why I'd avoid the noise of it, but no one thought about the smell.

If I could let the thundering noise of gunshots wash over me, I'd get used to it. Intellectually, I knew I was in no danger. These were professionals using tools they'd trained with. This was like dental work. Not pleasant, but I could get through it. I could pretend this was happening on a TV screen. This had nothing to do with me. *Fear is the mind-killer, I will face my fear, I will permit it to pass over me and through me—*

Oh my God, such macho messianic bullshit. Aphorisms weren't going to help me.

Almonte was a wiry Black woman with short-cropped hair and an intense gaze. She had served with Torres in the navy, and they related to each other with the ease of longtime friends. He passed a box of ammunition to her, and she accepted it without a word; they communicated with nods and gestures that were invisible to an outsider like me. She offered the occasional smile of comfort to me over her shoulder when she reloaded. If this mission had just been the two of them, I could almost feel good about it.

Wendell was also former military with an electrical engineering degree. Hacking and breaking high-tech security measures would fall to him. He'd shaken my hand with a distracted air and hadn't paid much more attention to me, as if I were a piece of equipment that he wasn't responsible for.

Rucker was the muscle, a white guy with a broad jaw, broad shoulders, and a broad way of moving. He was young, not much older than my students, which gave me a disconnected jolt. He ought to be writing book reports, not carrying a rifle like it was a beloved talisman. But he was old enough to have spent time in the army. He had not offered to shake my hand upon meeting me. He'd looked me up and down, managed a curt nod of greeting, and didn't say a word. Except to Torres, when he thought I couldn't hear.

"She's going to be a liability, sir." His voice had that brash edge of youth and certainty, even when he'd taken Torres aside and spoken quietly to him, before any of them had picked up a weapon.

"Not your call," Torres said.

"Then what's the actual objective? To take the target or babysit her? Sir," he added, after Torres gave him a stony glare.

"Your objective is to follow orders," he said, and Rucker shut up.

So that told me where I stood with the team. Sitting on the bench while they did the work.

Torres was the Ranger, calm and dangerous. Almonte was the Cleric, the team's medic and shepherd. Wendell the Artificer, Rucker the Barbarian. What did that make me? The one without any visibly useful skills.

The Bard, obviously.

I shut my eyes and focused on the feeling of breathing, of ribs expanding and air flowing in and out of my nose. Searched for a prayer that would work and found Alex and Dora. Their names had become something like a mantra for me. Remember them. Remember. They weren't just the friends I'd watched die, as Harris Lang had so bluntly described. They were my boyfriend and my best friend. My gaming nerds and cosplay peeps. Their deaths had punched a giant hole in my world, and I was still feeling out the edges of it. I would never know why the shooter, a disgruntled recent graduate with a grudge, turned the gun away from me at the last minute and used it on himself. These days, I could think about it without shaking, but I still cried when I thought of Alex and Dora and everything they'd missed. Fifteen years. Had it been so long?

Alex and Dora. Breathe.

I had the sudden idea that Dora would have thought this was *so cool*. A real-life video game. *Take notes,* she'd say, her grin wrinkling the freckles on her nose. Yeah, okay, if I could just pretend this was a game . . .

Even with the ear protection, my skull still thrummed after the guns went silent.

"Professor Cox?"

I let my face unclench, and my eyes opened. Captain Torres was standing over me. I hadn't realized I'd shut my eyes until he spoke.

"You okay?"

He didn't have to sound so condescending. "I'm not going to pretend that this doesn't suck."

"You shouldn't. It definitely sucks. But the odds of us actually using our weapons are small. The goal is to do this without firing a shot."

Odds? What if somebody rolled a one? Small wasn't zero. "Isn't that always the goal?" I asked. "How often do you actually accomplish your objective without firing a shot?"

He gave a wry smirk.

I drew my lucky twenty-sided die out of my jeans pocket, rubbed it between fingers. Didn't look like much; it was just your basic translucent plastic, pink with flecks of purple swirling around. Dom had given me that set of dice. I'm not sure why I was carrying this one around now. Torres had brought up odds, and I wondered what I'd get if I rolled the die right here, right now.

Odds were I should have died already. I wasn't going to burn my luck on an offhand roll here. I pocketed the die.

They all knew about my history. Almonte's expression when

she looked at me was always kind, if pitying. Wendell avoided looking at me at all. And Rucker—I was a chore to him. My past made me a liability.

I wasn't sure he was wrong.

As it raced ahead, the raft smashed through waves, sending up salt-smelling spray. I risked straightening a little, to try to get my first look at Insula Mirabilis. A wall of salt water crashed into my face. I spat and gasped, wiped my eyes clear, and shivered miserably.

Almonte stayed within arm's reach, like she assumed at some point she would have to grab me to keep me from flying over the edge. That was probably a good assumption.

"Five hundred meters to the shield, Boss," Wendell said. Even this far out, the purple glow reflected light off the water.

I huddled even more firmly at the edge of the raft. I didn't belong here. This had been a mistake. My gaze kept sliding over to the guns.

A wall of rippling purple light, pearlescent in the black of night, appeared in front of us, like a sunrise bursting into morning. Coast Guard analysis indicated that this was a dome, reaching all the way over the island and several dozen feet under water. Seeing it now, it couldn't possibly have been solid. It was a light show, an aurora. Some special effect. Better to think of it as light sparkling off cut crystal—pretty and very, very impenetrable. This wasn't the neat little magnetic particle barrier Dom's team had messed around with back in college.

The Zodiac raced toward the glowing wall.

Wendell had mounted a device at the bow of the raft, a metal box with wires, circuit boards, and a kind of parabolic dish pointing off the front. This was supposed to emit an electromagnetic pulse that would temporarily block the circuit that created the shield in this spot long enough for us to slip through. It would be like pulling up the corner of a tent flap and letting it fall behind us. Wendell worked furiously at the box as we drew closer.

"Wendell . . ." Torres said. He didn't sound nervous. Just, you know—interested.

"It'll work, it's fine."

Up ahead, purple energy pulsed in an undeniable barrier. As fast as we were going, hitting the intact shield would be like slamming into a brick wall.

"Wendell," Torres said, more urgently this time.

Wendell's device made a grinding noise, and the dish at the top sparked with electricity.

With a crackle of static, the space in front of us turned black. The raft raced through the opening. As the raft and machine sped past it, the shield snapped back into place behind us with a burst of light and crack of thunder.

We were inside. The pale glow arched up behind us and over to the dark silhouette of the island. The surf that broke against wave-rocked cliffs glowed purple with reflected light. The cliffs were dark, featureless, climbing up to forest-covered hills.

The raft aimed farther along the coast, toward a strip of pale sand edging a dense forest. Our destination loomed.

Suddenly, the Zodiac shoved past the breakers and straight onto a narrow, rocky beach. Wendell jumped out, splashing on shore and dragging the raft the rest of the way out of the water. The others quickly followed, hauling equipment. Torres grabbed my arm and made sure I didn't slip and fall, even though my legs had turned to rubber.

Despite Torres's grip on me, I fell as soon as I lurched over the rounded edge of the raft, struggling to get control of my legs. He dropped me next to the survival gear, recon equipment, and rifles that the others had unloaded, splashing in the surf.

When the raft was empty, Almonte and Wendell deflated it, wrestling it up to the tree line and covering it with branches and debris until even I, who'd been looking right at it, couldn't see it anymore. Rucker, rifle in hand, kept watch. They did it all without talking. With the raft's motor shut off, the quiet became immense. The shushing of waves against the shore sounded alien. The dark, overcast sky seemed very low. The purple shimmer of the shield overhead was ubiquitous, other-worldly.

I hadn't really done anything so far but sit in the raft. Still, I was exhausted. My lungs hurt, and salt water crusted my clothes. Now that we were here, surely we would rest. Surely we couldn't set out for the heart of the island until daybreak. But no, Torres and his squad didn't pause. Equipment got loaded onto shoulders and backs, and the four soldiers formed a line to march into the forest. I just had my little personal pack; they didn't expect me to carry any more than that, for which I was both embarrassed and grateful.

When I took too long to climb back to my feet—my legs were still rubber, my teeth still chattering—Torres came to me and took hold of my arm to haul me up. I jerked away, and that finally gave me the lurch I needed to stand on my own. Had to hang on to a tree trunk to do it, but I did it. I couldn't tell if his thin smirk was amused or annoyed. Or both. I couldn't read any of these people.

Torres took point; Rucker fell to the rear of the line. They put me right in the middle.

We marched away from the beach, into the forest. Into Mirabilis.

4

Dump Stat

We moved like something was chasing us, and maybe it was.

Torres led us on a slog through a dense forest of conifers with moss-covered trunks and undergrowth choked with ferns and vines. No nicely groomed trail led the way, but rather than hacking through the vegetation with machetes as I might have imagined, Torres carefully parted the growth and slipped through, creating a pathway that folded closed behind us. I strained to mimic his example, taking up the vegetation as the others did, every muscle tense lest I step on a twig.

I didn't step on a twig, but I gasped when I forgot to breathe, and Torres gave me a look over his shoulder. His face was wind-burned, rugged. His dark eyes had the kind of searching gaze that drew attention. He just had to stand there and anybody could tell he was in charge. This should have made me feel safer, but mostly I felt like I was going to disappoint him.

The squad kept watch, constantly looking out and around,

searching for—well, we weren't sure. Momentum kept me with the rest of them—it would take more energy to stop than to keep walking. But at some point I was just going to drop, and I wondered what would happen when I did. They might stuff me in a pack and carry me.

The sky turned pale; dawn broke. In sunlight, the force-field dome turned nearly invisible. I caught a sparkle of it out of the corner of my eye.

Finally, out of sight of the shore, we stopped to rest, and I sat. Breakfast was water and energy bars that tasted like sawdust, but I ate it all. When the squad was ready to move again, I was still uncurling, stretching cramps out of arms and legs. I sort of wished Torres would come haul me to my feet again— this time, I'd take the help. But I managed to stand on my own, wincing the whole time. Almonte gave my shoulder a quick pat as we moved out.

The sun rose higher; I felt like I should have been able to tell what time it was, the way characters in books always did so easily. We entered a boggy area, skirting around a pond that had collected in a low spot. Pitcher-shaped yellow blooms curled up from stems sprouting in the water. Ferns sprang above our heads from the middle of tree trunks, as if floating. Morning light filtered through an emerald canopy of leaves. The air smelled rich, and a mist rose up from the ground. Eddies of fog formed around our feet, stirred by our legs as we hiked. If I'd slept in a real bed the night before, I might have enjoyed the scenery more.

In one spot I stepped wrong; my foot slipped, a patch of mud grabbing me and pulling me into water. My high-tech boots were supposed to be waterproof, but water immediately poured over the tops. I probably fastened them wrong. In a desperate effort to keep from screaming, I clamped my mouth shut and squeaked instead. High pitched, nasal, the most undignified sound I had ever made in my life. Almonte grabbed my sleeve before I could tip over.

We had to stop so I could change socks. "No marching on wet feet," Torres stated. Almonte had made me pack a change of socks, and I had wondered why at the time. Now I knew. Everyone had this look in their eyes; I'd seen it from the very start, when we were back on the mainland and I couldn't figure out the buckles on my jacket. I was slowing them down.

At last, the ground became firm. Marsh gave way to meadow, the sky opened, and I imagined I could breathe easier because the air wasn't so damp.

Torres stopped and held up a hand—even before my haphazard training I would have known that meant halt.

I had to blink a couple of times to realize that the hulking form in front of us wasn't another set of trees but a structure. A tall, round tower with a conical, tiled roof stood in a clearing. Signs of recent construction lingered in the turned-up ground around it. Moss and lichens covered gray stone, as if it were ancient, but they must have been painted on, some kind of set dressing. Morning mist clung around its base. Like something out of a fairy tale.

"That's not on the map," Torres said. He knelt and dug into his pack. I did the same.

Because of the shield, GPS devices didn't work. Didn't matter—Torres had a laminated paper map marked with every building site and landmark established by the island's production staff at the time the place went dark. Lang Analytics had given us the maps, specs, and source material used by the island's design and production teams. With Almonte looking over his shoulder, he studied it, tracing the path we'd taken from the beach, glancing at the glare of the sun to mark our position, checking against a compass tucked in his hand. Wendell and Rucker stood watch, which made my back itch. What did we need to watch against? We didn't know—that was the problem. The tower looked deserted. I couldn't even see a door. But it loomed, sinister.

My own primary piece of equipment was a tablet loaded with the Mirabilis design team's files. Their sources included everything from Sumerian epics to Icelandic sagas to *Journey to the West* to the Mahābhārata. I'd added all the classic texts I could think of, dozens of modern fantasy movies and novels, and a bunch of gaming manuals, old school and new, from AD&D to Rolemaster to Pathfinder. Some Shadowrun and World of Darkness just to shake things up. And on the computer side, Zork all the way up to World of Warcraft and Skyrim. Lang warned us that we could face anything out here. *Anything.*

My own map was aimed at the island's theoretical future guests, showing castles, villages, roads, and lairs—most of them marked "future" or "in production." I set my map next to Torres's to compare, to make sure I was looking at the correct spot. He was right. According to our materials, this tower wasn't supposed to be here.

"Well, that's just great," Torres muttered.

"Our maps are wrong," I said, frowning. "Is that what this means?"

"We can't trust any of the information we got from Lang. Too much has changed." He shoved the map into his pack.

Wind rustled through the nearby copse of trees, and I flinched. Hard not to feel like something was watching us. I studied the tower. You didn't just put a tower out in the middle of nowhere. This had to be here for a reason. Part of the game, or some exclusive lodging option?

I said, "Then we just have to gather information as we go. Be even more careful. Mark up a new map. It'll be okay, right?"

Torres and Almonte pulled on their packs and re-slung

their rifles. The captain called, "Rucker, does that thing have a door?"

We had come at this from the back side. Guests—players on a quest—would approach from the island's interior. I marched ahead, to the other side of the tower, looking for a path, a sign, anything—

"Professor," Torres said patiently. "Stay back."

"There must be a path or clue. Some direction marker—"

A noise screeched through the clearing, like the scream of a hawk through an amplifier. I dropped to the ground, hands over my ears.

Something very large crashed through the trees across the clearing from the tower. Torres was suddenly at my side, weapon at the ready. The others spread out in a defensive half-circle. The earsplitting scream repeated.

A creature emerged, bounding into the clearing. As large as a bus, it sprang on golden lion's legs, paws wide and claws extended. Its head was human, tanned, with glossy black hair flowing down to a lion's tawny, muscular shoulders. Androgynous, its body was powerful, but its face was refined, teeth bared, jaw tight and angry. The bright gold feathers of giant wings stirred the air, washing a breeze over us. Their span cast wide shadows.

"It's a Sphinx," I murmured, disbelieving, amazed. I started to stand, to get a closer look. Torres put a hand on my shoulder and shoved me back to the ground.

Pictures were one thing—a stretched imagination, illustrations wildly different from each other and all of them somehow lacking. Artists reaching for the magical and not quite getting there. But this . . . the feathers rustled, the fur had texture. The tail twitched with an anxious flutter, just like a cat's. The eyes blinked and nostrils flared. This wasn't animation.

This was *right*.

Wendell pointed a device shaped like a radar gun at it. It combined a portable spectrometer, infrared monitor, and electromagnetic detector, among other instruments. A tricorder, basically, another one of Lang Analytics' gadgets.

Torres whispered, "What is it? Biological or mechanical?"

"Both. Neither. I don't know what it is." He banged on the side of the device. "I don't think this thing is working right."

Torres readied his weapon and said urgently, "Rucker, take the heart, I've got the head—"

"Wait." I got to my feet, holding on to Torres's arm, pulling off his aim. I must have been crazy.

"Professor, get down—"

Instead, I approached the beast.

"Hold!" Torres called. Guns turned away.

On the other side of the tower, a dirt trail curved along, leading away to the north. The Sphinx stood right on it, blocking it. No—guarding it. Of course.

Opening its impossible mouth, it screamed, a nearly human voice making a hawk's screeching cry, so the noise was like both and neither. Like the lion's body with the flowing black hair, that sound shouldn't exist, but it did. Biological, mechanical, both, neither. Whatever it was, it was convincing.

I fidgeted nervously, hands opening and closing, but stood my ground. The creature saw me, amber-colored eyes focusing. I met that gaze and could swear I saw intelligence looking back. Intention. That wasn't possible.

But I knew this story.

I called out, "Are you the guardian of this road?"

The Sphinx narrowed its eyes, flicked its long tail like a cat on the prowl, and settled into a crouch, clawed paws splaying. It licked its fangs. Then it spoke. "I am."

The voice was a clear alto, even as it shook the whole clearing. I could feel it in my sternum. This was designed to shock, to overwhelm. The muscles of the lion's flank flexed as a claw scratched a furrow in the dirt.

"What must we do to pass this way?"

It brought its head close to the ground, nearer to me. My heart pounded, my hands were sweaty.

"Answer my riddle," it said.

All right, so far so good. "Ask your riddle, guardian."

The Sphinx drew itself up, immense and impenetrable. Sternly, it recited, "What goes on four legs in the morning, two legs at noon, and three legs in the evening?"

My thoughts skipped, my held tilted. Really? I had been bracing for something difficult. Surely this ought to be more challenging. On the other hand . . . this place was originally supposed to be *fun*. Couldn't make the game too hard.

"Shit," Rucker grumbled behind me.

I said, "The answer is man. Humankind. In the morning of his life, as a baby, he crawls on all four limbs. In his prime, the middle of his life, he walks on two legs. As an old man, at the evening of his life, he uses a cane. Three."

There was an agonizing pause. I wondered—should I have answered in Greek? I could almost hear the firing of a circuit board in the Sphinx's head, the clicking of gears in its neck. Mechanical, it had to be mechanical.

The golden Sphinx bowed its head. "You are correct. You may pass."

I let out a nervous sigh. Nodding its head in what almost looked like a bow of respect, the Sphinx backed up a step, leaving the path clear. Folding its wings, it retracted its claws and settled into a comfortable seated position, where it froze, still as a statue.

According to myth, the Sphinx would fling itself off a cliff when someone answered the riddle correctly, but in this case the engineers wouldn't want their creation to destroy itself every time someone passed this way. The creature had to be there for the next group of adventurers.

Now, though, frozen in stillness, newly dull eyes gazing blankly at nothing, it didn't seem as real. A little of the magic had gone out of it, and it made me sad.

"The professor earns her keep," Torres said. He might have been smiling a little.

We crept toward the monstrous creature. The lion's fur looked so soft, so real . . . I laughed. The sound just burst out of me, and my eyes teared up. "Look at this. Just *look* at it!" I couldn't believe what I was seeing. I'd fallen into a movie, into my childhood mythology books. This *couldn't* be real. But it was totally real.

"Oh my God," Wendell said, approaching cautiously at first, then running even as he slung his rifle back over his shoulder. He slid to the ground at its front claw and started running his hands over it.

Rucker stormed toward it, and back, glaring. "What the fuck *is* this? I thought we were going to be up against, like, animatronic Johnny Depp. Not . . . *this!* This is *bullshit!*"

Wendell knelt by one of the big paws and started slicing at it with a knife.

"Um. I'm not sure you should be doing that." I watched the Sphinx's eyes, waiting for them to come back to life. For it to stomp us all to oblivion. Also . . . I didn't want him to cut into it and reveal how it worked. I didn't want to know how it worked. I just wanted it to *be.*

"I want to see what it's made of," he said. "If it's any consolation, I don't think it would have actually killed us. Assuming the safety protocols are still in place—"

Almonte said, "I don't think that's a good assumption." On alert, she searched the surroundings for the next attack.

A trickle of blood spilled into fur. Wendell peeled back the skin to reveal wires and steel struts. "Biomechanical. Thing's a cyborg." He grinned.

Advanced technology. Not magic. I ran my hands down the leg, feeling the soft tawny fur. Wishing for the magic of it. If I scratched it in just the right spot, would it purr?

"We're fucked," Rucker continued. "They should have sent a fucking platoon to do this."

Torres seemed unaffected. "Can it, Rucker. Wendell, pack up, we need to keep moving."

"There should be a prize. A clue to the next level," I said, scanning the clearing. From this side, a narrow wooden door with a simple handle and hinges gave access to the stone tower. There didn't seem to be anything hinky about it.

Above the door was a small alcove, a couple of feet or so tall. It held a statue of a man, his expression noble, gazing skyward. He was draped in an elegant robe and carried a scepter. I came closer, squinting to study it.

Short hair, gaunt features—I recognized him. "Is that Harris Lang?" Had the developers really put up statues of Lang? That seemed a bit much.

Torres approached. "Professor, maybe you shouldn't—"

I opened the door wide—it was flimsy, not very secure— and pressed in, hoping to find treasure, secret scrolls, ancient runes or a glowing inscription, a magic sword . . .

Nothing. Well, not nothing. Some construction detritus. A pile of two by fours and some Sheetrock lying against the wall. The place smelled dusty. The wood ceiling overhead was low but offered no way to access the rest of the tower.

Torres came up beside me, leading with his gun and efficiently shouldering me out of the way. After a moment of searching, he eased back. He hadn't found anything suspicious —or interesting—either.

My sigh must have sounded wistful. Torres looked at me like

I was a wayward toddler who'd just found the best mud puddle ever.

"Satisfied?" he asked.

"Yes? No? I don't know."

"Let's get moving."

We regrouped on the path near the immobile Sphinx. It cast a shadow, that was how large it was. It . . . didn't smell like anything. I thought it should smell like something, the lion enclosure at the zoo or some exotic perfume.

Farther on, into the next stand of trees, the path branched, the left-hand side heading north, the right-hand going south. Torres had his compass in hand, studying both it and the sun.

"Which way, Boss?" Wendell asked, squinting down one path, then the other.

"They—the design team—must have had a reason for building this way out here," I said excitedly. Left or right? According to the out-of-date maps we had, Tor Camylot—the great castle in the middle of the island, Insula Mirabilis's control center, the key to controlling the island—was north. We should go left. "This might be part of a quest, and if we can find the next step—"

"We're not on a quest."

"I think we should go left," I said. "This path might take us straight to Tor Camylot—"

Torres glared at me. "Marked trails mean people, and we're avoiding people. We head overland." He struck out, away from the path and into the trees.

The rest of the squad fell into line. Almonte, with her kind smile and infinite patience, waited for me to follow. Reluctantly, I did, glancing back to keep the Sphinx's immense golden flank in sight as long as I could, until the trees closed in behind us.

Mirabilis was real, I kept thinking, over and over. Mirabilis was *real*.

5

Though I Do Not Know the Way

I'd had ten days to get ready for this expedition. It wasn't enough.

Lang Analytics had filed a leave of absence from the university on my behalf, found a house sitter for me, and flew me out to their California headquarters for Torres's impromptu boot camp in survival basics and gunfire desensitization.

In addition to Torres's training, I spent those days in a windowless office with a computer, multiple monitors, a tablet, and stacks of books, looking at all of the design team's source materials, every scrap that had gone into their preproduction work on the project. The more notes I made, the more daunting the work became.

According to internal memos, the project managers had estimated they were a year out from a soft opening with actual guests—beta testing, in effect. There'd been a plan to offer raffle tickets for the chance to be the first guests. The price being thrown around for those tickets made my jaw drop, removing any question about whether Mirabilis could make money in the long run. The marketing department had already developed a raft of promotional materials, tour packages, and concept drawings of lodgings that I wasn't entirely sure existed yet. You could come as a tourist, explore the island and its many wonders independently, discover quaint fairy-tale villages, meet amazing creatures, join in feasting and revelry, and so forth, all for fun. Or you could sign up for a quest. Solve puzzles, answer riddles. Join a team—the island was divided into regions: the Realm of Sword, the Realm of Shield, the Realm of Arrow. Compete with other teams for points, win the chance to be king of the island for a day.

While the details of Mirabilis—the locations, setting, spells, ideas—clearly drew on dozens of sources, nothing was overtly familiar. This wasn't licensed from any established franchises —it was all original. All trademarkable. It all belonged to Lang.

So of course Insula Mirabilis and the Three Realms would have lots of branded merchandise available for purchase, everything from T-shirts to replica weapons. The tone of the marketing was breathless and exciting, and if I had encountered any of this as a potential customer, I'd have wanted to sign up immediately.

Nothing had prices listed, yet. This all seemed to be putting the cart before the horse—the marketing team was way ahead of the production team, whose memos seemed increasingly flustered about unrealistic timelines and overwork. Some things in game dev never changed, apparently. Then the memos and updates stopped abruptly. The information I had was old.

The Insula Mirabilis team had had years to develop materials and incorporate them into the final product. I had about a week to guess what they might have done with it. Especially after they didn't have the marketing department on the mainland looking over their shoulders.

But I knew what Dominic liked. I knew his fandoms, and I

could make a pretty good guess what he'd try to bring to life, given unlimited resources. At least, I could have guessed six years ago, when we were still together. Like our map, my information was probably out-of-date. Everything I thought I knew might be wrong.

A day before we boarded the cutter that ferried us near the island, a knock came at the office door. Before I could respond, the door opened, and I nearly jumped out of my chair when Harris Lang himself entered. I hadn't seen him since that day at the hotel suite in Boulder.

"Oh, hi," I said, standing abruptly, self-consciously snapping my pen over and over. I should have sat right back down, but by then it was awkward.

Lang studied the room, the stack of books, the ten different files open on the monitors, the messy pile of notes. Judging every last detail and finding them wanting, I was sure. "Do you have everything you need?"

"I don't know," I said, sighing. "I keep thinking of one more thing. I don't suppose they'd have tried to incorporate Mayan mythology? The Popol Vuh, journeys to the underworld accessed through cenotes—"

"I'd say you should expect anything." He grew a small, sly smile. Like expecting anything was the point. "I wondered if you could do something for me."

I shrugged. "Since I'm technically working for you now, I guess I can try. I suppose it depends on what it is."

"If you see Mr. Brand, I'd like you to deliver a message."

Not a request. A command. "Okay?"

"Tell him 'Bishop to king seven.'"

"You guys in the middle of a game or something?" I asked.

"Something like that."

Quizzically, I narrowed my gaze. "Can I ask . . . what happened? Dom was so excited to work for you. He really believed in you, in pushing technology as far as he could, that doing so would really help people. And now . . . this. What happened?"

Lang frowned, his brow furrowing. The expression damaged the serene calm he usually cultivated. Those of us on the Mirabilis mission were seeing a side of him he probably wasn't used to revealing.

"Clearly, Dominic doesn't believe in my vision quite as much as we all thought he did."

"You must have believed in him, to make him one of the production managers," I said.

"Yes, I suppose I did. But it seems the game got a little out of hand."

Frustrated, I shook my head, glanced away and to the monitors. "I'm sorry, but this isn't a game. Not if people have died." Lang kept skipping over that part.

His smile turned thin, smug. "My employees on the island —they don't know that anyone has died. They still think this is a game. So all you need to do is figure out the cheat codes. Happy hunting, Professor."

I hadn't thought much about it at the time, but looking back on that conversation, I should have been suspicious. Our maps were wrong, and Harris Lang hadn't told us everything we needed to know. Now we were here, and all my preparation felt useless. I was coming into this blind, like any other player, a wide-eyed guest just arrived on the island and ready for anything. Cheat codes and rules lawyering wouldn't matter if the code and rules had all changed.

But I would never forget that Sphinx as long as I lived. In spite of myself, I had already fallen in love with Mirabilis. My exhaustion vanished. Nausea and nerves—gone. My pace quickened. I desperately wanted to see what was next. I wanted to see *more*.

This was in contrast to the grim, professional resolve of the rest of the team.

"Professor, slow down," Torres said the next time I came abreast of him. I wanted to see the castles—the island's production specs said there were several. I wanted to answer more riddles. I wanted to see unicorns.

"But he did it. Lang did it. I didn't really believe, I didn't think—"

"This is a crime scene," Almonte said. "We're here to find out who activated that shield and killed those guardsmen."

Torres gave her a look. "We're here to return control of the island to Lang Analytics. It'll be up to the authorities to sort out criminal charges."

She pressed her lips together, a tight smile of acknowledgment.

Torres kept the squad's pace slow and steady. He and the others were examining every inch of the forest we passed through, on alert for the least sign of trouble. I could almost see them making continuous Perception checks.

The average stats for an average untrained human like me just weren't up to this. I wondered what the stats for someone like Torres would look like on paper, with his training and experience. Whatever they were, they were probably perfect for this situation. High constitution, proficiency in survival. I consoled myself that my Arcana would be off the charts compared to his.

After an hour or so, we rested. Almonte distributed foil-wrapped meals. The label on my package said "beef enchiladas," but I never would have guessed that, looking at the mash sealed within. At least there was also a package of M&M's.

What I really wanted was a cup of hot tea. And a comfy chair and a warm blanket. I felt like I might never be warm again.

Watching me, Rucker smirked, like he expected me to complain. He made me nervous, the way he looked at everything like he wanted to shoot it. Wendell left me alone, more concerned with tending to his equipment. Almonte checked in with me often. She was the unit's medic, and I gathered she was making sure I wasn't about to go into shock or collapse into tears.

Torres watched everybody, everything. He never seemed to blink.

"Think the rain'll hold off?" Torres asked.

Almonte glanced at the sky. "Not for long."

Rucker blew out a breath. "Can still get this shit done in the rain."

"Might be better," Wendell said. "If rain keeps the natives under cover."

I hoped it didn't rain. I'd already used my spare pair of socks. Torres had a tablet of his own, which he reviewed while eating from a foil-wrapped meal labeled "beef stroganoff." The aesthetic was so wrong. We should be nibbling on hard bread and cheese. Simmering stew in a cast-iron pot over the fire. The marketing materials had promised hot stew and home brew ale by a warm tavern fire. This wasn't it.

"Professor," he said, and I looked up. "Tell me about Brand."

I kept hoping that my relationship with Dom would turn out to be irrelevant. That we would reach Tor Camylot without ever seeing another person and walk right into the castle's control room without any trouble.

"You've got his personnel files there?" I asked back, and he nodded. "I'm not sure I know him anymore. I haven't spoken to him in years. He signed on with Lang Analytics right around the time we broke up. He just sort of vanished after that."

"Who broke it off, you or him? Would he be happy to see you?"

I blushed. Torres had memorized my dossier. I still thought it was weird that I even *had* a dossier. Torres knew everything about me, and I didn't know anything about him. I hadn't gotten to look at *his* file. "I did."

Rucker huffed, a brusque macho chuckle. "Then he's gonna be pissed when she shows up."

Torres threw him a quelling look before I could. "Why?"

"I suppose this is mission-critical information?"

"If it will help me figure out what kind of person he is, then yes."

Dominic wasn't—or hadn't been—that complicated. He was passionate, fierce. Working to help build Mirabilis would have been a dream come true for him, or at least the version of him I'd known. Would he have mutinied? Tried to claim it as his own? He might.

"If you asked him why, he'd say it's because I didn't understand him. That I think he picked Lang Analytics over me. That I couldn't handle him putting his work ahead of me. But that wasn't it, and he wouldn't listen to me try to explain . . ." I paused and took a breath. This was old news, but talking about it brought it all back. "That wasn't the reason at all. He just . . . wouldn't listen. Dom saved me, in some ways. He was my first boyfriend after . . ." Another deep breath, and I shook the memory away. "But that was part of the problem, I think. I was a supporting character in his story. The damsel in distress, the girl he saved. He would have kept saving me. It would have been easy to just let him take care of me. But that's not what I wanted, and I broke it off."

"So he believes in all this?" Torres said, gesturing to the trees and air around us. "Believes in the fantasy. The stories."

"Believe" didn't quite cover it. "He named his cat Elrond. He wanted to get married wearing a Highlander kilt. He . . . this whole place is him. He'd love it here."

"And he's not going to be happy to see you," Torres said, a wry lift to his brow.

"Maybe not. Unless he can rescue me from something."

"We could maybe arrange that," Rucker said.

"What about the other two?" Almonte asked Torres. "Will we be able to negotiate with them, if things go sidewise?"

The other two project managers she referred to were Tess Selvachan and Arthur Beckett. Selvachan was the chief engineer on the project; her teams made all this happen, bringing Dominic's team's design concepts to life. Beckett was the lead project manager; he was supposed to be the one holding everything together. If Lang's island had come apart, the fault might ultimately lay with him.

But again, what we'd been told and what was actually happening here might not be the same thing.

Torres said, "They're probably like Brand. Lang recruited people who would be passionate about this project. Real geeks, all of them. Any one of them might have gotten a little too passionate. The plan is still to avoid talking to anyone."

"Sixty-eight people were on the island when it went dark—what are the odds we can keep avoiding them?" Almonte asked.

"Let's find out." Torres grinned. The soldiers checked their weapons before we continued on, back in line, hiking through an exotic rain forest and wondering when the monsters were going to jump out at us.

I'd somehow landed in the middle of a summer action movie.

As we moved to the windward part of the island, the trees thinned and opened to a wide, rolling meadow. Wind rippled through the grasses in waves and tossed the ends of my short, salt-crusted hair into my face. I'd tried to finger comb it out. Hadn't worked so well, so it was just going to stay a mess.

According to the official map, this plain was destined to become an outdoor festival venue when the park opened, for seasonal special events. In this case, the map was accurate. The field was open, nothing had been built yet. We stopped so the squad could check our position, and I was practically swaying on my feet. My legs were aching blocks, and I wondered what would happen when I just got too tired to move anymore.

"Don't forget to breathe, Professor," Almonte said over my shoulder.

"Yeah. Thanks." Deep breath, and somehow even my ribs hurt.

Torres and Wendell consulted map and compass, and Wendell pointed across the meadow. They nodded, in the shorthand of people who were comfortable working together. We moved out again, cutting across the meadow. Grasses brushed up to my knees, and walking became even more of a slog, fighting against the vegetation. I didn't have anywhere to put my feet.

The meadow continued up a gentle slope that turned into a hill with a good view around us. Looking back, I could see the ocean, the white lines of surf crawling in to the rocky shore. I thought we'd walked a lot farther than that. When we reached the crest of the hill, we'd be able to see north, and get some clue about what was happening on the rest of the island. Maybe we'd get our first look at the castle of Tor Camylot.

"Do you hear that?" Almonte said.

My head hurt, listening for the tiny distant sound that had alerted her. Concentrating, I only heard wind rustling the grasses, a hint of the breeze that pushed scattered clouds overhead. Turned out, I didn't hear it. I *felt* it, a vibration in the ground under my feet. The others looked back, some of them cocking their heads to listen.

"Thunder?" I said. Gray clouds were gathering, but they were far to the north, out on the ocean.

Torres put up his hand to hush me. The sound grew louder.

"Hoofbeats," Torres said. "Get to high ground. Here." Jogging, the captain led us to the crest of the hill.

Rucker handed a pair of binoculars to Torres, who scanned the area, then pointed.

Pale animals, grouped in a wedge shape, galloped along the edge of the valley. The herd contained about a dozen animals, but it was hard to tell. At this distance they seemed a rippling mass of flesh and legs, impossible to differentiate.

"Horses, it looks like," Torres said.

I shaded my eyes. The herd came closer, taking a path that would lead them through the valley. The creatures were white, gleaming in the sun, with long manes and tails that rippled in the wind they created with the speed of their passage.

"No, they aren't," I said. Oh my God.

They had the bodies of horses, the sleek coats and graceful movements of horses, their powerful necks supported delicate horse heads. And in the middle of their foreheads grew ivory-colored spiral horns.

They were artificially produced using genetic engineering and biomechanics. Cyborgs, like the Sphinx. I knew that, rationally. But Lang's engineers had gotten them right. More than right. *Perfect.* They were a million fantastical illustrations come to life, tails streaming like banners, necks bobbing with effort, their bodies lurching when they shifted direction to avoid colliding with one another. When they tossed their heads, their horns flashed in the sun.

I walked, paralleling the path they made as they skirted the hill. I wanted to follow them, to see where they were going, where they lived . . . and to see if I could get close to them. I hoped the designers hadn't been able to get the part about virgins right.

Not watching where I was going, I stumbled and dropped to my knees. I didn't care. I blinked and tears fell. Quickly, I wiped them away.

"Down," Torres said, then again more urgently, "Down, everyone down!"

I hadn't been paying attention to him; I was now.

The squad practically melted, lying flat and merging with the grass to disappear. As usual I felt clumsy and useless, scrunching down, trying to flatten, shifting to hide my pack, then realizing my feet were sticking up. Next to me, Torres put his hand on my arm, and I stilled.

We were high enough up the hill that even lying flat and peeking through the grasses, I could follow his gaze and see what had set him off. The herd of unicorns was running for a reason.

They were being chased.

Two hulking dark figures the size of horses themselves loped up the valley. They had rough outlines, ragged fur over lupine bodies and crooked shapes, long and twisted hind legs that made them seem to rock downhill as they ran. Their heads were small but their mouths wide, snarling, revealing long tusks. And they had riders. Human figures dressed in rugged tunics and cloaks sat in black saddles, hanging on to bulky reins as their mounts raced across the valley with bouncing strides after the herd of unicorns.

I gasped, just a short hiss. Torres gave me a warning look, so I shut up, holding my breath.

The unicorns with their long horses' legs and smooth strides were faster and quickly dispersed into the woods on the other side of the valley. The dark monsters didn't seem bothered, continuing on at the same pace as if the unicorns weren't their target. They'd just happened upon them, and chasing them must have seemed like a good game.

The riders seemed to be in a hurry and so didn't see the five strangers huddled in the grass on the hillside. The monsters passed by us and finally disappeared out of the valley.

We stayed still for a long time, just in case they came back. Finally, Torres signaled the all clear, and the others straightened, watchful, hands near their weapons.

"You know what those were," Torres said.

Stiffly, I climbed to my feet, needing a little longer than the others to unkink my limbs. "Unicorns," I breathed. "Real unicorns." I wanted to get close to them. I wanted to touch one of them so badly, even though that sort of thing never turned out well in the stories. I'd get close and then there'd be darkness, goblins, Tim Curry in demon horns . . . just a mess.

Torres regarded me patiently. "Not them. The other things."

Oh. "Wargs. Wolf, dog, pig, *things*." They were hard to explain if you hadn't actually read Tolkien or seen the movies. The word had a mythic origin, based in old Norse and Germanic. But it was hard to ignore the operative sound: *war*. These creatures were meant for battle, for violence. I hoped the unicorns would be okay. I hoped they weren't being hunted. That would be horrible, but there were gamers out there who would think it was awesome.

"Did anybody get a look at who was riding them?" Rucker asked. "Were they just people or another whacked-out engineering job?"

Nobody could say. We didn't know.

But there were unicorns.

6

⟵ ▬▬▬◀◀◀

Twisty Little Passages, All Alike

It was clear why Lang and his team had chosen this island, off the coast of the Pacific Northwest. It contained a whole world, with so many different natural landscapes. We'd gone from beach to marsh to forest to grassland. And now back to forest, but this one hilly, with trees and upended boulders left over from some ice age. Ancient pines stretched up for a hundred feet, and great tangled roots crawled over the earth. I had to watch where I was going every step. On the other hand, the soldiers went smoothly, not making a sound. They were used to this kind of thing.

I wanted to go back and follow the unicorns, but the herd had been running away from Tor Camylot. Maybe later, after this was all over. I would so love to come back here as a tourist. I'd tell Lang he could keep his payment, if I could get a free pass here forever.

Every mile was a new opportunity. What else would we find? What else had the production team built that wasn't on the map? Unfortunately, or fortunately, depending on the point of view, Torres had plotted a path specifically to avoid the possibility of meeting any dragons, wyverns, lamia, rocs, enchanted villages, mysterious temples, merfolk lagoons, or treasure hoards. Anything, really.

But he'd been using Lang's maps when he plotted the route. Maps we couldn't trust.

Torres stopped, arm raised. The others halted immediately, watchful. I continued on another step before I was able to get my legs to stop walking. At first, I couldn't see what had caught his attention. The faint birdsong sounded natural—real birds just doing their thing. No footsteps, no voices, no roaring creatures. Here, a dozen trees grew in a perfect circle. These weren't the soaring pines of the ancient forest we'd been trekking through. These were different, strange. Artificial.

The ring of them was about twenty feet across. Each tree was different—one had the heart-shaped leaves of poplars, another had the lobed leaves of an oak, one had smooth gray bark, another gnarled brown. All of them had been designed, straight trunks, stylized sculptures of trees rather than the real thing, with graceful boughs, curving up like dancers' arms . . .

Arms. The branches looked like arms.

"Is this on the map?" Wendell asked.

"Yeah," I said. "'Grove of Dryads.'" I'd wondered what that meant. I hurried into the circle.

"Professor!" Torres called, in a tone that suggested he was getting tired of calling after me like that. I didn't slow down, and he marched after me.

Women's faces showed through the bark. Half-lidded eyes, the shape of pursed lips, bodies held mid-movement, merging with trunks and roots so you couldn't tell the body from the tree. One, the oak, had her arms spread wide, as if stretching after waking up in the morning. Her face was upturned, her lips parted. The curve of a breast was just visible, merging into the texture of bark. Another seemed as if she looked over her shoulder, and yet another gazed down, as if studying where her feet would have been if she had them.

"Okay, this is fucked up," Rucker observed.

"Dryads," I murmured. The glade was solemn and so beautiful.

A whisper breathed through the circle of trees: "Go back." Rucker leveled his weapon outward, but he had nothing to aim at.

"There is danger. Go back." It sounded like leaves, rustling in autumn.

Wildly, I looked around. "It's the trees. Which one is talking?"

"Go back . . . danger."

We went to each one while the murmured warning continued.

"Here!" Wendell said, standing in front of the willow, leaves drooping around her spread branches as if she stood out in the rain.

"Go back . . ." Her lips moved, the bark shifting. I pushed past Wendell to stand directly in front of her. Her eyes were blank. I couldn't tell if she could see me; she had nothing to focus with.

"Hello?" I prompted.

"There is danger . . ."

"What kind of danger? We're trying to get to Tor Camylot. Can you give us any hints? What's the fastest way there? Where's the danger?"

"Go back . . ."

"Please, any help you can give us." I was talking to a tree, and it felt like the most normal thing in the world.

Torres said, "Professor—"

"This is a game," I said to him. "This whole island's a quest

—if the designers put this here, it's a clue. You never know what's going to be useful." The dryad had a classically beautiful face, a piece of artwork perfectly merged with the wood and bark, leaves dripping around her. "What danger?" I asked again, sadly, futilely.

"It's a recording," Torres said. "There's nothing there."

"I just haven't found the right way to ask. If I just ask the right question—"

Wendell said, "The game's still in beta. They didn't get around to putting in the clues."

"Danger . . ." she whispered. The same words, over and over.

I brushed part of the branch, what would have been her wrist if this was really her arm. Nothing happened, and the bark just felt like bark.

"We keep moving," Torres said.

"And the warning?" Almonte asked.

"Stay sharp, like always," he said.

We walked on. "Danger . . ." The word whispered through the air behind us.

7

Too Deep We Delved

The forest closed in around us, and it was hard not to feel claustrophobic. The sky was gray and weighed down on us.

Torres had estimated half a day's walk to get to the castle from the shore where we'd landed—*if* we didn't run into problems.

The Fellowship of the Ring traveled for months, just to get from Rivendell to Moria. A lot of people missed that bit. The books never really went into the slog, getting from point A to point B in a pre-industrial world on foot. Because it was *exhausting*. No one wanted to read about how much the hero's knees hurt or finding a tree to pee behind. Forget the wilderness survival skills of building fires and setting snares to catch rabbits. How the hell did one pee in the wild without getting anything on your boots? I can see it now, the Dungeon Master says: "Roll to save not hitting your own boots with pee." Difficulty: girl in fatigues. Disadvantage: exhaustion.

Who would ever decide to do this for more than a few days, unless the fate of the world was at stake?

Ahead, Torres slowed, and I moved up beside him to get a look at what he'd seen. He put out an arm to hold me back. This was becoming a familiar pattern.

A pair of stone pillars marked some kind of gateway, camouflaged among the trees. Ten or so feet tall, made up of dark stone blocks, splotched with green and gray lichens to make them seem ancient, some monument from a previous age. As if some ancient civilization had once inhabited the island. An illusion of a fantasy world with a history reaching back thousands of years.

"We aren't even following a trail, how the hell do we keep running into stuff?" Rucker exclaimed.

"Random encounter," I said. "They want to keep the guests busy. Part of the quest."

"You know who's been busy?" Wendell said. "The design team. I don't remember this being on the map, either."

"They didn't tell Lang about any of it," I said. "They were holding out on him."

"Which suggests they'd been planning the mutiny for a long time," Almonte said.

No ominous voices foretold doom, no riddle-wielding creatures jumped out at us. I pushed past Torres to get a better look at the structures. "It might have directions on it, or instructions."

"Professor, we need to keep moving—"

The pillars had inscriptions on them in some invented language, characters meant to look ancient but still legible to the average modern person. Except, buried among the strange figures was a sentence I recognized. Latin alphabet, invented words.

Wendell was studying the other pillar. "Hey, this one's in English! I can read it!"

I frowned. "Let me guess. It says, 'That is not dead which can eternal lie.'"

They all stared at me. "How did you know that?" Wendell asked.

"Because this one says, 'Ph'nglui mglw'nafh Cthulhu R'lyeh wgah'nagl fhtagn.'"

"Wait—what did you even just say?" Rucker said.

"'In his house at R'lyeh, dead Cthulhu waits dreaming.' Welcome to a shrine of the Elder Gods. Dom, you just couldn't resist, could you?"

Wendell chuckled. "So do we need to be on guard for animatronic Cthulhu?"

"Maybe?" I said. The pillar had lines, straight cuts in the stone that at first I thought were the mortared space between bricks. But there wasn't mortar. They were meant to open up.

"Wendell," I said. "I think there may be some trapdoors in the stone." I started running my hands along the lines, searching for gaps. Pressing on runes and characters, looking for some kind of button.

"Are you sure you should be doing that?" Torres asked.

"There might be a clue," I insisted. "Treasure. Something we'll need for the next round."

"I thought we established that this isn't a game," the captain said.

I might have been grinning. "Except this place was designed by gamers, and when we get to the castle, we might need a key, or a code, or a password, or . . . or . . . I don't know, a gold coin to pay the doorman. A ring of power. We can take five minutes to look here, and maybe make things easier later on."

Wendell had come to join me, looking over my shoulder. "I didn't see any doors on the other pillar. Not like this."

I paused a moment, steadied my breathing. This, I knew how to do. "If it's part of the game, we won't open it by pushing things at random. There's got to be some kind of pattern." I went back to studying the inscriptions.

I thought back to the Sphinx. The game designers added various challenges for the players to figure out. But they didn't want them to be too hard. Challenging, but not frustrating. Fun. Escape-room hard.

At various points on the round pillar were a series of circles. O's. They could be mistaken for part of the inscriptions, except the other characters were angular, jagged. These didn't fit. Because they were buttons. The highest was over my head, almost at the limit of where I could reach. I pushed it first, then the next one down, then the next. Seven in all. Nothing happened. So I pushed them again, this time starting with the lowest.

"Klaatu barada nikto," Wendell said grandly, and chuckled.

"Nice," I said approvingly.

He added, "Maybe if you—"

I hushed him. Tried a more complex pattern. The highest, then lowest. Then next highest, next lowest. Then the last, right above the line marking the trapdoor cut into the stone.

And the door opened. A curved lid slid back into the stone, revealing a shoebox-sized alcove lined in red velvet. And resting on the velvet was a simple gold ring. Its warm, polished color nearly glowed against the cloth, enticing one to touch it.

"You've got to be kidding me," I muttered. Next to me, Wendell barked a laugh.

"That's it?" Rucker said.

"You never know, this might be the thing that controls everything on the island," I said, and took the ring out of the alcove and held it up to the light. It was just a plain gold band that probably wasn't even real gold. A man's ring, it was too big for my fingers. Otherwise I would have totally put it on, just to see if Lang's engineers had figured out a way to make someone invisible.

A mechanical *whump* vibrated under our feet.

"What was that?" Almonte said, moving her rifle to the ready.

A metallic slam clanged resoundingly, then another. A sudden, horrified realization came over me, and I looked back at her, wide-eyed.

"You know," I said, "I didn't check for traps."

The ground under us dropped away, dirt and debris falling into a pit along with all of us.

8

$$\longrightarrow$$

Critical Fail

Torres reacted instantly—he lunged for me, grabbing my arm as we fell, as if he could save me. It was kind of flattering. It didn't help.

We didn't fall far, a dozen feet I guessed, and the floor at the bottom was cushioned with thick, soft mats. This was designed to let us fall through and land safely. I hit and bounced. Torres landed next to me with a grunt and rolled to his feet. Rucker and Wendell hit the mat and came back up to kneeling, facing out, ready for whatever attack they thought was coming. A rectangle of forest was visible above us.

One of the squad hadn't fallen—Almonte hung on the edge and swung up a leg to pull herself back to the surface.

"Boss!" she called down. "Torres!"

"Get a rope!" he called back.

She didn't have time. The trapdoor was closing, sliding shut with a mechanical rumble.

Rucker jumped, trying to reach the door before it locked out the sky and freedom, but we were just exactly too far away from it. From above, Almonte watched, lips pursed, a coil of rope in one hand as the opening grew narrower, narrower. So she jumped. As she landed on the mat and rolled to safety, the door above us shut with an ominous, air-sucking *whump*. Rucker shouted in rage.

We rested for a moment, taking in the new situation.

"Sorry, Boss." Almonte broke the silence and sighed. "I don't know if that was the right call."

"No, it's best we stay together."

Me, I was relieved she'd jumped. "Never split the party," I said.

A torch flared to life on one of the stone walls. It looked like a gas flame, set to ignite when the door closed. We could see just enough to know how trapped we really were.

"Shit!" Rucker turned on me from across the room. "What do we do now, Professor? Huh? You going to get us out of this one?"

He wasn't angry at me—he was just *angry*.

Torres said, "Rucker, stand down." Rucker sullenly crossed his arms and paced to the wall and back.

I was still clutching the gold ring, the one I'd stupidly taken and triggered the trap. "It's a puzzle. We just have to figure it out."

The single torch gave off a wavering light. We were in a square room. The floor was soft, dusted with dried leaves and forest detritus that had fallen when the trap opened. On the wall opposite the torch was a doorway. The way forward was obvious.

Holding the ring to the light, I studied it, looking for an inscription, markings, anything. I said, "Check the walls, see if there's a slot, or a carving . . . some kind of space this might fit into to unlock the door or something."

The walls appeared to be made of stone blocks, joined by

mortar, all neatly made, smooth. No inscriptions, no secret slots or spaces exactly the right size for a ring. Torres even got out his penlight, which provided a more steady light than the wavering torch.

"Here, one of you guys put this on. If it's biometrically activated, it might need to fit exactly."

"What the hell does that even mean?" Rucker said.

Torres held out his hand, I gave him the ring, and he slipped it on. It fit like it was made for him.

"Now what?" he said, glancing at me.

I shook my head. "I don't know. I thought something might happen." I rubbed my hand over my head. My hair itched. "It's got to be good for *something*."

He clenched his fist. Spread his hand flat and held it to the wall next to the doorway, gamely trying a couple of different positions. Nothing.

"Worth a try," he said, slipping off the ring and handing it back to me. "We might have to do this the hard way." He approached the doorway, looking carefully in either direction. He shone his penlight into the darkness. "Passageway leads off in both directions. Looks like there are more intersections farther on."

"It's a maze," I said.

"Can you solve it?" he asked.

Almonte said, "We won't have any idea where we are when we get out the other side."

"Island's not that big, we'll figure it out," Torres said. "Professor?"

"The inscriptions on the pillars are from the Cthulhu mythos, so the maze is probably pretty bad. Non-Euclidean, or trying to be non-Euclidean. Although that's always been one of the problems with anything Lovecraftian. No matter how much you try to depict the unseeable and the unknowable forces of cosmic evil, you can never really conceptualize outside the limits of your own human imagination—"

"Professor!" the captain said.

"—turns out the color out of space is purple." I shrugged.

Calmly, he said, "Professor. Do we know where this goes? Do we go forward, or do we try to find a way to open that trapdoor?"

I pocketed the ring, pulled my tablet out of my bag, and started hunting. "I think I saw something about a maze in the production notes. I can try to find the solution for it."

The squad waited and Torres kept watch on the doorway while I searched through encyclopedias of mythical creatures, classic sagas from around the world, pages of designer notes, looking for maps and diagrams. Hoping they'd designed the blueprints for this place well ahead of time so I could lead us straight out of here. Although, it felt a little like cheating to be consulting the module in the middle of the adventure . . .

When I found a section labeled *Eldritch Labyrinth,* I gasped and read closer. A handful of paragraphs, rudimentary—they looked like meeting notes polished into a memo. Yes, the production team wanted to build an underground maze, and the design team had started initial concepts. Make it part of formal adventuring campaigns, and wouldn't it be fun to drop adventuring parties in by surprise, so they'd have no time to prepare. A real adventure, right? That part worked perfectly, and I would have to remember to tell them if I got the chance. I also found this little tidbit: "Re: monsters, we will consult with Selvachan's group about what's feasible."

The production notes didn't include any maps or layout drawings of the maze. And didn't clarify what they meant by "monsters."

"Well?" Torres said.

I'd been looking over my materials for twenty minutes and

hadn't found anything useful. "I can't find a map, but they were planning on putting in some monsters."

"*Monsters?*" Rucker said, adjusting the grip on his rifle. "What kind of monsters?"

"Chances are they didn't get around to adding the monsters," I said, trying to sound confident.

"No, really," Wendell said. "What monsters?"

"Minotaur, probably," I said. "This being a maze and all."

"Well, fuck," Rucker muttered, predictably.

Wendell seemed fascinated. "You really think they made a Minotaur? Like a guy with a bull's head?"

"Sure, why not?" I said, a little more flippantly than I intended. "They made a Sphinx."

"It could be some combination of mechanical and biological engineering," Wendell said. "With autonomous programming."

"What's the solve?" Torres asked.

"Kill it," I said.

"Good. Nice and simple," Rucker said.

"But they probably didn't have time to implement anything. Not really," I pleaded.

"And no map." Almonte peered out the doorway.

"We'll just have to do this the old-fashioned way," Torres said.

"There might be a prize," I said. "If we can solve the maze, we might get something that will make the next quest easier."

"The only quest we're on is getting to Tor Camylot and shutting this whole thing down. Wendell, get the torch."

Wendell did. Whatever fueled it was self-contained, and it detached from the wall. Everyone took up their places, moving out with their precise military attention. They were ready, and they were waiting for me. And I stared at that black gaping doorway.

The truth of the matter was I hated riddles. The solutions

were never obvious. They never made sense even when you got the answer. At least in a maze, there were rules.

"We make a map," I said. "We keep track of where we go. Does someone have a marker or something? We mark every room, every doorway. If anybody sees anything weird—a different color stone or something odd on the floor, a symbol or a button or a carving, anything—say something. It could be another trap."

On my tablet I opened a sketch app. I drew a square—the room—and drew a line for the doorway. Drew out the tunnel on the other side, the passages going left and right. I tried to remember which way the Fellowship left Rivendell in the movie because it was the only clue I could think of.

Left. They went left.

We set off to solve the labyrinth.

"There's got to be an easier way to do this," Almonte said.

According to the clock on my tablet, we'd been going for forty minutes. It only seemed like more because we had made so little progress. We turned, reached a dead end, backtracked, tried the next turn at the previous passage. Another dead end, and another try. We marked every turn we made—Torres had a grease pencil to make waterproof notes and used it to draw arrows on the walls to show which way we'd gone so we didn't wander in circles. But every turn we made seemed to be a mistake. My map was looking very thorough, but I was starting to think the maze didn't have a solution and we'd be bumping up against dead ends forever.

"Well, yes," I said. "If I was the one designing this, I'd have made some kind of smart string. It would unroll straight for the exit. It would be the prize in some other quest. We just didn't get a chance to find it first, so we're stuck. We could start singing like David Bowie, that might work."

"What?" Torres's brow furrowed.

"Never mind."

Wendell thought a minute. "You know, I think I know how you could put together something like that string. Wrap a wire antenna, put some kind of transponder in the center, then mount a receiver at the maze's exit. Get them talking to each other on a Bluetooth connection, put a motor in it. Easy."

"That would be *so cool*," I murmured.

"Wish we had that right now," Rucker said.

"Well, we don't, so can it," Torres said.

Somehow, Torres was still letting me decide the path we took. However, I wasn't feeling at all sure of myself. The squad didn't seem to mind that I picked wrong every single time. Rather, they were treating this as a methodical search. Try a turn, mark it, keep going. They couldn't *all* be wrong.

The walls were all alike. The floor was clean, as if the maze had just been built and hadn't had a chance to acquire a lived-in look. I felt like it should have been dusty, worn, ancient. I looked for carvings, inscriptions, symbols, patterns, hidden doors. Secret treasures—like balls of string with transponders that might tell us the way out. I didn't find anything. We only had penlights and the torch. In the circle of wavering light, the maze seemed even more claustrophobic and impossible. The next passage stretched ahead. I wanted to see sunlight at the end of it. I wanted to get out of here.

An alien, monstrous roar echoed against the stone. Impossible to tell how far, or how close, the source of it was. The soldiers halted and studied the way both in front of and behind us. The echoes of the roar faded.

"Minotaur," Wendell stated. He handed the torch to me so

he could take hold of his rifle. I tucked my tablet under my arm.

So. The production team had gotten around to adding monsters.

"We can handle it," Torres said. "But let's get out of here so we don't have to."

The squad fell into place, putting me in the middle, watching the path ahead and covering the path behind. We moved faster. The roar came again. My heart pounded harder. I wished I could be braver.

The passage ended in a T intersection—we could go left or right. Left, again. I hoped I wasn't leading the squad in circles. But this turn didn't lead to a dead end. It turned, turned again. And kept going. Maybe this was it.

The beam of Torres's light revealed stone walls and floor, and more stone, and then—a hideous, hair-covered face with huge, faceted eyes and knife-like mandibles. Behind the head was a bulbous body, leathery, shining with moisture. Eight jointed legs filled the passageway. The creature was so large, its legs braced against opposite walls. It wasn't a Minotaur. It was a spider.

A spider the size of a pony.

For a moment, it stared at us, and we stared back, disbelieving. The spider didn't move. Maybe it hadn't yet been activated and we could just go around it—

The spider screamed.

9

No Memory of This Place

The traditional labyrinth monster was a Minotaur. Body of a man, head of an angry bull with long, curved, sharp horns, trapped in an underground maze to keep him out of the way. Straightforward sword battle—Torres's squad would have been able to handle it, easy.

I didn't know what to do when confronted with the dozen gleaming lenses of a gigantic spider's horrific eyes. I would rather be facing a Minotaur. And yet here we were.

Sighting along the beam of his penlight, Torres fired his rifle. I was ready for it, pressing myself to the wall, holding the torch like a shield. Sparks pinged off the spider's body—it was made of metal, and the bullet bounced off.

"We've got ricochet in here!" Torres called.

Screaming, the spider charged us. Then another scream echoed behind us. I swung the torch around, revealing another spider. In the close space, the screams rattled my spine.

The soldiers paired up, one pair for each spider. Standing

side by side didn't leave them much extra room to mount a defense—they brushed up against the stone walls of the passage. Torres used the butt of his rifle to smash at the first spider's face. Rucker went low, slashing at the legs and mandibles of the second with his utility knife. The monsters slapped at them with hair-covered legs, their mandibles twitching.

"Professor, stay down!" Torres ordered. He didn't have to tell me. In gaming terms, I had about four hit points and no combat skills. If I'd had something to crawl under, I'd have been there already.

Almonte followed Torres's lead and slammed at the second creature with the butt of her rifle; Wendell tried to come in from the side to knock the first off-balance. Suddenly, Wendell grunted and fell back, clutching his arm. His sleeve was torn and showed a splash of blood near the shoulder—one of the churning legs, tipped with metal, had struck him.

Now we knew: the monsters in Mirabilis didn't have safety settings. Snarling, Wendell adjusted his grip on his rifle and charged back into the fray.

I couldn't think of anything I could do that would help. I knew of a half-dozen mythical and literary versions of giant attack spiders, and most of them were just exactly that—attack spiders, awful and deadly. Some of them had razor-sharp mandibles they'd use to shred you; some of them would grab you and cocoon you in spider silk. These didn't seem to have silk spinnerets sticking out of their backsides—small blessing. Because the only way to escape once you got cocooned in evil giant spider silk was to hope that one of your party hadn't been captured with the rest and could sneak in later to cut you free. Usually the noncombatant, which in this case meant me, and I wasn't sure I was up to that.

Abruptly, half the screaming cut out. The spider attacking Almonte and Wendell collapsed, wheezing as the hydraulics went out of jointed legs and the metal body slumped to the ground.

Almonte called back, "There's a button! Right under the mouth—an off switch!"

Torres lunged in and up toward the first spider, stabbing forward with his rifle. Once he knew where to hit, the end was fast—with another wheeze and hiss, the spider dropped to the floor. The air smelled like oil and burned rubber.

"Everyone okay?" Torres called.

"Wendell took a hit." Almonte already had a first-aid kit out of her pack and was studying the wound while the soldier, still on his feet, tried to shrug away from her.

"It's fine, just a cut," Wendell said, then hissed when Almonte prodded.

Rucker kicked at the inert spider, bending the legs, poking at the body, which made a metallic scraping noise on the floor.

"Why now?" Torres asked. "We've been down here an hour, why are we getting monsters now?"

I was on the floor, trying to catch my breath. "We might have triggered something," I said. "Stepped on a pressure plate, or there might just be a timer—if you can't solve the maze in a certain amount of time: monsters."

"Could it mean we're getting close to the end?"

"Wouldn't that be nice?" I said. But yes, the spiders could have been set to guard the exit. I really wanted to get out of there.

"Let me look at something," Wendell said, kneeling by one of the creatures.

"Wendell—" Almonte admonished.

"I'm fine, just a sec—"

Wendell went over the corpses like good adventurers on a dungeon crawl. I peered over his shoulder. "Do either of them have anything like a map or a transponder or anything?"

"Let's check here," Wendell murmured, digging into the spider's innards. He found some kind of plate on the back of the head, opened it, and started pulling out circuit boards, grinning like it was his birthday.

A familiar scream echoed down the passage behind us. Torres and Rucker took up positions, standing at the ready when a third spider came barreling toward us, eight legs skittering against the stone. Its steely mandibles flashed in the torchlight. Torres punched at it from above while Rucker came in from below, stabbing the deactivation button on the first try. The spider shut down and collapsed. The series of movements was impressive, graceful—almost beautiful. That was what high DEX got you.

Turning back to his spider, Wendell carefully peeled an object from the innards, a small black box with some kind of metallic plug at one end. "There it is . . . you were right, there's a transponder, probably to keep it from wandering too far off track. I just need to hook it up to some kind of output . . ."

Using a mini tool kit, he twisted a couple of wires and connected the device to one of his tablets.

"Wendell, how's your arm?" Torres asked. He and Rucker stood guard, waiting for the next scream.

"It's fine, sir," he said, wincing.

"It needs stitches," Almonte said.

"Can it wait until we get out of here?"

"Assuming we get out in the next hour," she answered wryly.

"We'll get out," Wendell said, holding up his palm-sized tablet. The screen displayed a blinking red light. He pointed his cobbled-together device back the way we'd come, and the red light slowed to an occasional beat. But when he pointed it in the other direction, ahead of us, the beating turned frenetic, to almost a solid glow.

"Time to go, people," Torres ordered.

Having someone else — something else — make decisions about which way we should go was a relief. Now if we ended up at dead ends, it wasn't my fault. Not that anyone was blaming me, but, well, I was feeling a little superfluous. "What's that giant spider thing attacking us, Professor Cox?" "It's a giant spider." Yeah, not particularly useful there.

Well . . . I was holding the torch since everyone else was busy being competent. That was something, I supposed.

Next, we encountered a four-way intersection, offering three new directions. Wendell held the transponder device to each of them — the light flashed most insistently to the right. Then straight. Then left. Then right again. We didn't hit a single dead end. Torres was still marking our path, and I was still making a map. But finally, the end felt within reach.

After another turn, the light changed — instead of darkness, the soft glow of sunlight. I wanted to run toward what had to be the exit, but Torres slowed us down. He searched the walls, because it was a trap that had gotten us into this place and we shouldn't be at all surprised to find a trap at the end of it.

He was getting the hang of Mirabilis.

Cautiously, we moved forward, step by step, until we left the stone passage through a rounded archway and entered forest. Our feet touched soil; the light warmed our skin after the underground chill. I took a breath that didn't smell like torch smoke.

"Jesus fuck thank God," Rucker sighed. I knew how he felt.

Behind us, the maze's exit was set into the side of a hill, like a cave entrance lined with stone. The tunnel leading underground quickly ran to darkness. Studying the torch's handle, I found a switch, and the flame went out. I set the now-dark torch by the cave entrance, hoping we wouldn't need it again.

Grinning, Wendell tucked the transponder device in his

pack. He didn't seem bothered by the wound in his shoulder, but in daylight the torn fabric of his fatigues, the wet patch of blood spattered around it, seemed stark. Much worse than I'd thought. The blood made me queasy, and I looked away.

Torres held his rifle like he expected more spiders to come boiling out of the maze entrance. Looking up and around, he studied trees and sky. The forest here was much like the one by the stone pillars and maze entrance, pine trees and tumbled boulders, so however long we'd spent solving the maze, we couldn't have ended up too far off course. A poorly marked trail, little more than a path that many footsteps had scuffed across the forest floor, led away, around the next hill and out of sight.

Finally, Torres slung his rifle on his shoulder and pulled out his compass. The sky was overcast, and among the trees we had no view of the sun. The maze had turned us around.

"This path might go to Tor Camylot," I said, with more hope than confidence.

"Paths go to people," Torres said. "We need to find some high ground and get our bearings. Get some water, catch your breath. We move on in ten minutes."

I immediately sat, right there in the dirt.

"Wendell, let me at least wrap that," Almonte said.

The engineer seemed to suddenly notice all the blood on his arm and sighed. "Yeah, okay."

Torres looked at me. "Professor, drink something."

"Got any merlot?"

He smirked, and I pulled my canteen out of my pack and drank. I was almost out of water. We were going to have to find more soon. Ideally, we'd reach Tor Camylot by nightfall and be finished with this whole thing. But nothing about this was ideal.

Torres announced it was time to go. Unkinking my muscles

after these stops was getting harder and harder. Almonte offered me a hand up, and I took it.

We did not follow the nice, smooth, flat path. Instead, Torres led us uphill, through trees and brush, to this theoretical vantage point. I could hope when we got there, when we saw the lay of the land, that we'd find our destination, Tor Camylot, just on the other side of the hill.

But there was still so much of the island we hadn't seen. What little we had seen was so incredible—how much more was there to discover? I sort of hoped we wouldn't reach Tor Camylot *too* quickly . . .

And would we find Dominic? Did I want to?

I needed a nap and a cup of tea. I was inventing scenarios. The entire staff was waiting at Tor Camylot and would never let us take control of the island, or this whole thing had been a terrible mistake because some middle manager downloaded a virus on the mainframe. They had gotten locked out by entering the wrong password into a computer. If we actually found someone from the staff, found someone to talk to, they could explain, we could get the real story, clear up this whole mess—

"Boss, hear that?" Rucker murmured to Torres, and the squad paused. I held my breath, trying to hear.

Voices, too soft and distant to make out what they were saying. Torres gave hand signals; the others fanned out, stepping slowly. I stuck with Torres, clinging to the straps of my backpack to give my hands something to do.

The hill leveled out. Torres and the squad waited behind one set of trees, then moved up to the next, until we saw it: a village in a clearing next to a pond, a quaint storybook medieval setting. Little cottages had thatched roofs, and lush little garden plots lay between them, along with little fences and even a little old-fashioned windmill, the blades turning lazily.

It was all so *little*. At first I thought my perspective was just off, that we were still a long way away and some kind of forced perspective was playing tricks on me. But no, it was only a few dozen yards away and *really small.*

Then we saw the rabbit walk by.

It was wearing a calico dress and apron, and its ears stuck up out of a cute bonnet. It carried a basket full of greens. Another rabbit, this one in trousers and a tunic, was hoeing weeds around rows of lettuce almost as big as it was. A couple of hedgehogs, dressed in brown tunics with little belts and caps on their spiky heads, carried buckets of water down the lane and appeared to be having a conversation in a high-pitched, chittering language. A fox and a weasel were chopping sticks into little logs and piling them next to one of the houses. A badger in a vest and boots waved hello to a rat in a dress sweeping off a front stoop.

The indistinct voices we'd heard hadn't been far away; they hadn't been *human.*

The whole village was filled with medieval anthropomorphic animals just, like, living their lives? The place had a pleasant, bustling air to it.

The five of us stood mostly hidden behind trees and watched.

"That's . . . that's adorable," Almonte whispered.

Wendell shook his head. "But what's it *for?*"

"Boss. What *is* this?" Rucker asked.

"Don't know, don't care. We go around," Torres said, gesturing back the way we'd come.

"But they might tell us how to get to Tor Camylot," I said.

"Professor, do not talk to the rabbits."

"But Foxy Robin Hood," I murmured, searching the higher branches of trees around us. "Where is Foxy Robin Hood?" I was feeling startlingly conflicted now that the possibility of Foxy Robin Hood was in three dimensions. "They might be able to help, we just have to ask. Please."

"The fewer interactions we have with this BS, the happier I'll be. Odds are they'll report back to HQ and blow our cover," the captain whispered. He gave a couple more hand signals to the rest of the squad, who started backing carefully and quietly away.

This was stupid. This was medieval Richard Scarry—it wasn't dangerous. A game like this set up exactly these kinds of encounters to help the players.

So I left cover and marched straight toward the village.

"Professor!" Torres bit out in hushed anger.

I found a particularly small and adorable bipedal rabbit in a tunic, who looked like it was digging holes for a new fence. When it saw me, its big black eyes went round, and its long ears perked straight up. Leaning on its shovel, it rubbed a whisker and twitched its nose in a childlike gesture.

"Hi," I said, keeping my distance. It looked so real I had to remind myself that this was a computer operated by software and I just had to hit on the right algorithm to get it to help us. "My friends and I are lost, and I was wondering if you could tell me the fastest way to get to Tor Camylot?"

The little nose twitched.

"The castle in the middle of the island?" I pressed. "It can't be far. If you could just point—"

It let out a long sentence in its squeaky animal language. I had no idea what it was saying and my heart fell.

"I don't suppose you speak English at all?" I asked hopefully.

The rabbit looked past my shoulder. Torres and the squad had come up behind me, weapons in hand. The rabbit gasped, dropped the shovel, and ran back toward the main part of the village. It stopped next to the lady rabbit with the basket of greens. By this time, everyone in the village was aware of the strangers. A crowd had gathered. Not all of them had trembling ears and whiskers. Some of them, like the badger, had lips curling away from sharp teeth.

I tried again. "I'm sorry, I really don't mean to bother you. We're trying to get to Tor Camylot, and if any of you could point the way—"

Two dozen anthropomorphic critters stared back at me.

"We're just going to walk away now," Torres said. He took hold of my arm and pulled back. "Professor, come on."

The animals talked among themselves, and no matter how hard I listened, I couldn't make out any of it. The badger and the weasel gestured, little paws reaching toward us. Rabbits and mice conversed in clusters. I swore I saw a mole sipping from a cup of tea in the back. Then a tough-looking mouse in the front of the group—he had a leather shirt, a rakish cap, and held a sword—pointed at us and laughed. He spoke forcefully, appearing to chastise the others. But I kept looking at that sword. No bigger than a table knife. Everyone listened to him. Okay, maybe this was a little more *Redwall* than Richard Scarry.

The mouse gave a decisive nod, marched toward us, and stabbed Rucker in the foot.

The small blade didn't even penetrate the leather of his boot, but Rucker snarled. "Hey, you little fucker!" And he kicked the mouse, hard. Booted him so that he sailed in an arc clean over the village and smacked into the ground on the other side. The body let out a noise, like a squeaker toy deflating.

"Rucker, back off!" Torres hollered, just as Almonte yelled, "Rucker!" Wendell just shook his head.

"What, they're not even real! They're robots!" Rucker complained.

The rat woman with the broom buried her face against the shoulder of a fox man and appeared to be sobbing. A rabbit mother gathered six rabbit babies to her, hiding their faces in her skirt. The weasel, the badger—they just looked pissed off. Their whisker-twitching expressions of shock were shifting to rage.

"Captain," I said. "I think we need to get out of here."

"What can they possibly do—"

But the villagers were running now, scattering, shoving the children into houses and re-emerging with . . . spears. Helmets. Their chittering speech had turned into all-too-comprehensible shouts of defiance. The largest building, a sort of barn at the edge of the village, was open now, and the large door had swung open to reveal . . .

"Oh, look," I said. "It's an adorable rabbit-sized trebuchet." The badger and weasel worked with a couple of mice to roll out the siege weapon. It appeared to be loaded with stones.

"Captain . . ." I murmured.

"Yeah . . ." He gestured to the others. "Let's go."

Rucker didn't follow when we moved out. Scowling, he put his rifle to his shoulder. "Screw that, I can take care of these rats."

I screamed. Just screamed something primal and furious, and I put myself between the tiny village and Rucker's gun. Spread my arms as if I really could make myself a shield, as if his spray of bullets wouldn't cut me in half just as easily as it would turn all those innocent animals into mush.

Lots of swearing from the squad followed, shouts at Rucker and orders to stand down. Behind me, the animals were squeaking battle cries. And I was crying. Just crying, and I couldn't seem to catch my breath.

Rucker lowered his gun, at least. He glared at Torres. Glared at me. I wasn't sorry.

The rabbity trebuchet advanced, the animals around it angrily waving their weapons.

"Professor, let's *go!*" Almonte grabbed my arm and dragged.

Torres had Rucker by the back of his neck. Wendell brought up the rear, and we ran. The town full of critters charged after us.

Fortunately, our legs were a lot longer than theirs.

We ran past trees, down the hill, slipping and sliding until the yelling fell behind us. Torres kept us going a few minutes after that, putting more distance between us and the angry critters. Almonte was practically holding me up. My legs felt like bricks; they were moving out of panic, not because I was telling them to.

Finally, Torres called a halt, and Almonte had to drag me to a stop just like she'd had to drag me to keep going. I immediately collapsed, my legs folding up under me, and I slumped to the ground and pressed my face to my knees. My lungs hurt, and no matter how hard I gasped, I couldn't seem to get air. No matter how much I wiped the tears away, they kept coming. I could step outside myself and know this was shock, pure emotion bubbling over. That didn't mean I could stop it. The four members of the squad stood nearby, watching me like I was going to blow up. That didn't help at all. Breathe, breathe. Think of blue, think of water—

"What the fuck is wrong with her?" Rucker muttered.

"It's PTSD, you jackass," Torres shot back. Gently, like he was prodding a grenade, he turned to me. "Professor, how you doing?"

I finally drew a breath I could feel in my rib cage. "I just need a minute." To go through my calming exercises, I had to remember them first. Breathe, breathe, calm waters . . .

Almonte knelt nearby, but she didn't touch me. She'd probably seen this sort of thing before and waited until I straightened and was able to look around with semi-clear eyes.

My gaze fell on Rucker, his too-young face with his too-hard eyes. He held on to his gun, white-knuckled. "I couldn't let you hurt them," I said hoarsely.

He looked away.

Torres studied the sky, which was noticeably darker. Late afternoon; the sun would set soon. "This is taking too long," he said softly. Then he gave a decisive nod. "I want to get a little more space between us and rabbit town back there, but we'll stop for the night. Rest up, get our bearings in daylight, and wrap this up."

Rucker said, "Sir, we can press on through the night—"

"We stop."

I was slowing them down, just like we all knew I would.

10

I Attack the Darkness

few months after the shooting, I made the news, briefly. A feel-good, viral-for-one-second story about how I ran a fantasy RPG for some of the survivors. Most of the coverage was completely divorced from what had actually happened—it latched on to the gimmick, not the reasons the gimmick was necessary. *Look, isn't it neat how these kids use games to cope with trauma?* The stories had had quotes from psychologists who'd never even talked to me about how games can build community and help kids talk about their feelings and process what had happened and a few more nice phrases full of therapy jargon. And all that might have been true, but that wasn't why I started the club and ran the game.

It was escapism. Pure and simple. Games gave me a world that had rules and made sense, where violence had well-defined parameters, clear and specific reasons for happening. Where magic could save us.

This world that Lang had built . . . it had started to make me think I really could escape—if I knew the rules. If I knew the right questions to ask and could come up with the answers to the riddles. Find the button to press that would stop the monster. And then . . .

Torres studied me like I was another of the island's puzzles. What would break me next?

At sunset, we found a sheltered bit of forest, a stand of trees near some rocks at the side of a hill. The ground was soft, and the trees offered some shelter. Torres set a watch, just like in every D&D campaign I'd ever played, which made me want to laugh. You did it in games because if you didn't the DM would punish you with a random encounter. Here, it was real. The captain wanted to let Wendell off the rotation, but he complained, and they compromised: if he let Almonte stitch the wound the spider had given him, he could stand first watch. The engineer finally let her treat his arm properly.

I was not expected to stand watch, and I didn't complain. Not here, when I couldn't roll a Constitution check to stay awake. I was so tired; if I couldn't fall asleep, I would just stare out into the dark, not seeing anything. I touched the d20 in my pocket; rolling it would mean absolutely nothing here. We didn't build a fire, but we had more self-heating meals and some chemical hand warmers. I hugged mine close.

"We should look for water in the morning," Almonte told Torres.

"Put it on the list," he said, huddling with his back to a tree and closing his eyes. I couldn't tell if he was actually able to sleep. I'm pretty sure Rucker was already out, curled on his side, head pillowed on his arm. Nothing ever disturbed that man.

Almonte sat beside me and offered a small envelope. "This is presumptuous of me, but I brought something to help take the edge off, if you need it."

"I brought my own," I said, slipping my own envelope out of

my pack, shaking the Xanax pills inside. "I have a standing pre-scription, mostly to help me sleep. On bad days, you know? But I'm not sure I want to sleep here. I feel like . . . I don't know. I want to be ready."

"We won't let anything happen to you. You know that, right?" Almonte said.

"Yeah, but can you save me from myself?"

"Get some sleep, Professor."

"I'll try."

Some distance away, at the edge of the clearing where he had some line of sight, Wendell walked a slow and relaxed cir-cuit of our campsite. And, weirdly, that did make me feel bet-ter. Snugged up inside my coat, gripping hand warmers, I man-aged to fall asleep.

A crack woke me, and I sat up, my heart racing. My hindbrain recognized that sound before I was even awake. Gunshot.

The sky was gray; light and shadows seemed vague, and I couldn't see anything clearly. The shapes of trees were black cutouts, the sky was featureless. My breath fogged in the morning air.

The rest of the squad was missing. They'd left me behind, to continue on their own so they wouldn't have to deal with me. Well, no. Their packs and gear were still here.

"Got it!" That was Rucker, his tone gleeful. He must have finally gotten to shoot something. I slumped back against a rock, my breath blowing out of me. My nerves were Jell-O. I really needed to pee. Hugging myself, I got up to see what had happened. I found the squad not more than twenty yards out, gathered around something slumped on the ground. Wendell crouched beside it, shining his penlight over it.

Torres glanced over. "Morning, Professor."

"I heard a shot," I said blearily.

"Drone," Torres said. "Shot it out of the air. You okay?" What he meant: Was I freaking out? Was I going to have another meltdown?

I pulled my jacket tighter around me, but it didn't help. "I could really use a cup of tea."

"Come take a look at this, tell me what you think." They made space for me around their prize, which lay in a lump at their feet.

The morning light was playing tricks with me, obviously. I must not have been really awake. "It's a monkey," I said, deadpan. It had gray fur, a mashed-up face that seemed oddly human but also reptilian, with leathery wings lying limply behind it. And it seemed to be wearing . . . clothes? The flying monkey was wearing a red bellman's coat with gold trim, buttons, and a fez.

"It's creepy is what it is," Rucker said, scowling with distaste.

A giant hole had been ripped out of its side where the bullet went through. Wiring and rotors spilled out. "'Surrender Dorothy,'" I muttered.

Torres ordered, "Wendell, take that thing apart, I want to know who's spying on us."

Worried, I looked up at the sky. It was noticeably lighter; full dawn was upon us. No more flying monkeys appeared.

The engineer was already picking through parts, peeling back the fur to reveal mechanical innards. Just a machine, nothing biological about this. The basis of the creature turned out to be a quadrotor drone, the engines cleverly hidden behind the wings and haunches.

"I'm really grateful they didn't make this big enough to haul up a person," he observed.

"Wouldn't put it past them," Rucker said, watching the skies.

Wendell set aside broken rotors and a looped wire that might have been an antenna, and finally drew out a box with a round lens in the side. He handed it to Torres. "I think that's what you're looking for. The shot blew out the transmitter. Whoever sent this isn't watching us anymore."

"And who sent it?" Torres said.

Wendell said, "It has the same basic circuitry and engineering that was in those spiders. I suppose it could have been anyone on the staff."

"And where is the staff?" Torres searched past trees, like he might have seen them there lurking, laughing at us. "We've been here a full day. Chances are they know we're here."

"Then where are they?" Wendell asked. "Why don't they show themselves, if they're so innocent?"

"They're hiding," Almonte answered. "They're not going to trust us, Boss."

"And now they're spying on us." Torres shook his head. "Let's get a move on. We need to pick up the pace. Sorry, Professor."

"I'm fine," I said, sighing. "I don't even have blisters yet."

"That's the spirit."

Wendell packed away a few components of the monkey— the transmitter, the camera, a couple of circuit boards. Almonte hid the rest of the remains in the underbrush while Rucker and Torres stood watch.

If I'd been in any mood to enjoy it, this would have been beautiful. All at once, the murky gray dawn gave way to crisp morning. Mist clung to the treetops; glistening moisture dripped from the edges of leaves. Unseen birds called out, the notes mysterious and echoing. The hair on the back of my neck tingled. This was exactly the kind of forest where fairy tales happened, where Snow White fled from her wicked stepmother, where animals told you your fortune.

Breakfast was energy bars and the last of our water. I consoled myself that there would be hot tea once we reached Tor Camylot.

"Professor?" Rucker was behind me. Once again, the squad kept me in the middle of the marching order. The others shifted, taking turns at the back or babysitting me, with Torres staying in the lead. Having Rucker at my back made my shoulders bunch up and my spine twitch.

"Yeah?" I glanced at him over my shoulder.

"I wouldn't ever hurt you. I'm not like that. You get that, right?"

He might have been a trained soldier; he might have seen action all over the world. But right now he sounded like a kid, one of my students explaining why his essay was late.

"Are you trying to apologize?" I said.

"It's just . . . I wouldn't hurt you. I'm here to look after you."

"Sure," I said, focusing on the way in front of me.

"But—"

"Let it go, Rucker," Torres said.

"Yessir."

A chittering call made us all jump. The guns all went up. I hit the ground, my arms wrapped over my head. The call sounded like it came from above, among the branches over our heads. It rattled again; the squad searched for the origin.

"There." Almonte pointed to a low-hanging branch. A gray squirrel perched there, scolding us, its bushy tail twitching.

I waited for it to speak some grand pronouncement. Like "Go back! You're all doomed!"

It did not.

"Is that an actual squirrel?" Rucker asked. "Or is it gonna shoot us with laser eyes or something?"

We waited. The squirrel scolded again. Twitched its tail.

"I think it's just a squirrel. An actual squirrel, I mean," I said.

The squad finally believed it and eased up.

"I think I hate this place," Torres muttered.

We walked all morning and still didn't reach the edge of the forest. Didn't seem to get any closer to Tor Camylot. When the next drone attacked, we all heard it. The mechanical whine was distinct, and it came at us through the trees, staying hidden until it dived straight down.

This one was small, and it wasn't disguised as anything. Just a couple of rotors with a box hanging under it.

"Who's got it?" Torres called, and no one did, though they all aimed their rifles. It flew behind a branch, zoomed up the trunk of an adjacent tree, came back around, almost moving too fast to follow, and definitely too fast to target. Rucker gave a frustrated snarl.

Then it buzzed Rucker. Came straight toward him; he pulled his rifle to his chest and ran to evade. With an electric ping, something shot out of it. Rucker froze; he seized, every muscle in his body clenching. Teeth bared, eyes rolled back, he collapsed. The rifle dropped from his hands.

I dived for the shelter of a low branch.

Torres shot at the drone and missed—it zoomed away, straight up ten feet before hovering back toward the ground and zeroing in on the next target—Almonte. She raised her handgun and fired. Pieces came off the drone, and it plunged straight down. I flinched, hands over my ears. I hated that sound so much.

"Wendell, keep watch! Almonte—" She was already crouched by Rucker, checking him. Wendell scanned overhead.

"He's stunned, Boss," Almonte called after a moment of examining the soldier. "Looks like some kind of remote Taser device."

My heart was in my throat until Rucker groaned and tried to sit up, but only got as far as flapping his arms. "Wazzat?"

Almonte pressed on his shoulder to keep him lying still.

"Stun spell," I murmured. It was just like a stun spell. A little awkward and mechanical, but it worked. I listened hard for any more whining motors and searched the trees.

That was when I saw the stranger standing behind me.

He was in his late twenties, with a full lumberjack beard down to his chest and a wild look in his eyes. He wore rustic-looking garb, a tunic of green and brown, a liripipe hood that covered his shoulders and had a tail hanging down, breeches, boots of soft leather. Straight out of the Luttrell Psalter illuminations, fourteenth-century England.

My eyes went round, I choked on a breath. And then I ran.

I didn't get very far. Medieval guy grabbed me, lunging to cover the few feet between us and catching the edge of my jacket. I crashed to the ground, and in the next moment he was on top of me, knee in my back, pinning me. My heart seared with shock.

There was a lot of shouting as Torres and Almonte closed in on us. Wendell—Wendell was nowhere to be seen.

In a straightforward American accent at odds with his outfit, my captor shouted, "Stop! Everybody stop and put your hands up! Put down the guns!" He lay a knife to my neck. At least I assumed the very hard, straight thing pressing under my jaw was a knife. I couldn't see it. And I didn't question. I froze, trying to suck in breath through clenched teeth.

Torres and Almonte fanned out nearby. Rucker sat up, a hand to his head. Torres hissed at him, "Rucker, stay still." Wonder of wonders, the young soldier stayed still.

"I mean it, drop your guns!" the medieval guy ordered. His

breath came in gasps; he was panicking. I prayed, Please don't do anything stupid . . . I realized he had targeted me because I wasn't holding a gun. Because I was clearly the weakest one of the bunch.

"Are you real or some kind of construct?" Torres demanded. "A robot like the others?"

The guy froze a moment. "What? No, none of us are robots! You want *Westworld*? Because that's how you get *Westworld*—"

A crashing, struggling commotion sounded behind us. I didn't dare shift to look, but I didn't have to because soon enough Wendell dragged another medieval forester into the clearing and shoved him to the ground.

Wendell grinned. "Caught us a spy, Boss."

"Wendell, back off," Torres said calmly, nodding at my own personal drama. My forester kept the knife pressed to my skin, just off the edge. It didn't hurt, yet. Please, I urged silently. Nobody shoot. Nobody do anything stupid. Nobody die.

Wendell didn't holster his gun. "You're bluffing," he said to the guy who was about to slice me.

I focused on breathing. I could keep breathing. I had stared down the barrel of a gun before. I had survived worse than this, and I could survive now if I just kept breathing.

The knife shifted—my captor adjusting his grip.

We had wondered about whether the island's creatures, its constructed monsters like the Sphinx, could kill us. Whether they'd been programmed with fail-safes that would make accidents less likely, that made the island less dangerous. But this wasn't an artificial construct. This was a person, a thinking human, unpredictable. Through the slight trembling of the steel against my skin, I could tell he was shaking. He was scared.

A second drone dropped from the sky.

Wendell didn't hesitate; he aimed his handgun and fired several times. The drone blasted apart.

His captive took the opportunity to scramble to his feet and run. At the same time, my captor's grip loosened—for that split second, he was paying more attention to the others than he was to me. I shoved him, wrestling out from under him, pushing the knife away from my throat, not even caring if the blade cut me just as long as I could get away. I put my hands on the ground, about to stand and run, when the forester stabbed down. Drove the knife through the back of my right hand, pinning it to the ground.

I screamed. The blade stuck out of my hand like something out of a horror movie, nothing that should exist in the real world.

At that scream, everybody froze.

"Oh, shit!" the forester said, sitting back, hands lifted in surprise.

Blood pooled around the blade, a rivulet spilling to my wrist. I was too shocked to even feel it much. Breathing fast, trying to suck up air that wasn't there, I was going to throw up. I clamped my mouth shut. My other hand was shaking when it pulled the knife out, and the blood poured from the wound. I pulled my hand protectively to my chest.

Wendell pointed his gun at my former captor. The guy froze, hands in the air. He didn't look like a medieval forester anymore, but a guy in a costume, afraid.

Torres shouted, "Professor!"

I whimpered. Assessed. I was alive. But my hand blazed with pain, and I was still gasping for breath.

"Oh my God, I am so, so sorry," the hapless forester said. His face had gone pasty. "I didn't mean to do that."

"Then why the hell did you hold a knife on me!" I shouted, my voice grating. My hand throbbed. Blood covered *everything*.

"I knew he was bluffing," Wendell muttered, disgusted. Almonte was now covering Wendell's forester with her weapon, and Wendell came over, grabbed this one's arms, and started handcuffing them behind his back.

He had handcuffs? I didn't know the squad had brought handcuffs.

"Boss, company," Rucker announced tiredly.

"Stop. Let him go," another voice called through the trees.

More commotion, and another shared flinch passed through the group as several more rustic-garbed folk entered the clearing. They blended into the trees surprisingly well and seemed to emerge from bark and foliage, perfectly at home here. They had bows and arrows drawn and pointed at Torres and the squad.

The squad held guns pointed back. Even Rucker, who was still on the ground, shaking from the tasing, had recovered his rifle. And I was in the middle of it all, clutching my wounded hand and hyperventilating.

"Stop it!" I burst out between gasps. "Just everybody stop being stupid and nobody gets hurt! Nobody *else* gets hurt!"

Almonte looked at me. "Professor. Breathe."

I did, and let out a shuddering sigh.

Torres lowered his gun first. That surprised me. Maybe he really was just that confident. He might have had enough levels of Monk that he could catch arrows. "Who are you?" he asked.

One of the newcomers stood a little ahead of the others. He lowered his bow, easing the tension on the string. He had a green tunic, a feathered cap. Among those flanking him, one carried a staff, another had a red cap and red sash around his tunic. Putting them all together, they made a picture.

Robin Hood.

An Errol Flynn curl to his lip, he said, "I'm the one telling you to let my men go."

"Robin Hood" seemed to be in his thirties. A few laugh lines touched the corners of his lips and eyes. I recognized him as one of the personnel from Lang's files, but he had a full beard now, and a tired look. I couldn't remember his name. His *real* name.

Torres gave his squad a look. Didn't even need to say anything, and they all lowered their guns. Even Rucker, though he scowled. The foresters kept their bows ready.

"We lowered ours," Torres said. "Now you."

"Not until you tell me who you are and where you came from."

"No. You've already hurt one of us. No more," Torres said.

"I totally didn't mean to do that," my former captor said to what must have been his boss, like he had to explain himself to this guy instead of me. He seemed to be right on the edge of hyperventilating, too, and all that had happened to him was getting handcuffed.

"Craig, settle down," Robin Hood said.

Craig? The hapless forester was named Craig? Not William or Edmund or . . . or Much the Miller's son?

"I said I was sorry!" said Craig the Hapless.

I whimpered again. My hand was still bleeding. I got dizzy looking at it.

"Almonte, go," Torres said. She slung her gun over her shoulder and brought her kit over to me.

That seemed to release some kind of spell. The foresters lowered their bows and replaced arrows in the quivers at their backs and belts. Wendell and Rucker holstered their guns; Rucker had gotten to his feet, and if he still felt wobbly, he didn't show it. Craig was still in handcuffs, but he seemed to be the only one bothered by that.

"Addie, you have to let me see it," Almonte said. I clutched my hand to my chest like it was glued there. Moving it would hurt.

I managed to kneel, trying to cradle my hand while Almonte

gently pried it away. "I'm okay," I said, weak and unconvincingly. I wasn't okay *at all*. I was about to pass out.

"You're going into shock," Almonte said, finally getting my hand loose and pressing gauze to it, front and back. "Breathe slower. That's it."

Breathe, right. I wasn't breathing. I sucked in a lungful of air.

Robin Hood finally got a look at me and the blood smeared all over my jacket. His eyes widened. "God, Craig, what did you do?"

"I don't know, she just moved, and I didn't think!"

"He *stabbed* her," Almonte said flatly.

"I'm sorry, I'm sorry!" Craig really did seem about to cry, his face scrunched up in anguish. I wanted very badly to kick him.

"You're not helping. Be quiet," Robin Hood ordered, and Craig shut up.

"Who the hell are you people?" Torres demanded again.

"I might ask you that question," Robin Hood said. "Let me guess: Special forces? SEALs?"

"Independent contractors," Torres said flatly.

"That really hurts," I choked out when Almonte started wrapping the bandage with tape.

She passed me a pill and a canteen. "Take this. Ibuprofen."

Torres said, "I'm guessing you sent those drones?" He nodded at the wreckage.

"Just trying to level the field a bit," Robin Hood answered. "How the hell did you get on the island? Nothing's gotten through for months."

"*We* did," Wendell said, leering, and giving Craig a nudge with his boot. Not quite a kick, but close.

"Ow!" Craig said, glaring.

"Let's start over," Torres said. "Who are you?"

"It's Robin Hood," I murmured. "And the Merry Men. Merry People, I mean." Because yes, there were two women in Robin Hood's company, also wearing tunics and hoods in green and brown. One had short hair, another a long braid over her shoulder.

Torres gave me a look like he thought I was joking. "I'm not calling that clown Robin Hood."

Robin Hood flashed that smile again. "I don't need you to. But now it's your turn: What are you doing here? Since you're not supposed to be here at all."

Torres said, "That's right."

Wendell's former prisoner, the guy in the red cap, spoke in a low voice to Robin, "Beckett's gonna go ballistic when he hears about these guys."

Arthur Beckett. The island's lead project manager.

Torres said to the leader, "You work for Beckett? You can take me to him? Weapons stay holstered. We don't want to hurt anyone."

Robin Hood's earlier charm was a put-on. His jaw tightened, and the suspicion he'd been masking leaked through. He had to know that Torres and his squad could take them all out, even if more Taser drones arrived. The only reason they hadn't — Torres didn't want to.

One of the women standing guard behind Robin Hood said, "Art's going to want to talk to them."

"Yes. I know," he replied. To Torres he said, "Let Craig go and I'll take you to Beckett."

Torres thought for a moment, then nodded at Wendell. Reluctantly, Wendell unsnapped the cuffs. Craig scrambled away to take his place with his fellow Merry People. The two squads continued glaring at each other, but at least the weapons were stowed.

Almonte finished with my hand and helped me to my feet. She gave me a wet wipe from the first-aid kit to try to clean up the blood. I was a mess.

"Professor?" Torres asked.

This wasn't a game. Torres had kept saying that, and I kept arguing that it was. But he was right, those bows and arrows were real, Craig's knife was real. It wasn't a game—but did the production team on the island know that? *Really* know it?

"I'll be okay," I said. He nodded, satisfied.

"Just a second, Captain," Rucker said. "Something I need to do first."

He walked over to Craig the Hapless and punched him in the face.

11

Speak Friend

C raig fell over and writhed around, complaining loudly, hands pressed to his face like it was going to fall off. Funny thing—nobody got after Rucker for punching him. Torres gave the soldier an annoyed look, but that was it. When Craig finally pulled himself together, he had the start of a big bruise over his eye, and his lips puckered like he was trying really hard not to cry. After that, I tried not to look at him at all.

Robin Hood's company flanked us on either side while still keeping their distance, trying to look like they had us under guard. Pure illusion, since Torres and company still had their rifles over their shoulders and handguns in holsters. They led us in a more westerly direction than we'd been going, until the land flattened out and the trees thinned. A creek ran through a series of lush, grassy glades. Everything here was so idyllic, so beautiful. It was almost enough to distract me from the bandage around my throbbing hand and the blood on my jacket.

"How you feeling?" Almonte asked Rucker.

"That was bullshit," he muttered. "You ever been tased? This was worse."

Wendell craned around to ask Robin Hood, "What's the battery life on those things? Can you get more than one shot out of them?"

One of the others started to answer, "We're not really sure, we haven't—"

"We're not telling you anything," Robin Hood said curtly. "Not until we know who you are."

"Let's talk to Beckett," Torres said.

I studied the Merry People, trying to get a read on them. Were they capable of mutiny? Did they look like they were getting what they wanted, or more like they were in over their heads? Mostly, they looked tired. Eyes shadowed, shoulders slouching. They cast suspicious glances at us. And curious ones, too. We looked so out of place among them, like we'd landed from a different world. A different game.

Torres stayed near me. I discovered I was grateful for it. Him, I knew.

"You all right?" he asked softly.

"Yes. I mean no. I got stabbed."

"If you need Almonte to look at it again—"

"I'll be fine." Yes, it hurt and, yes, blood had started to seep through the bandage. But I didn't want to talk about it. I wanted to rest. I wanted a cup of tea. I wanted to know what was going to happen next. We were supposed to be at the castle by now.

Dominic wasn't among the Merry People, but I didn't expect him to be. Rustic Ranger wasn't his style. I resisted asking any of them if they knew where he was. I didn't want to let on that I knew him.

"What are you going to say to Beckett?" I asked.

"I'm going to ask him a lot of questions."

"If he's the one behind the mutiny, he could . . . I don't know. Just get rid of us all. Right?"

"They're not going to just get rid of us," he said. He sounded so confident. But I guessed if anyone could tell killers from not-killers, he could.

I'd only ever faced the one.

Torres moved off and took up a position walking near Robin Hood's shoulder, in his blind spot. The forester had to keep looking back to keep Torres in sight, and it left him off-balance.

"How did you know we were here?" Torres asked. "You monitoring the whole island, or did we trigger something?"

"I'm not talking until I know who you work for," he said.

"Was it the Sphinx?" Torres continued, pressing. "When we answered the riddle, did that trigger some kind of alarm? Or the spiders in the maze?"

"Oh my God, you saw the spiders?" another of the band asked excitedly, and Hood made an angry shushing gesture.

So it wasn't the spiders that had done it.

"Something triggered an alarm," Torres said. "You sent out the flying monkey drone to investigate—"

"What flying monkey drone?" Hood said, flustered, his brow furrowed.

"Well, shit," Rucker muttered under his breath.

Hood, Beckett, their people—they'd sent the stunners but not the flying monkey. Then who had?

"We'll talk to Beckett. He'll sort this out," Hood said, scowling, and marched off.

Almonte raised her brow at Torres, who murmured, "We've got factions. Interesting." His grin suggested he was looking forward to untangling the mess. Or just slashing his way straight through it. That seemed more in character.

One of the other Merry People, a young guy with very non-medieval glasses and a shaved head, sidled up to us and asked, "You saw the Sphinx? How was it? I mean—did it look good? Was it cool?"

Rucker rolled his eyes and cursed. Torres chuckled. "Not as cool as you might think, when you're sure the thing's about to kill you."

The guy seemed taken aback. "Oh, it wouldn't really have killed you. Everything's got safety protocols."

"Are you sure about that?" Torres asked.

"You want to tell him about the spiders or should I?" Almonte asked Torres.

"What about them? They're programmed to just keep people away from the exit, and the deactivation switch shouldn't have been too hard—"

"Oh, we found the switches," Torres said. "Ask Wendell about the safety protocols."

Wendell helpfully pointed out the bloodstains on his jacket.

"Oh, jeez," the guy said. "It's the legs, isn't it? The metallic legs. I knew they were too—"

"Don't forget about the people," I said tiredly. "You're out here with live steel and bows and arrows—the people don't have safety protocols."

"Well, this isn't part of the game, this is for—" He shut his mouth, as if he didn't want to explain what this was for. Clearly, it was for whatever was going on right now.

I didn't like it.

"You ask me, the whole island ought to be set fire to and sunk," Rucker said.

The guy looked hurt, then angry, the emotions twisting up his face and making him seem even younger. "Hey—"

"The riddle was too easy," I said to him, by way of interruption.

"What?"

"The Sphinx. It was too predictable."

His brow furrowed unhappily. "Oh. Well, we didn't want to make it too hard."

"I could tell. It might have been an easy obstacle to overcome, but that doesn't make for very satisfying game play."

"They probably didn't expect to get too many PhDs through here, Professor," Torres said.

"That wasn't a PhD-level riddle. Any ten-year-old with a mythology obsession or who'd read up on Camp Half-Blood would have gotten it."

"Rob," the guy called ahead to Hood. Wait, was his name really Rob? Or were they just that intent on maintaining character? "Rob, we should think about difficulty levels. They're right, different players will need different challenges based on their experience—"

"I'm not really thinking about game dev right now, to be honest," Robin Hood answered. Then I caught him muttering under his breath, "We'll be lucky if we get out of this with no jail time."

I glanced around and, yes, Almonte had caught that line, too. She met my gaze, and her frown was serious.

"PhD in what?" one of the other Merry People asked.

"Literature," I said.

Hood turned to me. "You're not a soldier like them? Then what are you doing here?"

I grinned. "I'm the Bard."

Craig the Hapless sidled up to us. I flinched; he didn't notice. He didn't even notice Torres and Rucker glaring daggers at him. When he talked to Hood, he was just a little too loud. "I think they're secret beta testers. I think Lang sent them to check on the work—try a few of the encounters, test out some of the tech."

"Shut up, Craig," Hood spat back, his voice low. "We are so

far past play testing and development memos, and . . . I don't even know where we are anymore."

"Robin Hood," Torres said. "Who started the mutiny?"

I had never seen a man look so unhappy. Like he was sucking lemons spiked with ghost peppers. "I'm not telling you anything. Not until you prove who you're working for." He bit off the words.

"Then the sooner we see Beckett the better." Torres's gaze gleamed, like he had cornered prey and was enjoying it.

Everybody stopped talking after that.

This bunch of middle-management types should have been uncomfortable in the roles they were playing, tromping through the great outdoors, not a smartphone in sight. They should have been fidgeting with their hats and tunics, awkwardly getting their bows caught on tree branches, itchy and tired and complaining of too much time in the wilderness. You know, like me.

But they weren't. They'd been living here for months, and they were comfortable. They stepped lightly and moved around trees with casual grace. They worked together, giving each other silent signals and nodding in understanding without speaking a word. They were at home in the woods. These weren't costumes and roles they were playing. They were here because they wanted to be. This was who they were. Not a game.

Eventually the trail widened and the trees thinned, opening to a clearing. The sound of voices traveled, along with the smell of smoky cook fires. Up ahead, a handful of buildings clustered, one- and two-story timber-frame cottages lining the path. Some of the windows even had flower boxes hanging from them, dripping with petunias. This I recognized from the marketing materials. This had been one of the first sites developed on the island. There were people dressed in generic medieval garb and doing ordinary tasks like carrying buckets and feeding the chickens that were scratching and pecking in one of the yards. If this were actually a game, I'd say we needed to look for the guy selling healing potions.

The only things ruining the image were the cluster of antennae sprouting from the roof of the largest building, and the series of solar panels that had been worked into the thatch of some of the cottages.

"This looks like a Renaissance Faire," Rucker said unhappily. For some reason, the idea that he had actually been to a Ren Faire surprised me.

"Bring on the turkey legs," I muttered. My injured hand had turned the corner from pain into a worrying numbness. I clutched it to my chest.

We walked up the dirt street like villains in a Western. Villagers stared. Set down the buckets they were carrying, stopped hoeing their garden and fixing the thatch on a roof. The ringing of hammer on metal ceased as a blacksmith paused at his forge. An actual blacksmith, an actual forge. No, not villagers, I reminded myself. These were Lang Analytics employees. Possibly mutineers. Whatever they were, they stared, expressions a mix of guarded and confused.

We must have looked impressively rough. The men's faces were unshaven, shadowed. Almonte's close-cropped dark hair was neat, but mine was a nest of tangles. Our fatigues were spattered with dirt and mud, and two of us were smeared with blood. We'd come from the field and we'd Seen Things. We might as well have been Black Riders entering the Shire.

In the middle of the village, on a stone plinth carved with grape leaves, stood a statue. A life-size man wearing a tabard over chain mail, gazing solemnly up the road. He held a sword, point down. I had to circle around and get closer to see the face . . . and, yes: Harris Lang, with his clean-shaven face and sharp features.

Pointing at it, I looked at Robin Hood. "Are the statues of Lang his idea or yours?"

"That wasn't us," Hood muttered, his face pursed in a sour expression. So not everyone who worked for Lang was awestruck by him. "The design team put those in. I'd have preferred something a little more St. George."

The design team was Dominic's.

"That's some grade-A ass-kissing right there," Torres observed.

"The rest of us have just been trying to do our jobs," Hood insisted.

Lowering my voice, I said to Torres, "Would Dominic mutiny if he liked Lang enough to put statues of him up all over the island?"

"You tell me," he said.

I didn't know.

"This way," Robin Hood said, guiding us to the large building with the antennae.

"You're self-sufficient here?" Torres asked, noting the chickens, the woman drawing water from a nearby well. The well had a round wall, waist high, built of weathered gray stones and topped with a quaint wooden frame and roof, with a winch, rope, and bucket. It looked just like I imagined a medieval European well would look, straight out of fairy tales. This wasn't about being efficient; it was about aesthetics.

"Does the well grant wishes?" I said.

"Beckett will tell you what you need to know," Hood said.

What were they hiding? No, scratch that—what made them so paranoid?

I could wander here all day. The thatch on the roofs was perfect, the little flower beds and herb gardens—they seemed mature, like they'd been growing here for a couple of years. It was all so clean, so pretty—and that was the real fantasy, wasn't it?

A robust waste disposal plan and well-maintained roads made all the difference.

One cottage had the prettiest flower box sitting under a window with painted shutters on either side, and . . .

I gasped and ran up to it, and to a serene black cat lying on the sill, framed by flowers, like this was some kind of storefront. The cat met my gaze and blinked, and what if it wasn't a cat? This was part of the quest, it had to be—

"Torres!" I called back over my shoulder. "Do you have any loose change on you? Does anybody?"

The captain watched me nervously. He was probably getting really annoyed with me wandering off every time I saw something shiny. But this was *important*.

I didn't expect anyone to say yes, but I had to try. I hadn't even brought ID to the island, much less cash, why did I expect anyone else to have any? "Coins! I need coins!"

The cat looked sleepily back at me, with half-lidded eyes.

The nearby door opened and a woman with a kerchief tying back her dark hair emerged. Saw me, saw the cat, and smiled wryly.

"Miss Eglantine doesn't have wares, even if you have coins," she said. "She's friendly if you want to pet her."

I winced. "So . . . Miss Eglantine is just a cat. An actual real cat and not a cyborg."

"You've been traveling around the Island, haven't you?"

"Uh, yeah." I offered my hand to Miss Eglantine, who tilted her head and let me scratch behind her ears. Warm, furry, entirely alive. "Sorry about that."

"Who are you?" the woman asked confusedly.

I shrugged. "That's classified. Sorry." Sheepishly, I rejoined the others.

The large building across the village square was something like a Viking longhouse, two stories tall, a steeply sloped roof, wings branching off to the back, making it hard to tell just how big it really was. It had a painted wooden sign hanging from an iron rod over the front door—a classic tavern sign, artificially weathered. It showed a picture of a fierce gryphon rampant, claws up, roaring through a beaked mouth. Gothic lettering read: *The Gryphon's Head.*

Robin Hood opened the door and stood aside. "After you, honored guests." We filed past him.

Just inside the doorway, I stopped to stare.

I was standing in a generic medieval fantasy tavern. Every tavern in every fantasy novel and game looked exactly like this. A dark wooden bar stretched along the left-hand side of the room, and rustic tables and chairs were arranged before a great stone fireplace. Pale beeswax candles in an iron chandelier offered light, but on second look the flames were really flashing LEDs. Because the designers weren't completely out of their minds and knew that open flame and thatched roofs together rarely ended well. There were pewter beer steins and wooden trenchers, the smell of hops and baking bread. All that was missing was a tavern wench with her boobs bursting over the top of her tightly cinched bodice.

A large stuffed head of a blue-feathered gryphon hung above the fireplace. It looked so real—the pale yellow eagle's bill gleamed in the light, glass eyes shone gold, and the feathers sweeping down its head were soft and silky. I wanted to run my hands over it. It didn't look like a prop—it looked like they'd really made a gryphon, then killed it and stuffed its head.

Sitting in the corner near the fireplace, leaning back in a chair, a figure sat with his arms crossed, a wool hood pulled low over his face, disguising his features. But he clearly watched us, appraising. He looked like he was about to offer a job to our adventuring party.

I laughed. Hysterically, uncontrollably, bandaged hand

covering my mouth. Everyone except the hooded man in the corner frowned at me. Torres and his squad spread through the room like they were ready to mount some secret attack I didn't know about; the Merry People grouped by a wall and re-arranged their grips on staves and bows. And me in the middle, just losing it. Robin Hood must have signaled ahead, to set up this scene.

"I'm sorry," I gasped. "It's just . . . I don't know . . . I don't think I can take much more of this. I mean, you—" I pointed at the man in the corner. "You, what do we call you? Strider? Or cut the bullshit and go straight to Aragorn?"

He pulled back the hood. He was middle-aged, with brown skin and short dark hair, streaks by his temples going gray. He studied me in a way that made me stop laughing with a gasp.

"Arthur will be fine," he said.

For a lurching moment, I believed. Arthur, King of the Britons. I hiccupped, scrubbed a tear from my cheek, and blushed, embarrassed that I believed.

Torres said, "Arthur Beckett. Harris Lang's been worried about you."

Arthur Beckett, chief administrator for the entire island. His mouth opened wonderingly. "Harris sent you?" Breaking into a wry smile, he ran a tired hand over his hair. "The messengers of the gods arrive at last."

I snorted laughter again. My eyes were leaking tears, and not just because my hand hurt. I was so damned tired.

Arthur seemed tired as well. "Sorry if that sounds dramatic, but this place rewards people who recognize good stories."

"Yeah," I said in a small voice. "I know. Welcome to Quest-land."

"You're hurt," Arthur said, coming over to study the bandage on my hand, now stained red across the back.

"One of your Merry Men over there stabbed her," Torres said. Craig had the decency to stare at his feet and blush.

"Oh *no*. Here, sit down. Someone get some water. Katie, you want to get the medical kit?" Arthur guided me to a chair, which I melted into. One of the foresters went behind the bar, where I heard water run from a tap—so, not totally medieval rustic around here. One of the women ran through a door in back.

Torres watched all this, scrutinizing. Assessing. Trusting, for now. Searching for a reason not to. We, his squad, waited for a signal from him. What was our next step?

And how did I feel that among King Arthur's and Robin Hood's people, I was clearly part of Torres's team? I hadn't felt like it before now.

"Arthur, can we trust them?" Hood asked. He'd taken up a guard-like position by the door. Several of his people stood around the room—one near each of the squad members. As if they could actually do something against the soldiers. "How do we know they're really working for Lang?"

"One thing at a time," Arthur said.

The woman, Katie, brought in a box from the next room. A nice fairy-tale-type treasure cask, wood with iron hinges and fittings. Beckett opened it to reveal a series of corked jars—a medieval-looking apothecary. Classic D&D healing potions. I wanted to laugh again, to keep myself from falling any further out of reality.

When he uncorked one of the bottles and scooped out a lump of leafy mush, I pulled away. Almonte and Torres both strode forward, ready to push him back. Everyone in the room flinched as if they expected a fight to break out.

"It's okay," Beckett said. "This'll help, I promise." He raised his brow, as if to ask permission.

What could it hurt? I'd already been stabbed through the

hand. I unwrapped the bandage, now stiff and sticky with clot-ted blood. Underneath it, the wound was still oozing, and it turned my stomach. Gently, Arthur held my hand and started packing the wet, green mush onto the wound, front and back.

In moments, my hand hurt less. The throbbing faded. I must have looked astonished. Almonte asked, "Professor?"

"It's better," I said, my voice creaking. "Healing herbs?"

Arthur smiled. "It looks like an herb for the sake of appear-ances. It's actually a mixture of antibiotics, clotting agents, and an epidermal regenerative solution. Oh, and a topical pain-killer. All-purpose first-aid ointment. Or healing herbs, if you prefer. Can you move your fingers?"

The swelling had kept me from wanting to move at all, but now I tried—and was relieved that, yes, my fingers moved.

Almonte approached and took my hand, studying it. Arthur explained, "The knife seems to have slipped past the bone and tendons. It'll probably be stiff for a while. But you're lucky." He left the healing mixture in place and wrapped a fresh bandage loosely around the wound.

"Could I maybe get some of that?" Wendell said, nodding at his shoulder.

"You got stabbed, too?" Arthur said, raising a brow.

"Giant spider," Wendell said.

"I want to hear that story," Arthur said. Wendell took off his jacket and unwrapped his bandage, and Arthur applied the salve on the still-bruised stitches. "You're the island's first play-ers, and we have a forty percent injury rate? We're going to need to work on that—"

"We're not players," Torres and I said at the same time. I glared at the soldier, and he smirked back.

"Right," Beckett said, noting the guns, the weapons, the professionally watchful stances. "You have proof Harris sent you?"

Torres unzipped his jacket and produced what looked like a USB drive, a little longer than his thumb. He handed it over.

"You've seen this?" Beckett asked, gesturing with the drive.

"No. It's keyed to your thumbprint," Torres answered.

Beckett set the drive on the table and pressed his thumb on a depression in the plastic. The round glass circle on the end of it that I thought was decorative turned out to be a projecting lens, and with a crackle of static, a beam of light fanned out against the wall and showed Harris Lang's face, about a foot high, smiling out at us like a benevolent overlord. A whisper passed through the gathering, murmurs of recognition, of hope.

"Help me, Obi-Wan Kenobi!" someone in the back said with a chortle, and Arthur glared.

The image spoke. "Arthur. I hope all is well. Though probably not as well as we would like. This is Captain Octavio Torres and his team. I request that you give them any and all assistance you can. I'm sure this has been a misunderstanding and we'll get it cleared up in no time. I'll see you soon."

Arthur nodded. "Captain Torres," he said. "Welcome to Insula Mirabilis."

Torres nodded. "I'd like to leave for Tor Camylot within the hour. I could use some help finding the way."

Arthur Beckett ignored him, which I thought was a bit daring of him. Instead he looked at me, noting the lack of weapons. "You're not a soldier. Professor . . . ?"

Torres shook his head ever so slightly. So no, he didn't want to give that information up just yet. I asked the question that still hadn't been answered. "What's been happening here? Lang wasn't sure if anyone was still loyal to him."

"My team is loyal," Arthur said firmly.

Torres didn't seem convinced. He said, "Then you'll help us get to Tor Camylot and reboot the control center."

"Yes, absolutely," Arthur said, standing. A man more than ready to head into battle. "Lang gave you the codes, then?"

Torres looked blankly at him.

Arthur explained, "We figured that must have been what took him so long to send help. He needed to program override codes for the control center."

"Mr. Beckett," Torres started impatiently. "Lang has been out of contact with the island for five months. He has no idea what's going on here. He hired us to break in and do a hard reboot from the inside. There are no codes."

The project manager seemed to go boneless and sank into the nearest seat. He ran a hand over a face that seemed to age as we watched. "That's it, then. We're skunked."

Torres said, "Sir, you get us to the castle, we'll take care of the rest."

Arthur looked at him. Chuckled. "You think it'll be that easy?"

"Are you going to help us or not?"

"Mr. Beckett," I said, because the tension had spiked, and there was something happening here I didn't understand. Something that we were missing. "What aren't you telling us?"

He said, "To do what you want, I would have to control Tor Camylot. And I don't."

"Then who does?" Torres asked.

Arthur spread his hands and gave a tired laugh. "I don't know."

12

Bag of Holding

Torres loomed over the seated Arthur, who didn't seem at all bothered by the difference in stances. Like he was past caring.

"You've just been sitting here on your ass for five months, waiting for Lang to come rescue you?" Torres said. He hadn't lost his temper yet, but I suddenly wondered what it would look like when he did.

Arthur shook his head. "You don't understand the situation here—"

"Then explain it to me. From the beginning."

"The beginning is six years of interpersonal drama in a Silicon Valley pressure cooker," Beckett said. "You want all that, too?"

Torres nearly snarled. "Start with when the energy shield went up. You lost contact with Lang Analytics. When did you realize something had gone wrong?"

"The force field wasn't in the specs. That was probably the first problem. I knew the design team was working on some kind of energy repulsion, but not anything on that scale. They were talking flying carpets! Then suddenly we lost communications, GPS—"

"How could you not know what they were working on?" Torres said with admirable calm.

"Part of what Lang wanted with Mirabilis—it's not just a resort. He set the whole thing up as an accelerated R&D lab. He encouraged engineers and designers to experiment. Come up with their own devices, algorithms. Their own magic. We'd have meetings once a month to show off what we'd done and give a thumbs-up or thumbs-down. Like some kind of wizard academy. If something got incorporated into the island's overall design, there'd be a bonus. It's a huge incentive. Not just the bonus, but seeing your work be part of the story. I don't know if you can understand that."

I could. I totally understood. They weren't just following a corporate directive—they all had some intellectual ownership in what was happening here. That . . . that could be powerful.

Arthur went on, "And if an idea led to a patent that could be marketed commercially, that made it an even bigger deal. So it's not surprising that there was tech being developed that I didn't know about. Lang didn't just excuse people for going over my head—he encouraged it. It's *him* people had to impress."

"You're the lead project manager," Almonte said, disbelieving. "You should know what's going on with your project."

"There was a lot of incentive to keep things secret until the monthly meeting. Easier to make a big reveal that way."

Torres said, "That means Lang didn't even know—"

Almonte pressed. "Who developed the energy shield? Who actually gave the order to activate it?"

"And when did you know that the shield had gone up?" Torres added. "When did you realize you'd been cut off?"

Arthur looked back and forth between them, his brow furrowed, his expression screwed up. He gestured toward the bar, and a woman there began lining up beer mugs. "I could use a drink. What about you all?"

Torres glared. "Beckett. Talk."

He sighed, as if he'd hoped to have that beer in hand first. "About a week after the April development meeting. I could check my calendar for the exact date. We'd been on the island for almost a year by that time, building and establishing atmosphere, starting to work on game play. I didn't think anything was wrong. Nothing seemed out of the ordinary. We had arguments and personality clashes, but we always did. And then . . . it just happened."

"I take it you weren't actually at Tor Camylot at the time."

"No, my team was all here. We were working on setting up some of the remote encounters. I think that must have been part of the plan. I have a question for you. Why are you here now? What happened that Lang sent you now?"

The answering pause was heavy.

I was the one who explained. "A Coast Guard cutter came to investigate and crashed into the force field. The crew died." My tiny injury was nothing compared to that.

"Jesus," one of the others in the room murmured. A gasp, some rustling. We were messengers of the gods, indeed, pronouncing doom.

"I'm sorry," Beckett said. What else could he say? "It's got to be either Tess or Dominic who's behind this. I would never—"

"And where are they?" Almonte asked. Torres threw her a glare; this was his interrogation.

"I don't know. Probably in their own HQs. I don't know who was at Tor Camylot when the comms went down."

I almost asked about Dominic. His name was on the tip of my tongue, but Torres was on a tear.

"I don't care who controls Tor Camylot," the captain said. "My job is to get there, get inside, and shut it down. Just show me an accurate map and we'll be on our way."

"It's not that easy," Beckett said. "The castle—it's the centerpiece of the whole island. The boss level. You can't just walk in; you have to solve it. It's full of puzzles, challenges. I'm certain whoever activated the shield also triggered the castle's defenses. And if the safety protocols are off . . ." He shrugged as if to say he couldn't be responsible.

Torres looked around the tavern's front room, assessing. Always assessing. I sighed tiredly because this probably meant I wasn't going to be able to sit still—on a real chair, even—for much longer.

"I want to see your office," Torres said finally. "Your production files, notes. Everything."

"I can't just—"

"I've signed all Lang's NDAs, and I need to see anything that will help me get into Tor Camylot. Are you going to help, or do I get to tell Harris Lang that I suspect your motives?"

"Fine," Beckett said coldly.

"Wendell, Professor, with me." Torres gestured toward the doorway in the back of the hall.

"Now, wait a minute—" Beckett got to his feet, and the whole room tensed with him, Robin Hood and his folk coming to attention. Almonte and Rucker ended up in the middle of the room, looking out. Standing guard for Torres, who just smirked at it all like it was beneath him.

"You heard Lang," Torres said. "All I need is your cooperation."

If Beckett said the word, right now, his people would fight. I didn't doubt it. I looked for doors, for exits. For a table to hide under. Katie behind the bar had paused, a mug under a keg's spout mid-pour, her eyes wide.

"You heard Lang, folks," Arthur said finally. "We're cooper-ating."

His people didn't relax, but they didn't go for their weap-ons, either.

Wendell and I followed Torres; Almonte and Rucker waited behind, casual-like. They didn't seem to mind that they were outnumbered, as if that detail was irrelevant. They had the high-level stats, after all.

Through the door, a wooden staircase led up. Arthur Beckett was right on our heels. "I don't think you'll find anything that can help," he explained.

"I'm looking anyway."

"It's to the left," Arthur said, when Torres reached the top of the stairs and looked back and forth down a hallway lined with tapestries, iron sconces placed between them.

"This is beautiful," I said, murmuring at the artwork, ceil-ing-to-floor replicas of medieval tapestries showing hunting and feasting scenes. Light from clerestory windows shone down, giving the air a hazy, golden light. Construction dust, I told myself.

"Glad you like it," Arthur said. "You should see what we've done out at—"

"Is this it?" Torres said, knocking on a door at the end of the hall. It was made of some dark wood, carved with a tree, roots reaching down and branches reaching up, mirroring each other. The handle and hinges were equally intricate. The detail was astonishing.

Torres pushed open the door.

The office was almost entirely mundane. Almost. The desk was an antique with weight and heft. The laptop and scattered papers on it ruined the effect. It needed an inkwell, quill pens. An Oxford don in his robes writing something in Latin . . .

Torres and Wendell started pawing through the papers and schematics, and Arthur looked like he wanted to scream. His cheeks puffed up as his jaw clenched, and he crossed his arms.

I studied the walls. A large painting of the island on what looked like parchment hung on one wall. The different regions —the three weapon-themed realms—were clearly marked, outlined in their designated colors, stamped with their symbolic weapons. This village was in the Realm of Sword.

This version matched the maps we'd gotten from Lang. But then, Beckett's information might not have been accurate anymore, either. Did any of these boundaries mean anything in real life?

Off the northwest corner of the island, among stylized ocean waves, neat calligraphy read: *Here Be Dragons*.

"Are there really dragons?" I asked Arthur.

"European and Asian," he said proudly. I let out a sigh of wonder. I wanted to see dragons.

Another tapestry hung on one of the other walls and, above it, a replica of Excalibur was displayed. The one from the Boorman film, with its clean lines and aura of importance. Even in the natural lighting of the room, it seemed to produce its own lens flare.

I pushed back the tapestry, because you always push back the tapestry in a room like this, and revealed the square, gray-colored face of a totally mundane safe with a digital lock. Again, the contrast of mundanity in the middle of the well-crafted immersive fantasy jarred me. Hard to find my footing when the genres kept mixing.

"What's in the safe?" I asked.

Torres looked up, interested.

"Nothing important," Arthur said, trying a little too hard to sound disinterested. "Just odds and ends."

"If it's not important, why do you need a safe?" Torres pressed. Beckett didn't have an answer for that, and Torres said, "Show me."

Arthur looked like he might argue. Then, shaking his head in what seemed a dispirited moment, he went to the safe. I tried to get the lock code by looking over his shoulder, but he shifted just so, and I wasn't tall enough to look past him. I gave Torres a little shrug, and he smiled his wry "I can kill him with my bare hands" smile.

The door to the safe popped open, and Arthur stepped aside. Eagerly, I looked in.

Empty. It was . . . no, not totally empty. I reached in and pulled out a piece of clear plastic in the shape of an equilateral triangle, about the size of my palm. The more I looked at it, though, the more intriguing the object became. It seemed to glow with its own light. The edges had a golden tinge when I held it one way; reddish, when I held it to sunlight.

"What is it?" Wendell asked, stepping toward it, his curiosity plain.

"'It's dangerous to go alone,'" I murmured.

"Data storage," Arthur said. "There's hidden fiber-optic circuitry, invisible to the naked eye—"

"I don't think I want to know how it works," I said. "It's beautiful. If it's data storage, there must be a place to plug it in, or it's the key that unlocks something. This might bypass the obstacles at the castle—"

"It's a prototype," Arthur said defensively. "It doesn't do anything."

I might have let out a little disappointed sigh.

"But you have it locked up," Torres observed.

"For safekeeping."

I pocketed the piece, just because. Met Arthur's gaze squarely, daring him to call me on it and make me give it back.

He didn't. I almost asked him about the ring I'd found in the pillar at the entrance of the spider maze. But suddenly, I didn't want him to know I had it. It was still in my pocket, along with the glowing triangle and my lucky d20.

Surely I'd be able to do something with all this.

"Boss, here," Wendell said, riffling through papers on the desk. He unrolled a long sheet that had a map of the island. A more practical, detailed one than the stylized medieval version on the wall.

"This up to date?" Torres asked Arthur.

"As far as I know—"

"Which hasn't been very far, but okay," Torres muttered, rolling up the map, tucking it under his arm. "We'll make do. Anything else you two want to look at?"

"I'd love to take the whole hard drive," Wendell said, nodding at the computer. "But probably not feasible."

"Everything," I said, sighing. "I want to look at everything."

"Back downstairs. We'll study this, get some rest, and move out in an hour. I want to get to the castle by nightfall."

This corridor had other doors. At the other end, another staircase led down into a different part of the tavern complex. What else was here? Was this just for food and lodging, or was it part of the game? A stop on the quest?

"Professor?" Torres's tone of command was getting irritating. He and the others were already on the staircase back to the main hall, and I was still studying tapestries.

"Yeah, okay." Reluctantly, I followed.

13

Half as Well as You Deserve

At least let us feed you before you go," Arthur said as we left the staircase, returning to the tavern's main room. "A real home-cooked meal."

Food that looked like food and hadn't been inadequately warmed by chemicals? Oh, yes, please. And some of that beer, which I was betting was home brewed by people who knew what they were doing. These guys had probably started the beer before they even laid the foundation for the tavern.

Torres seemed reluctant to agree. Easy way to kill a bunch of ex–special forces mercenaries—put something nefarious in the stew. Except these people just didn't seem capable of it. If Torres looked at me wanting my opinion, he got it. My eyes were wide with begging, *Oh please oh please* . . .

"Fine," he muttered.

"Katie, do we have something we can get started for lunch?"

"Yes, give me half an hour or so," she said. A couple of others joined her through a doorway. A kitchen, presumably.

Meanwhile, Arthur helped himself to a full mug of beer on the bar. He sighed like he really needed a drink right about now.

"Would you like one? We make it ourselves."

Called it . . . "I could really use a cup of tea, if you have some."

He shook his head. "Not really period for the setting. Sorry."

"Period police will be the undoing of us all," I muttered.

"Almonte, Beckett, come help me with this." Torres spread his map out on a table, holding down the curled edges with nearby candlesticks. This was so . . . surreal. Appropriate.

This map was on a grid and had scale. We'd walked . . . miles. Not as many as it felt like. We'd done some circling. The spider maze was marked. So was the animal village and the tower of the Sphinx. None of them had been on our map. I searched for this village, and then found Tor Camylot, right in the middle.

"We're not that far," I said wonderingly. A few miles? We really could get there by nightfall.

"Yeah, but there's some rough terrain between here and there," Torres said. "Beckett, is that a trail?" He pointed to a dotted line that curved around terrain markings and offered a clear path between village and castle.

"That's the one. It's just a couple hours on foot. We've got some ATVs that'll get you there a little faster."

"We go on foot, overland. We assume marked trails are being watched."

"Monkey drone," Almonte agreed.

"Monkey drone?" Arthur asked.

"Robin Hood over there says it wasn't yours," Torres said. "We're being watched, and I don't want anyone waiting for us at the castle. So show me a good unmarked route from here to there." The pair bent over the map, discussing.

Meanwhile, the rich smell of wine-soaked roasted meat, spices, and garlic filled the place, along with the yeasty smell of beer. It was an actual adventuring tavern meal, right in front of me. My stomach suddenly felt empty.

"Oh man, that smells good," Rucker murmured. "Boss, can I have a beer?"

"No. Now show me where Selvachan and Brand are based."

Arthur pointed. "Before the blackout, Selvachan and her team were using a cave system in the Realm of Shield, here. Brand has his camp in the forests of the Realm of Arrow, here."

Dominic. Was the drone his? Had he gotten pictures? Did he know I was here, and if so, what did he think of that?

I sat down at the next table over. Word had gotten out about our being here, and more people filed in, coming to ogle the newcomers. Twenty or so of the rustic-dressed forester types, along with women in peasant shifts and bodices, kerchiefs over their hair, and at last the expected barmaid with lots of cleavage appeared. I could never get cleavage like that in my Ren Faire days, not even when I stuffed socks down my bodice. Torres and the squad looked them over. Yeah, just like in any fantasy adventure quest, it was real clear who the suspicious characters were.

We were a sudden wrinkle in this perfect medieval fantasy they'd created. The people who could either save them . . . or bring the whole edifice down in flaming ruins.

"Professor?" Almonte sat across from me. The map conference seemed to be over. Wendell rolled it up and tucked it into his pack. "How's your hand?"

"Huh?" I looked up, startled. I'd drifted off. Shook myself back awake. Studied the bandage, which was clean, though still oozing some of the green healing herbs. I was able to flex my fingers. "Surprisingly okay? I'm sorry I got myself stabbed—"

"That so wasn't your fault," Almonte said.

"Yeah."

"You're not a damsel in distress, if that's what you're worried about. Look, Professor—these people will listen to you before they'll listen to any of us."

I chuckled. "I can't think why—"

"You're one of them. They see that. We might be able to use that."

"Lunch is served!" Katie called from the bar, setting out a pile of wooden bowls and an actual cauldron with a ladle sticking out of it. Several loaves of bread came out as well. It all looked and smelled so good. I had that sense of displacement again. This felt so familiar . . . but it shouldn't have been. It was so *comfortable*. Like I'd done it all before. I supposed I had . . . or I'd pretended I had. Until now.

Someone put a log in the fireplace—the fire had been banked, and with new fuel the embers came back to life. Everyone collected food, found seats. Sounds of normal conversation rose up. Beckett went from table to table, talking with everyone, checking in. He ate his own meal at the bar, talking to Katie.

At our table, the four soldiers in fatigues sat tense, shoulders hunched, gazes watchful. They had stacked their rifles against the wall, next to Rucker, where no one else could get to them.

"Who does that dude think he is?" Rucker asked Torres, nodding at Beckett.

"He's Arthur," I answered for him. "King of the Britons."

Rucker huffed. "There's only one King in my book, and he's buried in Memphis."

I sighed at him. "Do you not have any sense of the profound at all?"

Torres grinned. "Rucker here is pure grunt, through and through."

"Yessir," he said proudly.

I was in the wrong story, for sure.

One of the foresters brought out a lute—an actual lute, not a guitar—and started playing old folk songs, familiar pieces that were part of the repertoire of any Ren Faire minstrel: "Wild Rover," "Whiskey in the Jar." And then he launched into "Her Sweet Kiss" from *The Witcher*. More than a few sang along.

For a moment, it seemed real. No, it *was* real. If I could just let go of everything else, the corporate politics and the rifles and my exhaustion—it would be real. But being part of all this —it was just out of reach. My eyes teared up, and not because of smoke from the fire.

"This is really good," Rucker said between bites, shoveling in beef stew like he was starving.

"It's good because it's *real*," I said. Torres gave me a look. He sat with his back to the wall, like he expected enemies to crawl up from between the cracks in the floorboards. His eyes shone in the firelight. A Ranger of the North. "What's wrong?" I asked.

"I gotta tell you. I've spent the night around a Taliban campfire, and this is making me more nervous."

This was *lovely*. Except for the part where the island was trying to kill us. "How so?"

He had to think about it, hand to chin, absently scratching at his stubble, and after a moment he said, "I don't know what motivates these people. I don't know why they're here. Is it the money? The power? Corporate loyalty usually doesn't make people take on a whole new life like this. You notice they haven't asked for any news? They've been cut off from the mainland for months, and it's like they don't even care."

I obviously saw something different, looking over the same gathering. But when I tried to explain it, when I tried to find a concise way to make him understand why people would put on wool tunics and sing at the fireplace of a fake-medieval tavern, I couldn't, really. You either got it or you didn't. I was more than comfortable here. I was happy. *You're one of them*, Almonte said. It was that obvious.

"It's love," I said. "It's just . . . love."

If anything, he frowned harder. "People will take a bullet for love. When they won't take one for anything else, they'll do it for love."

Yes. Yes, they would. I frowned and stared into my bowl. "Nobody *takes* a bullet. Bullets get delivered. Bullets get forced on people."

Torres ducked his gaze.

The lutist set down his instrument. The party broke up, people heading back out to their chores or whatever people in replica medieval villages did. Torres was right; they didn't seem at all worried that they'd been out of touch for months.

"How are you doing, really?" Torres asked. He turned a smile on me—a genuine smile, maybe the first I'd seen from him. Not a smile to impart confidence to his team or a badass smile to intimidate his enemies. I noticed he wasn't a young man. Not old, but he had creases at his eyes and weathering on his skin. It made him look like he knew what he was doing.

"I'm tired. Last couple of days have brought back some bad memories. But we expected that, didn't we?"

"I'm sorry," he said, and of all the people who'd said that to me over the years, he likely had the most understanding of what he was expressing sympathy for. "I really did hope we could avoid that."

"Thanks," I said.

"What's that about bad memories?" Arthur said, coming over to join us. He stood by my chair, a proud host showing off what he'd created. And why shouldn't he be proud? I had absolutely no idea what to say to him. Torres's expression was sad.

Bad memories, right. I should have said it was nothing, let the whole thing go. But the bandage on my hand made me angry.

"You remember the West Lake school shooting about fifteen years back?"

He had to think about it for a minute, sort out exactly which school shooting that was until the memory dawned. "Was that the one where the guy went through the lunchroom shouting that God made him do it?"

"I was there," I said bluntly. "Looked him right in the eye before he shot himself. I was seventeen." Alex and Dora, Alex and Dora. I wished I could tell them about this place. They'd have loved it.

"Oh my God," Arthur said softly, like people always did when they found out. They didn't mean to; it just came out. It was why I usually didn't tell people at all. "I'm sorry," he said. He sounded shocked and embarrassed—sorry for what had happened, but more than that, sorry for bringing it up. Not at all like when Torres had used the phrase.

"Yeah. I kind of don't like guns," I said.

He glanced at the rest of the squad. "And yet you agreed to play wizard for these guys?"

"I'm not the wizard. I'm the Bard."

"We'll see about that."

Torres pushed back from the table. "Wrap it up, folks. Time to move."

I collected the bowls, tucking them in my arm—my injured hand was still stiff—and brought them to the kitchen, where Katie and a couple of others were cleaning up.

"This was great, thank you," I said. "Can I help wash up or something? You've been doing all this work."

"Oh no, it's fine. You're guests!" Her smile seemed eager, genuine. She was here because she liked cooking for people.

"More like invaders. But thanks. Can I ask a question?"

"Sure."

"Why are you here? I mean in a general sense—how'd you come to work for Lang Analytics on this project?"

She paused, wiping her hands on a linen cloth and leaning up against a big tin washbasin. "I was already working for Lang Analytics in accounting. The call came through HR for a special project, and when I saw what it was, I jumped at it. Once in a lifetime, you know? I don't even have any particular skills they needed, except I do a lot of reenactment as a hobby. I'm the practical side of things, I guess. I could tell them what to actually put in the garden." She grinned, as if reminiscing. Those must have been some fun meetings.

"Not to mention the bookkeeping on a place like this must be amazing," I said. What had all this cost, anyway?

"'Spare no expense,'" Katie quoted, rolling her eyes a little.

I glanced out to the door to the main room. Torres and company were collecting gear, getting ready to head out. This . . . I wasn't ready to go. I wanted more beef stew and lute music. I'd only seen a fraction of the building.

I got an idea. "One more question—where's the privy?"

She gestured. "Out the back, at the end of the cobbled walkway. Can't miss it."

"Thanks." I ducked out.

I found the back doorway she'd pointed me to, and then the cobbled path and the quaint latrine building—so the plumbing hadn't gotten that far, and I wondered how popular the island would be with tourists if there weren't any flush toilets. But that wasn't where I went. Instead, I went back into the building by a different door, the first one I came to that was unlocked. I just wanted to see what else was here.

The plain wooden hall I found myself in ended in a doorway in one direction—from the sounds I was hearing, people talking and chairs scraping, my guess was this led to the common room. Next to this doorway, a set of stairs went up to Arthur's office. In the other direction, another set of stairs going down.

I went down.

This led to a simple corridor. Another flight of stairs went down, to a level that must have been belowground. Did this place seem bigger on the inside than it did on the outside?

At the foot of the stairs, a tapestry hung on the wall. I pushed it aside, to reveal a doorway. This room was mundane, with modern drywall and lighting. I flipped a regular modern switch to turn the lights on. It looked like a historic reenactor's dream warehouse. Replicas of suits of armor from all over the world, from classic European plate armor to Japanese samurai armor with lacquer plates, a rack of swords in a dozen different styles, another rack of spears, shelves of helms, shields piled against a wall.

I studied a spear tip, touched it lightly. Sharp. Everything here was sharp.

Decoration, I told myself. It was just decoration. No one was going to be using these.

A dozen tapestries lay piled on a table. A dozen chairs sat shoved in a corner, all in different styles but all of them ornate and antique-looking.

Around the corner from the storage room was a simple hallway lined with closed doors. The place was quiet. I tried the knobs of three or four of them; all locked. If I'd had to guess, I'd say these were crew quarters, employee rooms. I stepped as softly as I could, heading toward what now caught my attention: a set of double doors at the end, with faux medieval iron handles. Once there, I pulled. Not locked, so I went in.

This room had an LED torch in a sconce by the door that lit up when I stepped in. Motion activated, like the torch in the spider maze. The floor was wood; the paneled walls were bare. The room was empty except for a large antique wardrobe shoved up against the back wall. It looked scuffed and worn, as if had been moved around a lot. The edging was decorated with scrollwork and stylized leaves, and the handles were brass and looped like vines. They invited you to take hold with both hands and *pull* . . .

"Oh my gosh," I murmured, approaching. I couldn't not.

"Professor!" Torres's stern voice called.

I glanced over my shoulder. The captain had followed me and now stood framed in the doorway. I must have been gone just a little too long. I bit my lip, and my heart raced.

"Professor, don't you dare!"

The look on my face must have been full of longing and defiance. No, I would not stop.

Flushing, I threw open the wardrobe doors and plunged inside.

The wardrobe was full of coats, which was exactly right. I heard bootsteps—Torres, running across the floor after me. I kept going, shoving fur and felt out of the way, elbowing through, despairing that I would come crashing up against the back of the wardrobe at any moment—

This wardrobe had no back. The wall behind it, gone. And I could see light.

At last, I stumbled into the open. The back of the wardrobe dropped a foot or two, and I lurched out, catching myself from falling at the last moment. Gasping a little, I looked around.

I stood in a wide space with a high ceiling and steel walls with multiple windows. Stacks of lumber ran along one wall; a table saw and drill press stood against another, along with tool chests containing power tools, hammers, handsaws, and plastic bins full of nails and screws. The air smelled of musty sawdust, like the workshop had been idle for a couple of months.

Behind me, Torres stumbled out of the wardrobe, took a look around, and sighed with what sounded like relief. "You know, for just a split second there, I was worried Lang's people had invented teleportation and that you would end up on the other side of the island."

No such luck. "I guess I should have expected this," I said. "If you're already in Narnia and you find a wardrobe, where do you end up when you step through?"

"The hardware store?" he asked. "Professor, do I need to worry about you going native on me?" He sounded amused, making the question a joke. But not really.

I pursed my lips and thought about it. "I don't know."

He huffed. "At least you're honest."

"I love so much about what they've done here. But there's something . . . off about all this. It's a game, but it's not. If it's a game . . . who's running it? Who's the game master? And what's the game's ethos? Is the idea for everyone to have a good time, or to put everyone through the wringer? To make it hard? I've met GMs who weren't happy if they didn't kill at least a couple characters over the course of the campaign. Is that the game we're in? I can't tell."

He said, "Whoever launched the mutiny is controlling everything. Aren't they?"

Softly, I said, "I just . . . don't like playing in games where I haven't met the GM first."

"We need to get going. We'll figure this out soon and be done with it."

He pushed aside the rack of coats and gestured me back through the wardrobe.

"You know, Mr. Tumnus would have had tea for me," I said.

He raised a brow. "I've actually read that book. You can't trust Mr. Tumnus."

"Well, no. But still."

14

>>>———→

Cast Fireball

The road in front of the tavern became the staging area for the squad's departure. Robin Hood, several more foresters, and Arthur Beckett were gearing up for the journey as well.

"I'd rather you didn't come along," Torres told Beckett. "We'll get this taken care of faster on our own." Read: he didn't want Lang's staff looking over his shoulder.

"I'm not letting you break into my castle without me," Arthur said.

"As we've already established, it isn't your castle."

"I'm still coming."

"Fine."

Beckett was starting to sound like he was whining. "Look, I'm sure you're highly trained and competent . . . but I keep telling you, getting into Tor Camylot isn't going to be easy. Why don't we stay here while we come up with a tech solution? My guys can work with your guy—"

Torres shouldered his pack and rifle. "We don't have time to wait."

"We've been waiting for months. Another few days isn't going to make a difference."

"Yes, it will," Torres explained. "We already know we're being watched. There was the flying monkey drone this morning, and the . . . Professor, what did you call them?"

"Wargs," I said. I was standing by the statue of Harris Lang, my own pack over my shoulder, waiting. The statue seemed new—the stone was smooth, unweathered. In fact, it might not have been stone at all but some kind of molded resin. "We saw riders on two Wargs yesterday, back in the valley with the unicorns. Does it seem like its eyes are following you? Does anyone else see that?" I paced one way, then the other. It was probably my imagination. Lang's all-seeing gaze wasn't actually a thing. I hoped. I flexed my injured hand to keep it from getting stiff. Arthur had given me a pocket-sized jar of the healing herbs to take with me, and a short wool cloak to replace my bloodied jacket. I looked like some weird hybrid character.

"Wargs?" said Craig the Hapless, whose black eye had turned a really spectacular reddish purple. "Oh wow, Tess got the Wargs working?"

Arthur winced. "Actually, we can't call them Wargs because of trademark issues. We call them boarsts."

I tilted my head. "Boarsts? Boar and beast?"

"Something like that." He didn't sound happy.

"That's . . . hmm." I didn't want to come out and call it stupid, but . . . well. I backed up, paced at an angle—yep, the statue's gaze still seemed to be following me. Shivering, I turned away and did my best to ignore it.

"I tried to convince Lang to spring for licensing fees on some of the best-known properties, but that's the one place he wouldn't spend money. He wanted it to be all original."

"He wanted it to be *his*," Robin Hood added, glaring.

"So no Wargs, no Shire—"

One of the others chimed in, "No King's Landing or Alliance versus Horde—"

"Or Aretuza or Fire Nation," said another.

"No Hogwarts," pouted a third, a woman in her thirties. "I mean, we can have a wizard school, the concept of a school for wizards isn't trademarked, but—"

"Alice wanted to knit house scarves for everyone," Robin said.

She sighed. "I know this Realm of Sword and Realm of Shield thing is supposed to be cool—and it will be when we get the logos done and the merchandise out there. But it just isn't the same." Eagerly she added, "I still think we should make wands with Bluetooth remotes embedded in them—"

"We're walking a fine line here," Arthur said apologetically.

A little of the shine went out of the whole thing, thinking of the gift shops. "How about I just keep calling them Wargs and you can sue me later."

"So those were Selvachan's people we saw?" Torres asked, with admirable patience.

Craig and a couple of the others had moved closer. "What were they like? Were they AI—self-motivated? Or controller operated? How big were they? People were riding them, you said? Did they see you? Did they smell you? The original specs had olfactory tracking—"

Arthur waved them down. "The engineering department had the specs for the Wargs when we lost control of the island. So yes, they were probably from Tess."

"And Dominic wouldn't be caught dead riding a Warg," I said.

Arthur's gaze narrowed. "You know Dominic?" And once

again, everyone was staring at me. I didn't like it; it made me self-conscious.

"It was a long time ago," I said, slouching, as if I could back out of the conversation. I shouldn't have said anything.

"Mr. Beckett, this is Professor Adrienne Cox," Torres said, saving me from having to backpedal.

"Call me Addie," I said tiredly. "Hi."

"Wait a minute," he said. All the talk of Wargs and killer spiders, he hadn't looked this astonished. "Addie Cox? You're the Addie Cox Dominic talks about all the time?"

Why did that give me a sinking feeling in the pit of my stomach? "Surely he doesn't talk about me *all* the time . . ."

Arthur continued, "It's why Lang sent you, isn't it? You're not the Bard, you're the bait!"

Yeah, that was what I was afraid of. I squared my shoulders and tried to salvage my dignity. "And I can say the inscription on the Ring of Power in the Dark Tongue of Mordor. It's a pretty specialized skill set."

"Yeah, I guess so. I think the only other person on the island that hard-core is Dominic."

"Who do you think taught it to me?"

Torres asked Arthur, "Do you think Selvachan and Brand are working together?"

Clearly frustrated, Beckett shrugged. "I just don't know— I wouldn't have thought so. They don't get along. Brand's design team kept coming up with wilder and wilder projects, and the engineering team was fed up with it. But . . . who knows. I wouldn't have thought any of this was possible. We were all reporting straight to Harris, and Harris said everything was on track."

Torres's gaze narrowed. "Then you only had Lang's word for it."

And Lang had convinced himself everything was *just fine*.

Robin Hood put in, "When Mr. Lang says something, you learn not to question it. Anyone who questioned him openly was canned pretty early on."

The creeping realization over the last twenty-four hours that we couldn't trust any of the files Lang had given us landed with crushing finality. We were on our own. The whole squad looked like they wanted to collectively break something.

"Good to know," Torres said. "Now let's go. Keep up or don't."

We hadn't gone far outside the village when Torres and Arthur stopped abruptly and the rest of us piled up behind. For a long moment, they stared. I edged up alongside, just as the crowd of knee-high anthropomorphic animals—upright, wearing armor, carrying adorable tiny weapons—clustered on the path ahead let out a chittering, furious roar.

"Oh, fuck me," Rucker said.

"Well, then," Arthur said, his brow arched. "Whatever did you do to anger the folk of Furstershire?"

"Furstershire?" I glared.

A volley of tiny arrows sailed up from the crowd and rained down about ten feet off from us.

Torres rubbed his forehead. "We don't have time for this."

Arthur pulled out what looked like a mundane smartphone from his belt pouch. He apparently had an app for this. He touched a sequence on the screen, and the animal army simply froze. Mid–sword swing, bows half-raised, paws drawing arrows from quivers, other paws raised in defiance. Their righteous battle just . . . ended. Now they were a diorama, an impressive display of artistry and nothing more.

"That hardly seems fair," I said. A little sadly. Part of me believed that whatever algorithm was driving the creatures might have let them win and avenge their fallen comrade.

"Let's go," Torres said. We left the trail and the Furstershire army behind.

For future reference: a party of a dozen people couldn't really stay silent and stealthy while walking through the woods. No matter how quietly we each tried to move individually, or how little any of us spoke, all those sounds added up, shushing past trees and scuffing through grass. Not even birds stuck around, much less unicorns, gryphons, or anything else.

Torres assigned a new marching order with Rucker and Wendell taking point, Almonte following, himself in the middle looking after me and keeping an eye on Arthur. The foresters who'd come with us had their own marching order, spread out among the trees, walking with staves, bows, and quivers over their shoulders. Only a couple of Arthur's people had any military experience, and even those guys weren't inclined to listen to the stranger. Torres's carefully planned walking order didn't mean much, and he scowled.

Arthur said it would take three hours of easy walking to reach Tor Camylot. Torres chafed at this — on its own, his squad could probably cover the ground in half that time.

Arthur looked like a king, and once again I couldn't tell if he was playing a part or if he had this job because he was just like that. While everyone else wore simple wool hoods and tunics in solid browns and greens, Arthur wore a leather doublet and a black cloak held in place by a gold penannular broach with a large red gem on the pin and intricate design work on the ring. It probably matched something from a real Anglo-Saxon treasure hoard. He didn't wear a crown, but he held his head high, chin up, as if the crown he wore was simply invisible. His people deferred to him, and he greeted them all by name and had

kind words for them. They loved it. I understood why. Because
this was part of the fantasy: It wasn't necessarily to *be* Robin
Hood or King Arthur. It was to be part of their companies. To
follow them. To be judged worthy enough to follow them.

"Can I ask you a question, Arthur?" I said finally. "What's
your title in the SCA?"

Robin Hood snorted, a suppressed laugh. Arthur himself
looked a bit sheepish.

"Duke," he said. That meant he had won at least two crown
tournaments and served as king of an entire region. At least,
king within the context of those particular rules. I wondered:
Was playing King of Mirabilis more or less satisfying?

"Hmm, very nice," I said.

"And what's yours?" he threw back.

"Baroness of the Court, thank you very much."

"Your Excellency," he said, offering a truncated bow.

"Your Grace," I answered.

Torres gave us a look and shook his head. Rucker muttered
something under his breath that was probably an expletive.

I didn't have any of my garb or coronet or anything that
would have made me feel a part of this. Rather, besides being injured and tired, I felt ratty and underdressed. A hapless
monk, part of the bishop's train just as Robin Hood came along
to rob it. Because if we didn't trust King Arthur and Robin
Hood, what did that make us? The Sheriff of Nottingham's
men? Mordred?

We followed a trickling stream down gentle slopes into
glades filled with wildflowers. Craggy outcrops of granite stood
like castle walls. The air smelled earthy and rich, damp with a
recent rain. Exactly the kind of forest where you might expect
a guardian knight to step out from among the trees, or fairies
to throw sparks across a still pond.

Fairies. I looked really, really hard for fairies, for glints of light and color in the shadows, but if they were there, they must have been well hidden.

"Arthur," I asked, on an impulse. "Are there fairies here? Or fairy lights? This seems like a good place for it."

"Not yet, but it's on the list," he said, winking.

The stream led us down the next hill, the forest thinned behind us, and the sky opened up over a wide meadow. The path went past a stone pillar with a banner flying from a pole at the top: red, marking the Realm of Sword. The mood of the company shifted; Arthur and his people became palpably more nervous, glancing over their shoulders, clustering closer together. Even though this was artificial, all make-believe, it meant something to them: they were out of their home territory now.

We startled a deer that had come in to drink at the stream —a real deer, Arthur assured me. The island had a functional ecosystem, and one of their mandates had been to affect the local environment as little as possible. They hadn't gotten far enough along to see how they were doing with that.

Cutting through grassy fields, checking the maps and Arthur's memory, we hiked up a hill. The harder my heart worked, the more my hand throbbed. Almonte offered me another painkiller right before I'd gotten up the courage to ask her for one. Apparently I was looking pale.

Arthur stopped us at the top of the rise. "There it is," he said proudly.

In the distance, across more grassy plain and the edge of another forest, stood a castle: Tor Camylot. A tall gray tower, round and topped by a leaded conical roof, was hemmed in by a wall with crenellated ramparts. This was modeled on the big hulking edifices built to claim a frontier, with a moat, thick walls, and brooding atmosphere. It also had a big dose of Disney, a fairy tale in the height and slimness of the tower, the inviting landscape around it. This was the Ur-castle, the Platonic ideal of castle that children drew when they dreamed of princesses and knights in armor. Arthur should have been holding court there. I imagined a grand hall, wide and airy, with solid ceiling beams and silk banners hanging from them, rush-strewn floors and trestle tables, and roast pig carried in on platters. The only things ruining the picture were a series of solar panels along one side of the ramparts and a cluster of thin antennae mounted on the tower. They were partially disguised as a flagpole, but the illusion wasn't perfect. Realities kept creeping into the designs.

No banner flew from the tower, and even from this far, the place had a desolate, abandoned air.

The stream flowed into a moat that in turn fed a small lake on the castle's far side. Lac du Lancelot, according to the map, and I wanted to slap whoever came up with that one. A few white spots flashed around one of the towers, wheeled, then skimmed over the water. Seagulls in flight, gleaming in the sun.

"Like something out of a dream," I murmured, not realizing I'd said it out loud until Arthur answered.

"Straight out of legend," he said proudly.

"Or Monty Python," I said, blinking the stars out of my eyes. *The whim of a multibillion-dollar CEO is no basis for a system of government* . . . "Anyone going to be flinging cows at us?" Probably not, *Holy Grail* had never been one of Dom's favorites.

Torres pulled binoculars from his pack and studied the scene. "Where's the entrance? How is it secured?"

"The gate and portcullis are on the east side," Arthur said. "The gate has a code, unless it's been changed."

"And what's the code?"

Arthur pressed his lips into a line, and Torres looked like he was going to grab the guy by the collar and shake him. Finally Arthur said, "It's 'One Ring to Rule Them All,' no spaces, last letter in each word capitalized."

"Well, it's easy to remember, anyway," Wendell said.

"That's a terrible password," I said.

He spread his arms. "It wasn't like I thought anyone was going to be breaking in!"

"Boss." Almonte touched Torres's arm and pointed up. Following their gazes, blinking to focus against the glare of sky, I only caught a flash of movement. The dip of a wing, and then the object zoomed off, high and away, out of sight.

"Was that a crow?" Wendell asked.

"Too big."

"Raven," I murmured, flashing on the shape of black feathers and a tail streaking away.

Almonte said, "Bird's not that fast or stable."

I said, "Ravens are messengers. Omens. Magic."

"So that wasn't really a bird," Wendell said.

"Another drone, then," Torres said.

Beckett shook his head. "The specs for those hadn't been implemented five months ago—"

"But raven-shaped surveillance drones, someone on this island has them, yes?" Torres's glare would flay skin.

I thought Arthur was about to say he didn't know again, in which case I might just yell at him myself. But the project manager said, "Yes."

"That's more Dom's style than flying monkeys," I added.

"So now we can assume everyone knows we're here." Torres put away his binoculars. Almost as an afterthought he turned to me and said more softly, more reasonably, "Are you okay? Can you keep up?"

Like I was the baby of the group and needed to be coddled. Well, I sort of did. "I'll try," I said, which won me another of his wry smiles. I suspected the "I'll try" got me more mileage than an uncertain "Yes" full of false bravado would have. I took a long drink from my canteen and prepared to suffer. "Captain. Um, sir. We need to keep an eye out for traps. For . . . I don't know what. Like at the spider maze. We don't know what all's here, and Beckett clearly doesn't, either. So just . . . you know . . . make your Perception checks."

"Yeah." He and the rest of the squad exchanged nods, part of their secret silent language. Almonte's expression was grim as she studied the landscape with a practiced gaze. Rucker leered, like he was looking forward to taking down whatever jumped us next.

Moving out to the plain before the castle, the pleasant, bubbling creek widened, enough to cut a gulch in the landscape, grassy hills giving way to rocky walls. Trees lined the rim, and weathered boulders had tumbled down in places, making the way difficult but spectacular.

Landscape like this would be the perfect place to mount an ambush. An enemy would just have to sit on the edge of the rim and rain down arrows, and we'd be stuck, caught among rocks and river.

The only better time to ambush us than in the gulch would be catching us shortly after we came out of it.

"Torres—" I started, worried.

"Yeah, I know. How far does this go?" Torres asked Arthur.

"Not far. This leads to a field, and then we'll be just half a mile from Tor Camylot."

Not far now. Then I could sit down. Surely the castle had tea.

Beyond the gulch, the hills flattened. In the afternoon light, the gleaming plain was painted gold. Tor Camylot's tower rose like a beacon. There must have been such a view from the top of it.

The path to the castle widened at a sort of crossroads, intersecting with another path that appeared to loop around the castle. In the middle of this clearing stood a stone plinth. The statue that must have once stood on the plinth lay on the ground, broken into a dozen or so pieces. The face—masculine, wearing a crown—was shattered.

"Another statue of Lang?" I said. The features were unrecognizable, but I was willing to bet.

"Somebody around here really hates that guy," Wendell observed. He kicked at one of the pieces. I braced for some kind of booby trap to spring, but nothing happened.

Then someone screamed.

Short, sharp, it came from one of Arthur's people, who were strung out behind us along the grassy plain. Torres and the squad immediately crouched in defensive postures, guns facing out. Somehow, I'd ended up in the middle of their defensive circle without noticing, without even moving. I huddled on the ground.

One of the Merry People shouted a name and ran—toward nothing. Then he vanished, with his own short scream. Fell into the grasses as if a hole had opened under him.

This was why Arthur hadn't wanted to return to Tor Camylot.

15

⋙━━→

Halls of Stone

N obody move!" Torres called. "Stand still!"
A third member of Arthur's troop dropped to the ground, writhing as if he was doing battle with the grass around him.

"What's happening?" Arthur stood planted, dumbfounded, while his people fell around him.

A rustling movement progressed toward us, grass parting as it traveled. Folding back the vegetation to look, I saw a vine— a thick, rubbery, almost cartoony vine with flat leaves and tendrils winding off of it. It undulated like a snake, propelling itself forward—directly toward Wendell's foot.

I meant to say his name, shout some kind of warning, like *Hey, this creepy thing is about to touch you, maybe you want to do something about that.* But all that came out was a vast, embarrassing shrill scream, as I pointed to the ground.

Roll for initiative.

Wendell heaved back, drew his knife, and stabbed down.

When the blade pierced it, the vine threw off sparks. The tail end of it, about four feet long, slapped and writhed, curling around and yanking at Wendell's blade. Some mechanism inside it constricted, entwining around limbs and binding them, wrenching people to the ground and trapping them.

Dozens of these things were crawling through the grass. Another was coming toward me, and I backed away.

"Captain!" Rucker pointed up with his gun.

While we had been focused on the ground, more danger arrived from above.

Drones, little buzzy things, whirred over us. They seemed like the stunner drones again—but no. These sped over the area rather than diving. One hovered five or six feet over Robin Hood and dropped something. The package expanded into a fibrous net. Hood ducked and tried to run, but the net unfurled, its edges reaching around him, entangling. The man fell, struggling as the net constricted around him, and the more he struggled, the more bound up he became. The quiver over his shoulder made it all the worse.

A dozen of these drones sailed overhead.

"Scatter," Torres ordered, and the squad bolted in all directions. One of the drones had already found us, and it homed in on Wendell, launching its payload. The net got him, and he fell, the net tangling around him, but a second later he was on his knees, knife in hand, cutting the fibers.

Hand on my back, Torres pushed me to run for the trees at the edge of the meadow. He stayed close, my own bodyguard. Otherwise, I might have just stood still in shock.

Before I could get to safety, something grabbed me. Not a vine at my ankle, not a net from overhead. I would have sworn that they were hands, wrapping around my wrists, arms reaching across my chest, but nothing was there. And then

I was on the ground, invisible hands pinning my shoulders. Torres fell beside me.

He fought, shoving to one side and then swinging with a punch. The punch connected, someone grunted—and then a rope bound Torres's wrists. He shouted in wordless rage, yanking against the bindings that only grew tighter, the mechanism in them constricting further the more he struggled, just like with the nets and vines.

The air in front of me shimmered—and a petite woman swept back a cloak as she sat up. The cloak flashed with an electric aura, then settled into a plain, unassuming black fabric. The air next to Torres did the same, revealing a stocky man with a newly bloodied chin scrambling back.

Cloaks of Invisibility. They had honest-to-God Cloaks of Invisibility. I'd read about experiments with this using some kind of light-bending smart fabric. Invisible cloaks, and they worked.

The woman slapped a rope around my wrists; it constricted, locking them together.

"Hey!" I said, pouting, because there wasn't much else I could do. Pain throbbed in my injured hand.

The battle, such as it was, was all over after that. As soon as we were immobilized, a couple more people emerged from underneath Invisible cloaks and another dozen came out from the surrounding woods. The petite woman had a smartphone in hand, like Arthur's. The drones zoomed off, the vines unclenched from arms and legs and crawled away. Meanwhile, the newcomers had retrieved their prisoners, sitting us in a row in the middle of the meadow. All of us had our hands tied with the automated ropes.

This crew dressed differently than Arthur, Robin Hood, and the Merry People. Harder, heavier. Less authentic period sources and more fantasy novel cover. Leather doublets specked with chain mail, steel gauntlets and pauldrons, studded boots. The men all had beards, and they carried staves and axes strapped to their backs.

The Realm of Shield.

"Dwarves," I murmured. "They're Dwarves."

Torres grinned up at the woman, who pretended not to notice him.

The woman, our captor, was South Asian, her glossy black hair pinned in a bun with what looked like metal-studded bone. She had on a tailored leather vest, gauntlets, a double belt stuffed with pouches and tools, and thick boots. Her brow seemed to be perpetually furrowed. This had to be Tess Selvachan, head of the engineering team. Glaring, she stalked over to Arthur.

"Arty! What the hell are you doing? Who are these Call of Duty rejects?"

"Nice to see you too, Tess. How are things?" Arthur asked, as the woman loomed over him.

She crossed her arms. The brow unknitted a bit. "Better than you at the moment."

Arthur grit his teeth. "Tess, I'm trying to fix things. If we can just talk, compare notes—"

"*Now* you want to compare notes? Nothing from you for months, and *now* you want to talk? I think your hand's been forced." She eyed Torres.

I wanted to throw up. I clamped my mouth shut and tried to think happy thoughts.

"Tess Selvachan," Torres said, his grin ominous. "I have a message for you from Harris Lang."

Her mouth opened, but nothing came out. Speechless.

"How did they get past the shield?" one of her people asked, glancing sidelong at the squad. "Nothing was supposed to get through."

"Is the shield yours?" Almonte put in. "Did you activate it?" Torres hushed her.

"Tess, people have died," Arthur said. "They say a Coast Guard boat ran into the shield and killed the crew."

"Shit," she murmured, turning away. Put her hand to her head, thinking. When she turned back around, her expression was impassive. Hiding everything. "We're too exposed here. Let's discuss this back home."

"Can't you at least untie us?" Arthur asked, holding up his bound hands. "I swear, we won't do anything crazy. Well, *I* won't."

Raising her fist, she called to her people, the rest of the Dwarves, "Get our gear, we're going back to the Hall!"

Some of Tess's people went back in the woods and returned leading . . . creatures. Horse-sized but canine, covered in coarse black fur, tusks protruding from slavering mouths, glaring with red eyes. Wargs, up close. A couple of them were harnessed to wagons—simple wooden platforms with two wheels and rickety sides.

"Jesus, are those the Wargs? Like what we saw before?" Wendell breathed. "Ugh."

"Boarsts," Arthur corrected, uselessly.

"Wargs, Arty," Tess said with a grin.

The Wargs moved and licked their lips, shook out their fur, and blinked at their handlers. One scratched the ground and barked, and its handler patted its shoulder with affection. These things had *personalities*. It was amazing.

I wanted to pet one.

I was also terrified.

"Everybody up," Selvachan said. "We're out of here."

The Dwarves hauled the foresters up by their arms and guided them to the backs of the wagons. The foresters mostly complied. More than that, they called each other by name, and no one seemed inclined to throw punches or try to escape. Once upon a time these were their coworkers. They must have had company picnics together. How much of this seemed like a game to them?

"Should we try to get away?" Arthur said, leaning in to whisper to Torres.

"No." Torres glared.

"But—"

"I want to find out what they know."

Arthur said, "We don't know how dangerous they are—"

"Are Selvachan and her people any more likely to kill us than you are?"

Arthur sat back, mouth shut.

The rest of the squad didn't look happy about it, but no one argued. Me, I had to admit I was happy at the prospect of not walking for a while. And we were going to get to see the Hall of the Dwarves . . .

The soldiers didn't make it easy on their captors. Rucker alone was two hundred pounds of dead weight, and it took three of the Dwarves to haul him to his feet and over to the wagon. He didn't struggle or fight—he just *didn't move*. All four soldiers had a look in their eyes that made one question who had really captured whom. I wished I could manage something like that arrogance. To even pretend to have that confidence. When in fact I was so very proud of myself for just not crying.

Selvachan's people distributed the foresters among the different wagons, and they were very careful to separate the squad, putting Rucker in one wagon, Almonte and Wendell in another, and me and Torres in the third. Their gear and weap-

ons—rifles, pistols, knives—ended up with yet another Warg,
in panniers, far away from the soldiers. Torres didn't seem
bothered. He settled in and bided his time.

Finally, the caravan moved out. One of the Wargs tilted back
its head and let out an echoing howl. The wagons lurched, fell
into a line, and made their way slowly around the edge of this
section of forest. Selvachan and a couple of her lieutenants
went mounted, riding Wargs up and down the row of wagons,
supervising, keeping watch. She paused by our wagon to glare at
us. Torres glared right back. I was so tired I couldn't feel my face
anymore. I couldn't imagine what my expression looked like.

Torres muttered, "It's embarrassing, getting ambushed by
nerds like that."

"Don't be too hard on yourself," I said. "They've probably got
thousands of hours of World of Warcraft under their belts. You
can beat them up, but they have remote controls."

"That's not making me feel better. This whole island runs on
remote control."

"*Right?*" I exclaimed. "It really is like magic, just like Lang
wanted! And they're smart enough not to go up against your
guns. That actually surprises me a little. I think they figured
out they couldn't count on you to not just shoot them. So, they
dodged."

"Jesus," Torres muttered, and slouched back, disgusted and
disgruntled.

I woke up slumped on Torres's shoulder, the smell of sweaty
fatigues in my nose. Quickly I straightened, pulling away from
him.

"Sorry," I muttered. "Didn't mean to fall asleep."

"No worries," he said. "It's been a rough day. How are you
doing?"

"I don't know," I said, trying to scrub some wakefulness into my eyes. The bandage on my hand was stiff, but my fingers moved easier, like the swelling had gone down some.

We'd left the plains and entered a range of hills. They were young, craggy, filled with clefts where waterfalls poured down, covered with a searing-green carpet of foliage. The sun was setting; we moved into the shade. At some point we'd joined a road, a wide path of packed dirt made for carts. Someone came by on foot to light lanterns hanging from the fronts of the wagons.

The road sloped down, and we passed a stone pillar with a black and gold flag hanging from its top. The marker for the Realm of Shield. Torres twisted to see ahead—we were at the back of the caravan. A feeling of anticipation and anxiety hung over us.

Tess came up behind us, reining in her Warg so she could look at Arthur over the cart's side. "Arthur," she said to get his attention. "Wait till you see this."

The hillside before us glowed orange. Soon, we passed two big iron torches, blazing with fire. They were gateposts, markers for the wide mouth of a cave. The road sloped down into the cave and underground, into the realm of the Dwarf Kingdom.

16

Cheat Code

The cave swallowed us like a mouth. The bleed of torch-light from outside vanished. The rock walls were dry, rough, and clearly excavated. Mined, as if by Dwarves.

Just when the darkness closed in on us, the walls opened into a cavern. No, not a cavern, which implied rough stone and dripping water—this was a warehouse-sized space with carved pillars at regular intervals, decorated tile on the floor, and gilding on the polished walls, so that the light from dozens of sconces reflected and expanded until the whole place glowed. This was a palace, the pride of the Dwarf realm, one of the great halls under the mountain—

Arthur Beckett stared, awestruck. He hadn't seen the hall in its current form, I assumed. Even the soldiers of Torres's squad gazed up and around in wonder. The carts lined up near the wall, and the Dwarf folk worked to unharness the Wargs and take them through an archway. Did they live in some kind of pens or stables? Or did they just get switched off and put in a closet? Others unloaded the prisoners, sitting us on the floor in our respective groups, Arthur and the foresters off to one side, Torres and his squad to the other, lining us up as if for inspection.

"Oh, dude, Craig, what happened to your face?" One of the Dwarves leaned in close to Hapless Craig.

"Rambo over there punched me!" He jerked his chin at Rucker, who winked at him.

The captor had the gall to laugh. "I wish I could have seen that!"

"That's right, Ted, laugh all you want—"

Robin Hood finally elbowed Craig—awkwardly, given they were both tied up—and left him grumbling.

"You've been busy," Arthur said to Tess.

"Yes," she said curtly, and passed him by. She stopped in front of Torres. "Is it true? A Coast Guard crew died running into the shield?"

He considered her a moment, then answered. "Yes."

The word fell like a weight, and the silence in the hall grew heavy. "So there are criminal charges waiting for someone at the end of all this."

"That's not my concern. I'm a private contractor. Lang Analytics hired my team to return control of the island to the corporation. That's all I care about."

"You said you had a message from Harris."

"My inside jacket pocket, left side."

She made a show of it, keeping eye contact with Torres while tugging open the zipper of his fatigues, reaching inside slowly, feeling around. Like she could actually make him uncomfortable. Unperturbed, he wore this wry, inscrutable half-grin the whole time. When she finally drew back, she had the thumb drive in hand.

"You know what this says?" she asked. Exactly what Arthur had asked when he got his message, and I really wondered about what kind of corporate culture Lang had promoted. These people must have been paranoid before the energy shield ever went up around the island. How paranoid had they gotten after?

Instead of playing it right there, Selvachan pocketed the drive. I was disappointed. I really wanted to know if her message was the same as Arthur's. I had a feeling it wasn't.

Arthur interrupted. "Tess, have you talked to Dominic? Have you seen him?"

"Not since the shield went up. He's shut himself off in that little enclave of his."

Arthur said, "I'm thinking you helped him build the shield. I'm thinking you're working together—"

"You know nothing, Arthur Beckett! You played Lang's games with all this competitive R&D bullshit and look where it's got us! Dominic has spies in both our camps—"

"No, I would know if there was a spy—"

"What do you think all those statues of Lang are for? You thought it was just ass-kissing, didn't you? And you didn't dare knock them down because you didn't want to piss off Lang!"

Beckett gaped at her a moment, as if the thought had never occurred to him. I quickly reviewed the statues we'd seen, and the one that was broken. The one in the village—maybe its eyes really had been following me around. What a terrible thought.

If those statues really were for surveillance, and Dominic really controlled them—then he definitely knew I was here.

"Tess. Please," Arthur begged. "Take off the ropes. Let's talk."

"We're talking!"

"Lang is going to get back control of the island sooner or later, and if we don't figure out how this happened, we'll all be on the block—"

She laughed. "What? For manslaughter? Or for something else?" Her gaze narrowed, turning sinister.

I glanced at Torres. He gave a little nod, and I might actually have been learning to read the guy because I was pretty sure what that meant was let them talk. See how much they'll give away. I was rapt.

"It wasn't me," Arthur said, glowering. "I *swear*. You want to get to the bottom of this, talk to Dominic."

"Oh, I'm sure Dominic's up to his neck in this. The question is if he's under your orders."

"You'd be more likely to side with him than I would."

Torres said, "Are all your staff meetings like this?"

Something clicked, and I laughed. "Oh my God, you put Ravenclaws and Slytherins in charge—that's the problem with this place!" They turned on me, glaring, and I quailed, just a bit. I should have kept my mouth shut. Now, I had to explain. "I mean . . . you're both Ravenclaw, right? Arthur, you might be Ravenclaw leaning Gryffindor. But there's that micromanaging streak. And Dominic is Slytherin—"

"Dominic says he's Gryffindor," Tess said.

I shook my head. "He likes to think he's Gryffindor. He took the Pottermore test ten times trying to get Gryffindor. He's Slytherin."

"What does that even mean?" Torres asked me in a low voice.

"It means everyone thinks they're the smartest one in the room and they're all working on their own brand of logic."

"Now, that hardly seems fair—" Arthur started.

"And who are you? How do you know Dominic?" Selvachan stopped her pacing in front of me and glared. "You're not a soldier like them. What are you doing here?"

I couldn't think of what to say. Were we still being cagey? Would I be giving something away if I talked?

But Arthur said wryly, like it would make everything clear, "She's Addie Cox."

And yes, Tess's eyes widened in recognition, and I wanted to kick Dominic's ass for talking about me so much. What could he possibly be telling people about me?

"Dominic's Addie Cox?" she said, disbelieving. "For real?"

"I'm not *his!* I haven't spoken to him in years!"

"But Lang hired you because of him." Her lips curled.

"He hired me for my expertise in comparative literature and folklore—" I sighed. "And because of Dominic."

"I have a proposal," Arthur said, raising his voice. His brow was sweaty. I imagined he'd never conducted a staff meeting quite like this. "We send Addie—Professor Cox—to talk to Dominic. Find out what he knows."

"Oh, that's a bad idea—" I muttered.

Undaunted, Arthur continued. "She can mediate, work out terms for all of us to meet and finally get this straightened out—"

"No," Selvachan said. "I don't trust him, and I don't trust you."

Calmly, Torres said, "You want to talk to Lang first, tell him your side of the story? Then help me." He offered his bound hands, asking the question with a raised brow.

Selvachan didn't say yes. Which might have meant she didn't really want to talk to Lang after all.

Turning away, she called commands and pointed to Arthur and his foresters, then to Torres and the squad. "Take this crew to the Baldr Suite. Take them to the Freya Suite. Remove the ropes but lock the doors."

Robin Hood, Craig, Arthur, and their whole crew grumbled, calling the Dwarves by name as their captors hauled them to their feet and prepared to march them out. By contrast, Torres and his soldiers were very, very quiet. Rucker might have worn a small smile, like this was all going exactly the way he wanted it to.

"Not her." Tess pointed at me as my own Dwarf escort lined me up with the others. "She stays with me."

"Now, wait a minute—" For the first time all day, Torres looked actually angry. Really angry. He jerked out of his escort's grip, and even with his hands bound, the escort just let him. Did they realize how much restraint he was showing?

"Don't argue. Get them out of here," Tess said, holding me back from the group, even as I leaned after them. *Don't leave me, don't leave me, don't leave me—*

"Sit tight, Professor," Torres said, letting them steer him away.

He had a plan. The guy had a plan through all this. Glancing over his shoulder one more time, he caught my gaze, gave the briefest nod. Then . . . they were gone. Torres and his squad heading down one corridor, Arthur and his down another. Leaving me with the Queen of the Dwarves.

I said to her, "I can't believe I'm about to say something this cliché, but I think you're going to regret this."

She sighed. "Yeah, probably. I've regretted just about every decision I've made in the last six months." She made a gesture with a hand, and the rope around my wrists went slack and dropped to the floor. I stared, like I didn't quite believe it. It looked like a normal, everyday rope. She'd used some kind of telekinesis on it like it was nothing.

I tried to recover whatever dignity I had left. "You going to try to turn me to the Dark Side now?"

"What? Oh—I guess that does sort of make me the Emperor, doesn't it?"

Only if I was Luke Skywalker, which was a really daunting

thought. I wasn't the hero. I never had been. "Show me how you did that."

Tess spread her right hand flat in front of me, showing off four rings, two on her index finger, the others on her middle and ring fingers. Thick and ornate, they each had some kind of gem set in the metallic bands. Using her thumb, she flicked one of the gems, and the rope constricted, writhing like a demented snake into tight coils. She flicked the gem again, and the rope went slack.

That was *so cool*. "Wow."

"Would you believe I've started to take some of this for granted?" she said. "Like I don't even have to think about it, I just assume I can untie ropes without touching them."

"Arthur's been using a smartphone remote, but can you get all the park's systems into rings like that?"

"Rings, wands, you name it. That's the whole idea. The same basic tech has been in the commercial smart appliance market for years. We're just adapting it."

"And then turning around to sell it back to the commercial market," I said, remembering what Arthur had said about patents, and the island being an R&D pressure cooker.

"Mirabilis is supposed to pay for itself, in the long run," Selvachan said, with a sigh that suggested the thought made her tired. "You look exhausted. Let's go someplace we can sit."

She had separated me from the others on purpose. To butter me up. Win me over. But why? Did she think I would talk more without Torres looking on? I was too tired to be on my guard.

"I don't suppose you have any tea on hand?" I asked hopefully.

"No, but I do have the only espresso machine in Mirabilis."

Tess led me through the magnificent great hall. Designed to impress, it was large enough for massive medieval dinners on long tables filled with platters of exotic dishes. Huge, rowdy drinking parties. Vast enough for theater, for concerts —musicians could play, and the sound would expand and reverberate. There would be dancing and intrigue, sneaking behind columns, stealing kisses from noble suitors—

Most of the decoration on the stone columns looked to be based on old Scandinavian motifs, stylized trees looping into knotwork, sprouting leaves and whorls before ending in interlocking dragon heads. Images from Norse mythology, from the Icelandic sagas, Yggdrasil and the Nine Realms, pairs of ravens, Fenris gnawing on chains. The complex artwork of a culture that spent a lot of time indoors during long, frozen winters. The motifs continued up the pillars, floor to ceiling, and each of the dozen pillars had a different design.

"Did people actually carve all this?" I asked, brushing my good hand along the intricate stone as we passed it, feeling the slopes and angles. I hesitated before touching them, then reassured myself—this wasn't a museum, and they weren't old. They only seemed like they were.

"No," Tess said. "God, can you imagine? They're printed. Still—looks good, doesn't it?"

Somehow, they'd even gotten it to feel like stone, full of real weight.

The lanterns on the wall were iron, or something that looked like iron. Did it matter that it wasn't really iron, if it looked real enough? If the technology acted like magic, why not call it magic? Except that once I saw the seams, once I knew it was plastic and resin, I couldn't quite *not* know.

"So you're really Addie Cox?" she said. "Dominic talks about you all the time."

I scratched my hair and groaned. "I don't understand why

he'd talk about me at all. How do you all know so much about me?"

Her smile thinned. "He'd use you to make decisions. 'Let's do it this way—this is how Addie would like it. This would make Addie smile. This was Addie's favorite.' You're part of the design specs, hon."

"That is somehow both sweet and horrifying."

"Right? That's Dominic for you."

An ornately carved doorway led to a small, much cozier room, with tapestries hanging on brass rods, bathed in warm light from an iron chandelier in the center of the room. The scenes showed battles between armies, duels between warriors, wizards crafting spells, dragons launching from mountainsides and breathing fire. I could identify scenes from Pern, from Earthsea, from *Journey to the West*. That was the point, that thrill of recognition. Someone would come in here, have the insider knowledge of what all this meant, and know they belonged. I examined the stitches, the colors, the floral designs around the borders.

On the far end of the room stood bookshelves. Floor to ceiling on three sides, dozens of shelves containing hundreds of books. Thousands. A library. I brushed my hand along the spines. If I felt age and wisdom pressing out from them, it had to be my imagination. This place was only a year or so old. The books were replicas.

"You're one of those," Tess said.

"One of those people who goes straight to the books? Yeah." You could tell a lot about a place by the books on the shelves.

"Yeah, but you don't just look. You have to touch them."

These were leather-bound, gold embossed, made to look like old manuscripts though certainly printed. The titles were a mix. On the one hand, the shelves held all the texts I expected, titles I recognized from the production notes I'd studied before coming here. Classic novels and mythology guides, collections of folktales from all over the world. Garb and weapons manuals. Some were completely made up, customized for Mirabilis. Part of the setting. *Forest Trails of Insula Mirabilis* and *The Ways of Boarst and Dragon.* Made-up reference books with suitably mysterious titles and luscious gilded covers any fan would be happy to fondle. Adventurers would come here to research what they needed before embarking on their quests. This was a room full of clues. I searched for titles that might be immediately useful. Like *How to Knock Out That Force Field Surrounding the Island.* It would probably tell us we needed a couple of droids and an old Jedi Knight.

A wide table held a large map spread over it. This one had more detail than the one we'd taken from Arthur Beckett's office. Extra roads and trails, secret ways out of the Dwarves' mountain stronghold, camps and buildings added in. Corrections made in pen, circles in some areas, X's over others, notes added. And infrastructure: where solar panel installations were located, communications arrays and antennae. Electrical distribution stations. Wendell would eat this up. If I were a good adventurer, I would try to memorize this. Copy it into my journal. We would need this information.

Tor Camylot, a small stylized tower inked in the center of the island, had a big question mark written next to it. So did an entire region at the northeast corner of the island: the Realm of Arrow. The word *Riverhaven* was written there. The last homely house of the Elves of Mirabilis.

That was where Dom was, I was sure.

In the space marking a nearby cove, on the tangled coastline near the Great Dwarf Hall, someone had written: *Here Be Dragons.* The same place the phrase was written on Arthur's fancy stylized map. I wanted to go *there.*

One of Tess's assistants, a guy wearing a fur-trimmed leather coat, with brown hair down to his waist and braids in his beard, brought out a tray with cold cuts, slices of cheese, and a rustic-looking bottle of something that was probably alcoholic. The pair of cups next to it were made to look like they'd been carved from stone and polished to a sheen. He set the tray on the low table in the center of the room—anywhere else it would have been a coffee table, but I didn't know what to call it here—then bowed properly as if it meant something and exited the room.

"Come, try this," Tess said, pouring what smelled like mead and gesturing to the offerings.

"How are you doing this? All the food, the supplies?" I asked. I was hungry, and though it felt a little like I was betraying something, I started in on the cheese and bread.

She said, "We were set up to be self-sufficient. We have at least six months of food stored, but on top of that we have a working goat dairy, chickens, and organic gardens and or-chards. We've got hydroponics set up here in the mountain."

"I'm guessing the project specs had subsistence farming as part of the atmosphere. Part of the game. But you developed it with an eye toward self-sufficiency. You planned for people to live here full-time. The island isn't just a resort, but a way of life. That made the mutiny possible."

"Yes, we're all very aware of that now," Tess said.

I asked, "How did it happen? How did you know something had gone wrong?"

"You going to pump me for information? Report back to your Green Beret?"

"Navy SEAL, but yeah. I mean no. I mean, I don't know."

She leaned forward, so serious. "You're not like the others. Torres and his crew. I see the way you look at this place. You understand what we're doing here."

I sipped mead. I really shouldn't have. It went straight to my head and made me dizzy. My injured hand itched. As cozy as the library was, I could imagine it was just a room in a house. Then I would remember we were in a cave, under a mountain, and my breath caught. I was being buried.

"I admire what you've done here," I said. "The scale of it is incredible, the technology—"

"And it's all in danger right now. Lang can decide to shut the whole project down if he doesn't like the answers you bring him. Sunk costs don't bother him, especially when he's already gotten a dozen patents out of the team."

I shook my head absently. "Like Torres said, our job isn't to bring him answers, just get the project handed back to him. Especially me. I really am just here to distract Dominic if it turns out he's a problem." I set down my cup until I could control my breathing and get my hands to stop shaking.

"Addie." She lightly rested a hand on my arm; the touch wasn't comforting. "We're on the same side here, really. I need you to understand, I did not initiate the mutiny. I did not activate the force field. I'm not responsible for those deaths. You'll tell Lang that, won't you?"

"Then, you'll help us? Help Torres restore communications—"

"I don't know if I can."

"Why not? We just need to get into the castle—"

She straightened, took a long drink. "You can't get into the castle because you don't have the Ring."

I *almost* put my hand in my pocket. Almost.

"I hear the capital letter in that," I said carefully. "What Ring? The One Ring?"

"That's right. Like these." She held up her hand, the ring controls. "But this one overrides the whole island."

"Where is this Ring? How do we get it?"

"I don't know. I thought it hadn't been constructed yet.

We've got plans, specs. But then the shield went up, communications went down." She shrugged. "I started to wonder if someone had made the Ring in secret. You find the Ring, you find the mutineer."

The ring in my pocket was probably just a ring. Small *r*.

"Play the message," I said, trying to sound brave, like I was in control and not her. Like I was the one doing the manipulating. "Show me what Lang told you. If I'm going to help you protect the island, I need to know everything."

Pursing her lips, she drew out the device, set it on the table, and pressed her thumb on it. The projection lit up, and Lang's head appeared, blue and wavering. He offered a fatherly smile, condescending.

"Hello, Tess. If you're seeing this it means you've met Captain Torres. I expect it also means you don't have a lot of time. If you cooperate with the captain and his team, I can promise a fair—"

She grabbed the drive, clutched it in her fist, and the recording shut off.

I tilted my head, confused. "What was he saying?" I asked. "What . . . was he about to accuse you of something?" My eyes widened. She looked guilty as hell.

By the time she met my gaze again, her expression was back to haughty and impassive. The Dwarf Queen. Quickly, she drained her cup of mead.

"Can you trust Torres?" she asked.

I chuckled. "I'd better. He could kill me with one hand if he decided to." It didn't sound very funny when I said it out loud.

"That's not trust," she said. "That's fear. Are you sure you're both working on the same set of instructions?"

"Why wouldn't we be—" I started, then cut myself off. It had seemed innocent, Lang coming to see me. Give Dom a message. What if . . . what if he'd had a private meeting with

Torres as well? What would Lang have told Torres about Dom? About *me? Bishop to king seven. Checkmate.*

Lang hadn't given everyone the same instructions.

Tess continued, "When you work for Harris Lang, he makes it clear your loyalty is to him and no one else. That's why we never talked to each other, because if Harris ever got the idea that we were planning something behind his back . . ." She shook her head. "I don't know. Not for sure. But it's something Lang would do. He didn't like us meeting without him. He came out to the island as often as he could, but he couldn't be here all the time. He's paranoid, you might have noticed. It rubs off."

"But you kept working for him."

"Because I get to be part of . . . of this." She smiled at the room, sighing wistfully.

How many of us dreamed of going through the wardrobe to Narnia? How many of us vowed that if we got there, we would never come back?

There were no guns in Narnia or in the worlds like it. I told myself that a lot, over the years.

"It's getting late," she said. "We can talk more in the morning. You could probably use a good night's sleep."

"Yeah, we were under a tree last night. And then came the flying monkey. That was yours, wasn't it?"

Her grin said yes, it was. "What does it say about me, that one of my bucket list items was to *actually* release my flying monkeys?"

"That somehow isn't at all surprising," I said flatly.

Tess showed me to a room just off the parlor and library. Not a suite like the others. Just a room, like one of the employees would sleep in. For some official librarian in some future when this would be a game with guides and actors. It had a small bathroom and four-poster bed with a thick duvet and fur blanket. Tess showed me the lights, obviously proud of everything here. My appreciation, my delight, seemed to make her happy. Then she said good night and left me alone.

She didn't lock the door.

17

Riddles

I had some decisions to make.

I could sleep. The bed was amazing, cloud-like, warm. I wasn't sure I'd been totally warm since arriving on the island until this moment. I could just not think about anything and sleep.

Or I could sneak out and try to find where Torres and the others were locked up. Not that I trusted myself to find my way through the passages of the Dwarf realm. Even if I could remember which corridor they'd gone down—then what?

Tess hadn't told me everything. Maybe I could figure out what she wasn't saying.

The room included a small lantern, an LED made to look like a candle in an ornate box, so the light glowed atmospherically through scrollwork patterns. It was almost convincing, but that repetitive artificial flicker gave it away. I took up the lantern, wrapped my cloak over my shoulders, and instead of ranging farther out, I went back to the library to see what I could find—stocking-footed, hoping I'd be quieter that way. I wanted to try to make a copy of the map on the table. Compare it to the one we'd taken from Arthur Beckett's office. I should have asked for my tablet back. Tess's people had taken my pack and hidden it with the rest of the squad's gear. I bet she would have given it back if I'd asked for it. I wasn't so great at this whole subterfuge thing.

First, I looked in drawers. I wanted paper and pen to make a copy of the map, or at least write down as many details as I could. This assumed I'd be in a position to use them later. The library had a couple of desks and cupboards, but I didn't find anything inside. Most were bare, as if they hadn't yet been stocked. This was still new. Still waiting to be dressed up for their first guests.

I'd have to find paper somewhere else, like in the endpapers in the back of one of those books. In my time in academia I'd highlighted and marked up enough books I didn't even hesitate at the idea of writing in them. Holding up the lantern, I scanned shelves for something that looked slender, small, and easy to carry.

The gilt titles gleamed in the light. Like the books were speaking to me.

One title spoke a little louder than the others: *The Origin of Mirabilis.* When I pulled it off the shelf, I nearly dropped it—it was heavier than I expected a book this size to be.

Turned out that was because inset in the cover was a solid metal amulet of some sort. An intricate, knotted symbol showing a snake and a vine curled around one another, joined tail to mouth. I tried to remember if I had seen the symbol anywhere else on the island, or if I could suss out the meaning of it. I ran my fingers along it, feeling the texture of scales etched into metal. And yes, this was metal, not printed resin.

I flipped through a few pages to learn more and found the author listed was Harris Lang. At least, his name was on it. The text looked like an organizational document, not the public-facing resort literature they'd given me early drafts of. Charts and outlines and contractual clauses. Dense legalese about staff positions within the company, revenue models. Patent development was a big one. Codes of conduct for managers, for employees resident on the island. Temporary residents versus permanent residents — some of these people expected never to leave. Model waivers for guests, and wouldn't that be fascinating to parse?

But buried in the middle of the corporate legalese was a block of text labeled: *Game Master's Guide*. The tone was narrative, chatty. I could hear Lang's voice coming through, as if this was the draft of some future TED Talk. Then I came to this:

OWNERSHIP, AND PERCEIVED OWNERSHIP OF THE ISLAND AND ITS WONDERS, WILL BECOME MORE FRAUGHT AS TIME GOES ON. HENCE THE IMPORTANCE OF ESTABLISHING A RIGID LEGAL PARADIGM FROM THE START. THOSE WHO ARE CREATING THE MARVELOUS LAND OF INSULA MIRABILIS, MY MIDGARD, MY MIDDLE-EARTH, THOSE WHO ASPIRE TO MAKE LIVES THERE AS AN INTEGRAL PART OF ITS WONDER, WILL OF COURSE FEEL TIES TO THE PLACE AND ITS MAGIC THAT WE CAN ONLY IMAGINE IN THE ABSTRACT NOW. THOSE IN PARTICULAR WHO ALREADY EN-JOY RICH LIVES OF FANTASY AND IMAGINATION WILL BE PRONE TO, IF I MAY SAY THIS AS POLITELY AS I CAN, OVERSTEPPING BOUNDARIES. FEELING ENTITLED TO MORE THAN THEY ARE LE-GALLY BOUND TO. THIS IS WHAT WE MUST PROTECT AGAINST.

Why did I hear a "royal we" in there? This text didn't seem like it was meant for public consumption. How had it ended up here?

I ENVISION A KIND OF MODERN FEUDALISM. THAT WORD
HAS SUCH NEGATIVE CONNOTATIONS NOW, BUT WE FORGET
THE CONTEXT IT ORIGINALLY GREW OUT OF. AT ONE TIME IT
MEANT PROTECTION IN A PERIOD FRAUGHT WITH DANGER AND
UNCERTAINTY. AND SO IT WILL AGAIN. THE REWARD FOR THOSE
WHO GIVE THEMSELVES TO MIRABILIS WILL BE THE SAFETY AND
COMFORT OF THE KIND OF LIFE THEY ALWAYS WANTED TO LIVE.

How many people did I know who would give up . . . well, a
lot, for a place here? And Lang was clever enough to know not
everyone would buy in to his philosophy. He expected rebellion.
He expected someone to try to take Mirabilis from him. Maybe
not this quickly, maybe not quite like this. But he'd expected
it. And he might even have expected Dom to be the one to do
it. *Those in particular who already enjoy rich lives of fantasy and
imagination* . . . Oh yeah. I tried to imagine what Dom would
say if he'd read this—

Dom probably *had* read this.

Most of the books in the library seemed new. They smelled
of fresh glue and new paper, no matter how much they'd been
made to look old. Had any of them been read? I opened this
one, flattened it—the spine didn't crack. It didn't have that
new-book tightness in its binding. It had been opened before.

From over my shoulder, an arm reached, and a hand closed
over my mouth and pulled me off my feet. My scream never
had a chance to start.

Another set of hands grabbed the lantern and book from me
so they didn't fall. All of it done without a sound.

"Not a word," Captain Torres said at my ear.

A penlight blazed in my face, and I would have cried out, but
his hand was still clamped over my mouth.

"Understand?" he hissed, and I nodded, but not very much.
He let me go, and I grabbed for the nearest thing to keep from

falling, which was him. Beside him, Rucker held the penlight and glared. Almonte was at the table, examining the map. Near her, Wendell had a laptop out and was typing furiously. A cable connected it to a USB outlet in the table I hadn't noticed before. The map was uploadable. The soldier was shielding the light of the screen from the doorway.

"What—" I started, and Torres lowered me into a cushy chair.

"We got out. I see you did as well." He sounded almost proud, and I hated to disappoint him.

"She never locked my door," I said. "I'm just that harmless."

He gave me a side-eye at this. "Got on her good side? Maybe we can use that."

"What are you doing?"

"Hacking into the engineering team's files. We'll break this place apart from the inside if we have to. Keep the lights down and stay quiet."

Crawling back out of the chair, I carefully retrieved my lantern and Lang's book out of Rucker's hands. For a moment, I worried that he wouldn't let them go. But he did. I hid the book under my cloak. I needed to think about it and . . . I didn't want to have to explain.

"You okay?" Almonte whispered to me as I moved to the table. "How's your hand?"

"Not bad," I said. I held up my hand, showing her the fresh bandage I'd wrapped around it. "Aches some. Itches a lot. I hear that means it's healing."

"We'll get you in for X-rays when we get back to reality."

Reality. Right. "How are you?" She returned a wry glance. As if it didn't matter how she was.

"And we're in," Wendell said, and we gathered around.

My heart pounded against my ribs, I was so sure that someone would walk in on us.

"What have we got?" Torres asked.

"I think it's everything. At least on the engineering side. I mean, I'd love to get a look at the accounting spreadsheets on this place, but I don't think they're on this server. We've got schematics, floor plans, emails . . ."

"I want to get into the power grid," Torres said.

"Yessir."

Torres turned to me. "What did you find out?"

He took it for granted that I would have been able to collect information from Tess. And then he took it for granted that I would share that information.

I frowned. "Apparently Dominic designed everything based on whether or not he thought I would like it."

Torres let out a muffled chuckle. "Well, that explains a lot."

"I can't decide if that's romantic or creepy," Almonte said.

"Yes," I answered. "Most definitely yes."

"Did Selvachan tell you anything *relevant?*" Torres said.

"She started to play Lang's message, then shut it down. It sounded incriminating. Lang seems to think she's guilty of something, and if she cooperates he'll let her off. And she says we can't get into the castle without the Ring."

"Oh? What ring?"

Again, I almost reached for my pocket. It couldn't be the one. It just couldn't. "The One Ring to rule them all and in the darkness bind them. Did you notice the ropes are controlled by little remote controls in their rings?"

Wendell looked up. "So that's how they did that."

"Apparently they made plans for a ring that would override the whole island operating system. Tess says she didn't think it got made. But now she wonders if it did, on the sly."

"If we had that, we could just walk into the castle and shut it all down," Wendell said. "You still have the ring we found at the scary spider dungeon?"

"Yeah." I didn't sound happy. I sounded daunted. That story turned out *so badly* for the person actually carrying the ring around.

"Forget the ring," Torres said. "I like our plan B. We stick with that."

"What's plan B?" I asked.

He grinned. "You'll see in the morning."

"You don't trust me," I said. A statement. It only made sense that he didn't trust me. Perfectly logical. I tried not to care.

He ducked his gaze for just a moment, seemed to consider. "Professor, can you step over here a moment?" He nodded to another part of the library, a nook with a couple of armchairs, away from the others. Rucker kept watch by the door. Almonte and Wendell continued working at the computer. They glanced up, but their expressions remained neutral. Professional.

I could be professional. Except there wasn't really anything in university guidelines about dealing with mercenaries and a rogue corporate R&D project. I'd never been in a gaming campaign quite like this.

Torres indicated that I should sit, and I did. He took the chair opposite . . . exactly how Tess and I had been sitting earlier. Torres had that same stance, cautious and making an appeal at the same time.

"You know why Selvachan separated you from the rest of us?"

"Yeah," I said, leaning back, looking away. "To try to win me over. Suborn me. Pretty classic move."

He chuckled. "And?"

"I told you everything I picked up from her. You know I'm telling the truth because I'm a terrible liar."

"If you were a good liar, you could say you were a terrible liar and I'd believe you."

"But if I really am a terrible liar . . . I could say I was and you wouldn't believe that I'm a terrible liar and would decide I'm a good liar, and—I don't think that riddle works out. But I'm pretty sure there's way more going on here than we've been told."

"Those are the worst fucking missions, when they don't tell you everything." His sigh sounded tired.

"Can I ask you a question?" I asked.

"Please."

"Do you have one of those message drives for Dominic?"

"I do," he said, nodding once.

"And you have no idea what it says?"

"None whatsoever. Lang likes his games, doesn't he?"

"He really does," I murmured. I tried to work out the tangle. In the dark room, the bookshelves were featureless and offered no clues. The ceiling was invisible. The faint, half-hidden glow from computer screens made Wendell's and Almonte's faces seem hollow, ghostly. "I think . . . I think Dominic probably initiated the mutiny. But I'm starting to think that Lang knew he was going to do it." Torres raised a brow. "Lang gave me a message for Dominic. Verbal. It would only really work verbally, given the reference. He said to tell him, 'Bishop to king seven.'"

"That sounds really familiar," Torres said.

"It's from *Blade Runner*. It's the chess move Roy gives Sebastian, to get them in to see Tyrell. The checkmate."

His brow furrowed thoughtfully. "So which one of them is Tyrell?"

"I think it's Lang's way of telling Dom that he knows. That he knew all along."

"And Lang didn't tell us." His tone went dark, but his eyes gleamed in the faint glow nearby. As if this detail made him eager.

"He might even have wanted Dom to mutiny? But then Dom took it too far. I don't know."

"Why not tell us?"

"Maybe he wanted to give everybody a fair shake to come clean." I shrugged. It didn't really sound in character for Lang to give anyone a fair shake. More likely, he had a plan. "This is an experiment. Radical playtesting. Lang wanted to see if his world could function in isolation, if it was self-contained. That was his parameter for testing his hypothesis. We're just another set of pawns on the board, a control group who wasn't in on it from the start . . . Sorry, I'm just thinking out loud."

"We're all being played," he muttered. "Good thing the paycheck just about makes it worthwhile."

I was just about to ask him again what plan B was when Almonte called softly from the desk. "Boss?" Torres immediately went over, moving between them to study the screen. I followed, listening in. Almonte explained, "We found a folder of personal correspondence buried under a couple of layers of encryption."

Wendell said happily, "We cracked it. Thought it might be important."

"Does that say what I think it does?" Torres said.

I read over their shoulders. While I couldn't say I was an expert in corporate-speak and politics, this looked like a corporate recruiting letter, from Garamon Tech to Dr. Tess Selvachan. The gist of it was, they were either trying to hire her away — or bribing her an obscene amount of money to divulge Lang's secret project on his private secluded island.

"Isn't Garamon one of Lang Analytics' primary competitors?" I asked.

"Yeah."

"So Tess is a spy? Did she initiate the coup so she could hand everything over to them?"

Almonte added, "Or someone else on the team figured out

what she was doing and locked down the island to stop her. They wanted to flush out the corporate espionage—"

"Not our job to sort all that out," Torres said. "Finish downloading, Wen. We've been here too long." Torres patted Wendell on the shoulder.

"And . . . done," the engineer said.

"Right. Pack up. Professor, anything else in here you think we'll need?" He gestured at the shelves of books, as if I could somehow just *know*. If I had a couple of weeks I could go through it all . . .

"I—I don't think so," I said.

He said, "I want you to get some sleep. Keep making nice with Selvachan."

"I'm not any good at this spy stuff."

"It's not spy stuff—just talk to her. And don't worry, this'll be finished soon."

I hissed a pained breath, and he stared. "What?"

"Don't ever say something like that out loud. You might have just doomed us all."

"Professor. Get some sleep."

They gathered up their gear, did a quick sweep and recovery of the room, making it look like they'd never set foot in it.

"Good luck," I murmured, watching them slip back into the darkness outside the library, skilled and soundless. Spy stuff. *They* knew what they were doing.

I returned to the room and sat on the fluffy, too-comfortable bed for a long time. By the faint LED glow of the lantern, I spread out my treasures. The stuff I'd found that I'd been shoving in my pocket for the last two days: a plain gold band; a transparent plastic triangle that seemed to have its own faint glow; a book with a twisted knotwork amulet; and my lucky d20.

The ring couldn't be the Ring. It didn't have anything special about it, didn't seem to have any markings or circuitry. It weighed what I'd expect it to weigh. The triangle — it was probably meant to slot in somewhere, be part of some other device. I hadn't seen any other triangle-looking shapes, nothing that looked like this should fit into. And the book. There might have been a code written into the text somewhere, or the amulet matched some other symbol on the island and would reveal all . . .

My d20 was the only object here that I really understood. I turned the book over to give myself a hard surface to roll the die on. I just wanted to see where it would come up. Shook it — awkwardly, using my left hand — and rolled . . . 11.

Well, that was ambiguous enough.

I shoved my very questionable stash back in my pockets, folded the book in my cloak, turned out the light, and buried myself under the covers.

18

>>>>>——————→

Area of Effect

Professor, wake up."
    A banging rattled the door. The lights came on, way brighter than the atmospheric candles from the night before.

"Ungh." I'd slept in my grubby fatigues, and now I was sore and sticky as well as exhausted.

"Did you know about this?" Tess stood over me, fuming.

"Know about what?" When I thought about it half a second, I assumed she meant did I know about Torres and the squad —and me—sneaking around in the middle of the night. Reflexively I reached for my cloak, which still had *The Origin of Mirabilis* wrapped up in it. This was what we'd come to—I was stealing books from libraries.

"Come on. Get up."

Last night's adventure came back to me in a trickle. It didn't seem quite real. Was Tess a corporate spy? A turncoat? And did Lang really see himself as some kind of feudal lord of the island . . .

"Just a sec . . ."

She waited while I used the bathroom and washed my face because I didn't give her a choice. Unfortunately, the bathroom had a mirror. I was a mess, my bleary eyes staring, my brown hair sticking up everywhere. I itched. My boots made my feet feel like blocks.

"Can I get a cup of coffee first?" I asked as she led me back to the great hall, then out the front passage.

She glared. So, no.

We emerged from the cave to the outdoors. The cloud cover had broken; the sky was clear, and the sun was just starting to gleam over the edge of the hills. The fires in the iron torches had gone out; they were simple black frameworks now. The courtyard space between them was half in shadow, half in light. I winced, blinking away the stabbing feeling in my tired eyes and trying to ignore a new headache.

Near the cave entrance stood yet another medieval-ish statue of a regal warrior, this one holding a halberd planted on the ground. Or it would have been standing, if the statue hadn't been knocked over, the face smashed. In the dark last night, I hadn't seen it.

"You did that?" I asked Tess. "And the one outside Tor Camylot?"

"They're cameras," she said simply.

Across the courtyard, Torres and company had set up a workshop with a defensive perimeter. They had retrieved all their gear, packs, equipment, including guns. Rucker stood casually on guard, glaring at a half-dozen Dwarves armed with spears and swords and what might have been Tasers. A couple of drones hovered menacingly overhead. The remains of one lay scattered on the dirt road, shot to pieces. They were at a standoff, which didn't seem to bother Rucker one bit. Almonte and Wendell were building something that looked like a Frisbee with claws.

Torres stood overseeing it all. "Morning, Professor," he said with what passed for cheerfulness with him.

"Hi," I said, rubbing my eyes again.

"Did you know about this?" Tess asked again, and I stood with my mouth open, not sure what to say. Evidently this was plan B.

"What . . . what is it?"

"How'd they break out of their rooms?" she demanded.

"Are you kidding?" I said to her. "This is the real world, they're all super high level with massive bonuses in, like, *everything*."

Just then Arthur, Robin Hood, and the foresters came barreling out of the cavern entrance, only nominally escorted by Dwarf guards.

"What the hell is going on here?" Arthur demanded, looking warily at the squad's guns.

Tess pointed. "Call of Duty over here is running amok. You know, we outnumber them. If we team up, we could stop them."

"I don't want to stop them!" Arthur exclaimed. "Whose side are you on?"

"Mine," she muttered under her breath, just out of hearing.

Arthur went on a tear. "They have guns, Tess! And training!" He looked wildly at me. "Professor Cox. Addie. What are they doing?"

I looked at Torres. He nodded once. "I think they're building their own override system to bring down the shield and bypass Tor Camylot entirely."

"*Fuck* Tor Camylot," Rucker added happily.

"They're making their own One Ring." I shrugged.

Arthur blinked, startled. "Tess, I thought you said you couldn't get the Ring to work."

Torres raised a brow. So Arthur knew about the Ring and hadn't said anything.

"I couldn't! I didn't! It doesn't exist!" she exclaimed desperately. She turned on the squad. "You can't just build your own Ring. It took us years to develop the tech—"

Wendell looked up and grinned. "Yeah, see, the thing is, it's a lot easier if you don't have to make it look like a ring." He gestured at the mash of wires and circuitry with the soldering iron he was using.

Both Tess and Arthur looked at me, as if I could do anything about this. I said, "Do you know what I would do for a cup of tea right now? A lot. I would do a lot."

Arthur paced for a moment. He seemed to be muttering some kind of meditation exercise to himself. "I still think that if we can get Dominic to talk, he'll shut down the shield and we can clear all this up in no time. We just need to send Professor Cox to Riverhaven with a message—"

"We're not sending the professor anywhere," Torres said.

"Never split the party," I added.

"That's right." The captain gave a mock salute.

"You'll never be able to bypass the shield control," Tess said. "The power grid is all centralized at Tor Camylot."

The squad ignored her.

Arthur turned to me. "Can they do it? Can they build their own Ring?"

"I have no idea," I said. Looking around, I found a nearby rock at a comfortable height, wrapped my cloak more firmly around me, and sat.

A couple of Dwarves and foresters, who obviously knew each other from before the island went rogue and were happy to be back in contact, put together a breakfast of muffins, fruit, and coffee. A bitter and stabby substitute for tea, but it scalded my throat and woke me up. The squad had their own rations and were careful to maintain a perimeter between themselves and the natives.

I sat right in the middle, and neither group seemed eager to take me in. I didn't belong anywhere. The spine of Lang's book, nestled in the waistband of my fatigues, was digging into my ribs, and I couldn't stop thinking about it.

I didn't like Harris Lang. I hadn't liked his arrogance, his smug assurance, way back when Dom dragged me to that presentation. His declaration that he could unilaterally save the world seemed the definition of hubris. I'd been a little hurt when Dom was so eager to go work for him. There were other ways of being part of something bigger than yourself. The longer I spent on Mirabilis the less I liked Lang, but maybe I wasn't being fair. I was taking this too personally. He owned the island —he'd paid for it, paid for everything that had been built here.

But the ideas behind it weren't original. The ideas themselves couldn't be trademarked or patented. But once they'd been made real, once the technology had been developed, *that* could be patented.

Harris Lang was trying to patent magic.

More than that, he thought he owned the people. If he could get them to behave the way he wanted, if they behaved the way he predicted . . . Lang had sure manipulated me into doing exactly what he wanted. I began to see why someone here would want to mutiny, just to deliver a couple of big middle fingers to the guy. Except . . . no one should have had to die for any of this.

Tess slipped beside me, and I flinched, startled. I wanted to just come out and ask her what contact she'd had with Garamon Tech, but then I would have to explain how I'd learned about the emails.

"Addie," she whispered. "I want to show you something. This way." Her eyes were alight. She seemed perfectly in earnest. And she was clearly trying to avoid drawing the attention of Torres and the other soldiers. "It's nothing bad, I promise."

And wasn't that exactly what someone would say if they were about to do something bad? "What is it?" I asked.

"You want to see a dragon?"

It was a trick. Why was everyone trying to manipulate me? And why was I so easy to manipulate, anyway?

Glancing back to make sure Torres was looking somewhere else, I followed her out of the courtyard.

Nearby, a footpath branched into the rocky hills. It was well hidden, unless you knew what to look for. Beyond the courtyard, the landscape was even more beautiful in the early morning light. What had been shadowy and brooding at dusk was now painted gold. The path had a lot of up and down, and on the higher parts the ocean became visible. Frothing white waves crashed against rocks, jagged and treacherous, a perfect place for shipwrecks and mermaids. A colony of swallows dived and skimmed, chittering. The air smelled of salt water and moss.

"Can I ask you a personal question?" Tess said as the path flattened out to a stretch of grassy hillside.

Now that didn't put me on guard. "I guess? I reserve the right not to answer."

"Oh, of course. But . . . were you really going to marry Dominic?" Tess asked.

Oh. That question. "I broke up with him when he proposed.

There . . . were a lot of reasons." *We grew apart* was the cliché. I didn't fit in his story anymore . . . and he never noticed.

"That must have *killed* him," she said, grinning like she would have enjoyed being there to see it. I suddenly wondered what it had been like, the months of Dom, Tess, and Arthur working together as colleagues. Like the three races yelling at each other during the Council of Elrond. Nobody wanting to stick their necks out, and no Hobbits around volunteering to throw themselves into a volcano in the name of peace.

"He is a bit of a romantic," I murmured, and she spit laughter.

"Yeah, you could say that. A lot of women seem to like that sort of thing."

I looked at her sidelong. Did that mean Dom had a girlfriend here? "Oh, I'm absolutely certain he has fans around here."

"But not you?" she said.

I smiled wryly. "He wanted to zig and I wanted to zag. It would have come apart sooner or later. In the end he just wouldn't listen to me." We walked a little farther and I ventured, "So. Were you and he ever . . . ?"

"Oh, ˙God no. Dwarves and Elves? No way." She shook her head with enough vehemence to make me suspect she'd actually thought about it. I tried to come up with a witty joke about Legolas/Gimli slash fic. But no, I had nothing.

The path wound down to a cove where seawater came in at the high tide to form a pool. From the water, a scree of gray rockfall sloped up to a cave. My breath caught. The space was quiet, primal. The sounds of distant waves and the calls of seabirds enveloped it in calm.

"This way," Tess said, gesturing me from the trail to a flat platform of rock, a couple of dozen yards from the cave entrance. Unlike the symmetrical, carved entrance to the Dwarf realm, this was natural, flattened, formed by centuries of waves and erosion. The darkness within was like a mouth into some other world. Carefully, I found a seat on the rocks edging the pool, my whole body tense. Not sure what was going to happen. Hoping for what I wanted to happen.

She pulled up her sleeve to reveal a bronze-looking wrist cuff—not a ring like the other control devices, but still a piece of jewelry with buttons and wires hidden in the design. Her finger brushed the pattern. A noise emerged from the cave, a bellows-like whoosh of air, as if the earth itself had started breathing, deep and slow. I could almost feel it under my feet, in my sternum. The ground seemed to be moving.

Steps rumbled; the breathing shook us. And the creature emerged, face peering from the cave, blinking into the light, nostrils flaring as it sniffed and whuffed. Eyes of reddish gold gazed over a fierce canine face, covered in thick white fur with orange tufts sweeping from its ears. Its lips curled over sharp teeth, and long whiskers draped gracefully from its muzzle. With those teeth and claws, it could tear me apart without thinking. But it gazed at me with what seemed like intelligence.

More of it emerged from the cave, and then even more, a snake-like body as long as a bus, full of white shimmering fur and pearlescent scales. Its legs were short, keeping it low to the ground. Lion-like paws gripped the rocks, balancing the undulating body much more gracefully than should have been possible.

Amazed, I listened for the hum of electronics, some clicking of gears or a buzzing motor. The in-and-out pumping of lungs, suggesting this thing might have been engineered from biological material. I couldn't tell. I honestly couldn't tell how they did it.

This was a *dragon*.

Now fully in the sunlight, it bounded forward to splash

in the pool, pawing to make waves, shaking water off fur the whole length of its body. I laughed—you'd have to be heartless not to at least smile at this powerful creature behaving like a puppy. Washed and invigorated, it trotted back to shore, then turned its attention to us, its huge eyes blinking.

My tears fell, and I held my hands over my mouth to hold back whatever astonished noise was waiting to burst out. It was so, so real. As if I had crept secretly into this cove and happened upon a dragon, a real dragon, just going about its business.

Tess pulled a baggie out of her belt pouch and handed it to me. "Pork and ginger dumplings," she explained. "It seems to like them."

I stared at the handful of dumplings in the baggie. Was she serious? How did an artificial creature *like* anything? How did that algorithm work? I crept forward, holding out one of the dumplings. The dragon leaned in, nose working. In the end, I wussed out and tossed the dumpling toward it, rather than waiting for it to come to me and bite my hand off.

The dumpling splatted on the rocks, and the dragon pounced on it like a puppy with a sock, hooking the bit of food in its fangs, tossing it in the air, chomping down. Shaking out all its fur, it whuffed again. I tossed the next one a little closer.

Again it devoured the bite with glee. When it looked up next, it focused, fur standing on end. Stepping forward, its claws scratched on rock. Its gaze showed curiosity and playfulness as it came right toward me.

I should have been scared. I should have backed away. Instead, I reached out. I was ready. It was a Chinese dragon, a sign of luck and fortune. Auspicious.

I crept forward to meet it, and in turn it stretched toward me, sniffing, its nose working. We inched closer and closer, until I could see the fur ruffle, until the whiskers quivered, tasting the air around me. Then, it ducked its head to press up under my hand, and I was petting it, stroking the fur, scratching behind its ears. It purred, rumbling deep in its throat, a pleased ripple passing down its snake-like body. It pushed closer—just lightly enough that it didn't knock me over. Just exactly like a cat asking for more scritches. I obliged, and it flopped over, purring louder, stretching its short legs in the air. I laughed and hugged its whole head, wiping my snotty, messy tears in its fur. It didn't seem to mind.

"How?" I asked, breathless. "How did you do this?"

"Software and response algorithms," Tess said. "But it's awfully convincing when you're in the middle of it."

Yes, it was.

Behind us, voices called out to Tess. A commanding shout cut through them. "Professor!" It was Torres.

The dragon reared up, cocking its head. Its back end curled around, as if it was preparing to spring. Tess quickly tapped out a pattern on her wristband, and the dragon calmed, settling back to the rock.

Torres ran into the cove, followed by a couple of Tess's assistants who were screaming at him. The soldier paused, took a fraction of a second to look over the scene—and holstered the handgun he'd been holding.

I started hyperventilating, my heart racing in my throat. My hands shook. I couldn't control any of it. Unthinking, I embraced the dragon's head and bent over it, shielding it. I wasn't going to let anything happen to it. I buried my face in its fur, trying to control my breathing, to steady my heart. It was okay, it was okay . . . I couldn't stop shaking. The memories only came screaming back after I couldn't see the gun anymore.

I should never have come here to Mirabilis. But it was all worth it, to spend five minutes with a dragon.

It nuzzled into my arms, as if it sensed I needed comfort. But how could it? The shush and crash of the nearby waves broke the silence.

Torres finally said, "Dr. Selvachan, can you give us a minute?"

"Addie?" she asked warily.

"It's fine. Go on." I wiped my face, then laced my fingers in the dragon's fur.

Tess led her assistants out of the cove, leaving Torres and me to stare at each other. He came forward slowly, like I was some kind of wild animal that needed caution. Or more likely he was responding to the dragon. The creature watched him with glassy eyes that still somehow managed to glisten with simulated life.

"That's really amazing," he said. "It seems so real."

"It is real. If it walks like a dragon and responds like a dragon —does it matter what it's made of? What does 'real' even mean here?"

"I don't know anymore." He settled on a nearby rock.

"You want to feed it?" I still had some of the dumplings Tess gave me, and I offered him one.

"It eats?"

"Well, it takes food in its mouth. Probably stores it somewhere and dumps it out later. I didn't really ask."

He held out the dumpling, remaining crouched and braced, ready to react in a moment. The dragon stretched forward, stuck out a pink wet tongue, and daintily wrapped it around the bite. Torres wiped the spit off his hand. The artificial tongue actually had saliva on it.

"You shouldn't go off alone," he reprimanded. "I thought you knew that."

"I just wanted to see the dragon."

Torres sighed, scowled, but I didn't think he was angry

at me. Just at this, at everything. "I don't trust any of these people. They'll get themselves and everyone else killed without even meaning to. This . . . this thing has very big teeth."

The dragon tilted its head questioningly at Torres. I scratched its ears harder, and it arched its back and purred. Settled its length on the rocks and seemed to fall asleep.

"I'm sorry about the gun. I wasn't thinking," Torres said.

"Thanks."

"You love this. This whole island." It seemed like a declaration, like he had just figured something out.

I sighed. "What you said before. About people taking a bullet for love. That day at West Lake, Alex got in front of me. The shooting started, and we all got down under the tables just like in the drills. But it didn't matter, the shooter looked under the tables. Alex pushed me down. I didn't realize what was happening, and if I had known I wouldn't have let him get in front of me. But what . . . what does it matter, knowing he loved me, if he isn't here anymore?"

"It matters," Torres said immediately, no hesitation. "It has to matter."

"I'm . . . not sure I'm worth what he gave up? How am I supposed to live up to that?"

This was where my friends and family and therapists and everyone said of course I was worth it, Alex knew I was worth it, survivor's guilt was a thing and I had to keep living, and that was how I made the sacrifice worth it . . .

"None of us is worth it," Torres said. "But we keep trying, anyway."

That might have been the most honest thing anyone had ever said to me. It . . . lifted some responsibility off my shoulders. As if, suddenly, I had nothing to prove.

"If things go really sideways and it comes to that, please

don't get in front of me. I don't think I can go through that again."

"Can't promise that, Professor." He smiled.

The dragon sensed my mood had changed, and it snuggled closer, licking my hand. Its tongue was soft, like a dog's. I pressed my face to its fur again, hugging it close. I couldn't forget, but I could at least let myself be distracted. There was a whole world of distractions, and I indulged, because I was living for Alex and Dora, too. That was what I kept telling myself.

Torres looked lost, or sad. His guard was down, making him seem younger somehow. Vulnerable, and that wasn't a word I thought I'd ever associate with him. But then the expression disappeared, so quickly I wondered if I'd even seen it.

"Wendell's almost finished. We'll take the new Ring to the antenna array over the Dwarf Hall. This will all be over soon."

"Then what?" I asked.

"Then it's not our problem anymore."

"But we haven't heard Dominic's side of it . . . What if, what if he knew one of the others was a spy, what if—"

"Professor. Addie. It's not our problem. I'm not sending you to talk to Brand because it's too dangerous."

"But what if—"

"That's final. You were hired to do a job. Just keep your head down. You think you can do that?"

"I can try."

He scowled again, gave the dragon a last skeptical look, and marched out of the cove.

Tess returned, giving the man a wide berth as they passed each other, treating him with as much caution as if he was one of the island's monsters.

"Are you all right?" she asked.

I must have looked a mess, face red and puffy from crying,

clinging to the dragon, who had snuggled its head in my lap. "Yeah. You guys programmed some amazing responses in this thing."

"It'll make for great photo ops with kids," she said.

That took some of the magic out of it. "And how much extra would guests have to pay for those photos?"

Scowling, she touched another command on the control bracelet, and the dragon seemed to grow sleepy, stretching out, yawning wide. It gave me one last snuggle, then turned away, back to the cave, where it slipped underground and presumably curled up for a comfortable sleep. My arms felt cold, empty after it was gone.

"We should go," Tess said. "Mr. Green Beret is anxious to move out."

"Navy SEAL," I murmured, but I hauled myself up, brushed myself off, and followed her back to the others.

19

>>>———————→

Elven-Kings Under the Sky

Back in the courtyard, the squad was packing their gear. One of the Dwarves led a Warg out of the tunnel, and Torres barked back, "No, we're not taking those things."

"But—"

"On foot, quietly." He jabbed a finger.

Tess and Arthur argued with him. Rather, they argued with each other while he looked on. Like he was letting them wear themselves out.

"This is a waste of time," Tess insisted. "Arthur is lying to you—he could get into the castle the whole time if he really wanted to."

Arthur huffed. "You're just trying to cover your own ass, sitting up here pretending like you don't know what's happening, waiting for me to come rescue you!"

She laughed. "You haven't rescued anybody! It's your fault any of this happened! If you hadn't let Dominic go off by himself for weeks at a time, all because you thought he was Lang's golden boy and were afraid of pissing him off—"

Arthur set his jaw. "How about we let the lawyers decide whose fault this is, hmm?"

Torres didn't say anything about Tess's communication with Garamon Tech, or that this really did look like she was desperately trying to cover her ass.

I raised my voice to ask, "Are you guys really so afraid of Dominic that you couldn't just go talk to him?" During all this I'd been waiting, sitting on one of the rocks ringing the courtyard. Torres had liberated my simple pack with my tablet, canteen, a few protein bars, and odds and ends. No tea, though. I should have brought even just a few tea bags. All these fantasy LARPers and how had no one packed tea? I hugged the pack and felt small.

The pair exchanged a look and deflated some. Some kind of truth settled heavily on them. Torres ended up answering instead. "It's probably best they stayed away. No telling what Brand would do to protect his interests."

"Dom wouldn't hurt anyone," I insisted.

All three of them gave me a look. An accusation of rank naivete. I ducked my gaze. Dominic had so admired Lang, it was hard to think of him doing anything to betray Lang or his interests. But the evidence all pointed to him. What had happened?

"Boss, we're ready," Almonte said. The squad was waiting, rifles stowed, packs secured.

"You coming?" Torres asked Tess, who stood gripping a spear and glaring.

"Do I have a choice?"

"Not if you want to be there when we get Lang on the line."

She grumbled. It was disconcertingly Dwarf-like. "You've met Lang, right? Do you think he's going to do anything but bury us under NDAs and pretend like none of this ever happened?"

No, he wouldn't. He wanted to control them. To control everything. He would give them all a second chance—if they groveled enough.

"Not my problem," Torres said.

But it was. It was all our problem. We were trying to decide who the villains were, and who the victims were—and it wasn't so clear as it was in the stories.

"Tess," I said, thinking out loud. Aware that everyone was glaring at my interruption. "You ever read the Prose Edda?"

"The what?"

"Or any of the Icelandic sagas?" I continued. These were the basis for just about everything we knew about medieval Scandinavian mythology and culture. Tolkien had definitely read them all, was one of the foremost scholars on a big great chunk of northern European medieval literature. I turned to Arthur. "Have you read Geoffrey of Monmouth?"

"Why are you asking this?"

"Robin!" I called over to the lead forester, whose people were gathered at one end of the courtyard. "Have you read *A Gest of Robyn Hode*?" This was a fifteenth-century English text, one of the earliest written versions of the Robin Hood story.

He looked over at me in confusion. "No, I watched Errol Flynn. Oh, and Disney."

Oh, Foxy Robin Hood . . . we probably hadn't met Foxy Robin Hood because he was totally trademarked.

Tess put her hands on her hips. "Are you asking if we're geeky enough for you? Are you *gatekeeping*? This isn't a classroom—this is real life!"

There was something genuinely absurd about that statement given the context.

"Just . . . the source material. How far are we removed from the source," I murmured. Lang's secret manifesto was still tucked in my jacket. "Never mind."

Torres narrowed his gaze at me. "Let's get the hell out of here."

"Yessir," I replied.

Torres invited Tess and Arthur along, but he only allowed them each one assistant — preferably someone who knew how the island's tech worked and could help with the antenna override. He was keeping an eye on the numbers of this expedition — the island's residents would always outnumber his squad, but he could keep his people from being overwhelmed.

The team leads grumbled about it, but in the end they agreed. The rest of their people would probably follow at a discreet distance. Torres didn't seem to care. Arthur chose Robin Hood as his second, and Tess brought Ike, one of her specialists in communication hardware. We traveled light — this was only supposed to take an hour or two. Almonte led; Wendell hauled his gear, the weird-looking device full of projecting wires and hastily bolted pieces, strapped to his backpack. Torres followed along after Tess, Arthur, and their people, so he could keep an eye on them. I tagged along with Torres.

As we headed out of the courtyard, Rucker sidled up to me, eyeing me warily.

"You okay?" he asked.

I was so sick of that question. "Yeah," I sighed, unable to think of a more clever response.

"I was wondering . . ." He scuffed his foot, seeming for all the world like one of my awkward undergrads come in to ask for an extension on a paper. "Torres says I should research mission sites. He's a good guy, I learn a lot from him, so I thought you could tell me what books I should read or whatever to start to understand this place? Like the ones you were just talking about. The source material. For next time."

That was so . . . sweet. And earnest. "You're probably never going to have a mission site like this ever again."

His shrug came off as boyish, belying the rifle slung over his shoulder. "Yeah, but still."

Gosh, where to start . . . "Every couple of years I teach a class, Introduction to the Fantastic. We start with *The Epic of Gilgamesh* and work our way up. Once we get back home, I can send you the syllabus and a few texts to get you started. How does that sound?"

He seemed uncertain. The badass paramilitary guy, intimidated by books. "Okay. Thanks."

"Happy to. I'll find stuff you'll like, I promise." I was already thinking about what to send him. *The Odyssey* for sure. Rucker would get a kick out of Odysseus.

"Did you put him up to that?" I asked Torres, after Rucker had gone off to keep a watch over our trek.

"Nope. Kid's taking some initiative." He grinned, apparently amused.

I suddenly wondered what it would be like to play actual D&D with these guys. It would either be hilarious or terrible. Hilariously terrible. I should set that up.

A maintenance trail branched off the main road to the Dwarf realm. The thin dirt track circled around the hill and led into the woods. A couple of miles ahead, a cluster of antennae rose above the trees. According to the specs, Wendell explained, this array had enough power to be one of the broadcast nodes for the force shield. If he could cut the power, it should break the shield's circuit and deactivate it. Then the squad could simply use their satellite phone to contact the outside.

This would all be over soon. A few hours, Torres had said. I paused a moment, surveyed the scene. The day was sunny, and the ocean spread out from the rocky coast. The grass around us was emerald, the forest rising beyond. The iron torches of the Dwarf Hall were just visible, a gateway promising mysteries.

We might as well have been at the edge of the world. The illusion was perfect.

And we were going to destroy it all.

Torres urged me forward. The line of us was strung out along the trail now; I was holding us up. I pushed on.

We kept looking up, studying the sky, stepping carefully as if we expected the ground to open up under us. After a couple of hours, late morning, we reached the antennae array. A steel shed housed the equipment. The building had some ivy and ferns growing along the base, beginning a slow climb up the walls. Obviously intended to disguise the modernity of it, but they hadn't had a chance to mature. The path kept going, climbing toward the summit. The views must have been fantastic up there.

"Do you have the key?" Tess asked Arthur. The latch on the door was padlocked.

"My keys are all back at the village; I didn't know I was going to need them. Don't you have an extra?" he replied.

"No, I don't have an extra," she said angrily. "You're the lead project manager, keys are your job!"

"This is on your land!"

"It's not any of our lands, we're all just hired help here—"

I said, "All you Rogues and Rangers and not one of you can pick a lock?" That got me some scowls.

Torres nodded at Rucker, who produced bolt cutters from the squad's bag of gear and wrenched the lock off the door without any ado. Tess and Arthur gaped.

"That works too," I said.

"Jesus," muttered Robin Hood, and sank to the ground with his back to a tree trunk to wait it out.

Torres and Rucker kept watch while Wendell and Almonte went to the shed to hook up their device . . . the Ring bypass. The Anti-Ring. Tess and Ike squeezed in to help, nominally.

More arguing ensued. The soldiers mainly ignored the engineers. At one point there was a loud hiss, a shower of sparks,
and some cursing.

"Wendell?" Torres asked.

"It's fine, it's fine, just trying to get the hookups to match."
More cursing.

Arthur was sticking close to Torres. "What are you going to
tell Lang when you contact him?"

"I'm going to tell him to get over here and clean up his
mess," Torres said.

"He'll be expecting a report from you."

"I suppose he will."

"And?"

"I'll be sure to answer truthfully any questions he has."

Arthur heaved a sigh and looked at me. "Addie? Professor?"

"I don't know, I'm just the consultant," I said.

"I'm sure you have nothing to worry about, Mr. Beckett,"
Torres said, his contempt undisguised.

"I just want it on the record that I'm fully cooperating—"

"It's on the record."

Another bout of sparks and cursing came from the shed.

I had set down my pack and moved away from the others—
still within sight of Torres and the shed, of course, but I needed
space. To catch some of the sunlight coming through the trees.
Take in the last bit of clean, wild air before rescue came.

Behind me, there was more cursing and engineering—hard
to tell the difference sometimes—and Arthur covering his ass.
Before me, forest. Light filtered through the branches of towering conifers, with enough space between them for a dense
undergrowth. Even in midday, a mist touched the air. Just
enough to add an otherworldly sheen.

Then I saw motion through the trees. A flash of white. The
flicker of a horse's tail. Oh, oh no. I glanced back at the crew;

they might be at this for hours. I shouldn't wander off. I really shouldn't, I knew that. I could almost hear Torres yelling after me.

I wandered off.

Focused on the spot where I'd seen the movement, I crept on, around trees, past a giant stand of ferns. I spotted it again. A snowy white flank, a clear black eye, vanishing as a head tossed and disappeared around some foliage. I kept after it, moving as quietly as I could. Leaned up against a tree and peered around it.

The unicorn stood in the misted green light, head raised, ears flickering, gleaming so silver that it almost hurt to look at it. And its horn. That impossible horn, glistening with the colors of mother-of-pearl, spiraling in a perfect line as long as its own neck. It shouldn't have been able to even move its head under that weight, but here it was. It nibbled on leaves, its silken mane draped across its shoulder, its thick tail reaching almost to the ground.

Gripping the edges of my cloak, I crept forward, step by careful step.

The unicorn raised its head, and I froze. It saw me, flicked an ear, and went back to grazing, undisturbed. I continued, closer. Any moment, I expected it to turn and race away, kicking up dirt in my face. But it didn't. I came close enough to see the hairs on its muzzle, its fine dark eyelashes. Each strand of mane was perfect.

I'd seen *Legend* a dozen times. I knew how badly this sort of thing could go.

I did it anyway.

Crouching, I reached out my hand, coaxing the creature forward. Assuring myself that Tess's engineers couldn't possibly have programmed it to be able to tell virgins from non-virgins.

The unicorn stretched its neck. Somehow, it knew exactly

how to hold its head so the horn didn't stab me but aimed precisely, daintily, upward. The velvety muzzle touched my hand. It stepped forward, my palm rubbing along its cheek. And the creature froze. All four legs braced in place, the neck locked into an arch.

Suddenly, it was just a statue. A machine following a command.

I should have run then, but it was too late.

On both sides of me the air shimmered as newly revealed arms threw back the edges of invisible cloaks. Masked figures reached for me. One covered my mouth before I could scream, the other grabbed my arms. And a third, behind me, wrapped a blindfold over my eyes and put a cloth gag in my mouth.

They didn't say a word.

20

Split the Party

My captors tied my hands in front of me and manhandled me onto the back of a horse. Probably one of the unicorns, except the illusion had been destroyed. The mount stood too still and then moved too steadily to be a live animal, and as we rode I was sure I could hear the clicking of gears and whirring of motors underneath its smooth coat that wasn't nearly warm enough to belong to a real horse. At least I was allowed to sit astride, and not slung over its back like a bag of potatoes. I couldn't guess how many mounts and riders there were—I heard hoofbeats both in front of me and behind me. Listening for clues was exhausting, and my mind wandered as my back muscles cramped and my legs grew sore. I desperately needed a drink of water.

Blindfolded, I couldn't keep track of time, but we must have traveled for a couple of hours. The flavor of the air changed; the salty mist of the coast turned to the earthy scent of pine forest, and a muggy warmth settled over us, as if we had entered a valley and were now sheltered from the breeze.

Finally, we stopped, far enough away that my screams wouldn't carry back to Torres and the others. I listened hard: around me, thuds of feet on ground as riders dismounted, accompanied by soft voices. I couldn't make out what they were saying, and it wasn't just because they were whispering, trying to keep me from overhearing. They weren't speaking English.

Were they speaking . . . *Elvish?* Sindarin Elvish?

A hand touched my thigh. After so much exhaustion, the touch was a shock and I flinched. I wanted to get away. Whoever it was pulled back, then took my arm and guided me off the unicorn. I wasn't that high off the ground, but the drop was enough to jolt my knees, and my captor held me upright to keep me from falling.

He tugged at the gag. "I'll take this off if you promise not to scream. Nod if you agree."

I nodded quickly. The taste of cotton had filled my mouth, and I had started choking on it. When the cloth loosened, I spat. Pulling away, I yanked off the blindfold and finally got a look around, squinting into afternoon light.

We had indeed been riding unicorns. Gleaming white, they had magnificent pearlescent horns and black eyes. Six of them waited, feet planted, unmoving. Machines, they were only machines. They didn't have anything like the response algorithms of the Wargs or the dragon. The illusion was lacking.

A stone pillar stood at the spot. A silver banner hung from a pole at the top. Gateway to the Realm of Arrow, like the other markers that stood at the borders between lands. It was made up, it shouldn't have meant anything, but my heart sank. We had crossed a boundary, into another land, and it felt momentous. Like I had traveled hundreds of miles away from the others, instead of just an hour or two.

A life-size statue of a man stood at the base of the pillar, gazing serenely over his domain. This version of Harris Lang wore the leather doublet, leggings, and boots of an Elvish Ranger, bow and quiver on his back.

The man at my side saluted the statue—but he wasn't saluting Lang. The eyes had cameras, and Dom was looking out of them. I stared. The expression of the stone didn't move; nevertheless, I imagined its smile growing wider.

The five men standing next to the unicorns were Elves. Or seemed enough like Elves that it made no difference. They wore doublets of soft leather, tunics in forest green and dark gray, supple pants in brown, close-fitting boots, all subtly decorated with embroidered knotwork, with clasps and buttons shaped like leaves. Their hair was long, pulled back from their faces. Their attitudes were solemn, serene—totally Elvish. They wouldn't so much as break a smile.

One of them offered me a leather waterskin. I accepted, awkwardly gripping it with my tied hands, and drank eagerly, trying to get the taste of cotton out of my mouth. I finished, coughed, and glared. Tried to stretch my fingers—the bandage was coming off my hand.

"Where's Dominic?" I asked.

The Elves exchanged glances.

"All in good time," my immediate captor said formally.

I might have rolled my eyes. The dialogue in this movie stank.

We were in a forest of tall ancient trees, widely spaced, creating the sense of being in a cathedral, grand and solemn. Did I hear distant, ethereal singing in an invented language? Probably just my imagination.

The man reached behind me, and I flinched. Didn't matter. He got the blindfold back over my eyes anyway. There was no point in struggling; the group had me hemmed in.

"Hey," I complained. "You don't have to do that, it's not like

I have any sense of direction. You think I'd actually be able to lead anyone back here?"

"It's so you can't find your way out," he said matter-of-factly. He and the others proceeded to haul me onto the unicorn.

"So where'd you guys learn how to kidnap? It's like you've practiced."

"We did, actually. Practice, I mean," he said. "Dom wanted to make sure we didn't hurt you."

"Oh."

Over the next hour, we traveled downhill on what felt like a well-packed trail. What should have been a magical journey, riding unicorns in the company of Elves, was thoroughly ruined by the fact I was blindfolded, tied up, and my whole body was becoming one big cramp. The movement of the creatures was jerky, mechanical. I didn't believe they were unicorns. Not anymore.

Finally, we stopped, and I was once again guided off the back of the creature. This time, my knees buckled. I sank to the ground and heaved a sigh. The Elves—the kidnappers— exchanged a few words in Elvish. I recognized a word or two, could almost understand what they were saying. Then my head started pounding and I couldn't listen anymore.

A hand took my arm. "Just a little farther," my captor said, and pulled me up. My legs still weren't working right, and soon I had someone on each side keeping me upright. I heard hoof- beats—the unicorns, moving away. Awkwardly, I reached my bound hands to yank the blindfold off so I could look.

I was in heaven.

Unicorns, their coats gleaming and long silken tails rippling, walked off through an arch of vines and roses into a pasture ringed by trees, all of it glowing gold in the misty sunlight. Ahead, a dirt path faded, replaced by slate paving stones that formed a patio bounded by gray stone pillars. At the top of the pillars, copper braziers in the shape of lilies bloomed in graceful, flowing lines. At night, fires would blaze out of them, a second roaring bloom. Beyond this elegant gateway, the wild forest gave way to gardens. Roses climbed trellises; honeysuckle dripped from the tops of covered walkways.

I stepped forward to see more, expecting they would stop me. Instead, one of them touched his ring, and the rope around my wrists loosened and dropped away. I was free, I could finally run . . . but now I didn't want to.

Across the patio, paths branched off. One continued straight to a bridge made of ivory-colored stone, standing on arches above a gorgeous grotto, forest sloping down to where a waterfall poured into a crystal pool. All around the glade was a village. Cottages, walkways, halls — all in pale stone, built with arches and pillars made to look like looping vines and flowers. The structures climbed from the edge of the pond, up the surrounding hills, as if they had grown there, stairs and curved pathways flowing naturally. Silver edging on the roofs made the buildings gleam. I almost missed the handful of antennae rising from the highest point, a rounded alcove with arched windows overseeing it all.

This was Riverhaven. Home of the Elves. I might have let out a little mewl of disbelief. I'd never seen anything like this outside of a painting.

The guards stood with me, taking in the view just as I did. Like they didn't take it for granted — they knew how amazing this was.

One of them said, "My lady, if you'll come this way."

My knees went weak and my mind was dizzy, just for a mo-

ment. I blinked, unable to tell which world I was in. *My lady*.
Not *ma'am*, or *miss*, or *Professor*. Nothing mundane or ordinary.
No hint of the prosaic world, as if I wasn't wearing grubby fatigues, as if I hadn't been bashing my way through wilderness
for days.

My lady, as if I was beautiful.

They guided me down a series of stone steps leading to another arched bridge. This one connected to the main cluster of
structures on the other side of the glade. I moved slowly, trying to take it all in, the pool stretching below filled with water
lilies and paddling ducks, the waterfall raining and splashing
over rounded boulders.

As we moved across the bridge and to the stairs leading
down the other side, I ran my hand along the railing, tracing the carved leaves and flowers that made it look like it had
grown in place rather than being carved. Probably all created
with molds and 3D printing, like the columns in the Dwarf
halls. However much I wanted it to be handmade, for the spirit
of a creator to shine through the work, this was all manufac-
tured. None of this represented a living culture—it was a piece
of art, yes. But it wasn't organic.

We descended a set of delicate stairs, leading through a
carved arch that looked like trees, branches intertwined overhead, welcoming us in. My muscles felt like soup and I wanted
to cry. But I didn't. I was determined to hold on to whatever
pretended nobility held my spine straight.

The patio at the end of the walkway had a lattice pergola
over it that filled the space with dappled light. The floor was
tiled, soft colors forming images of leaves and flowers. Again,
the walls were carved to suggest trees rising up to support the
roof, so this didn't feel so much like a room as a glade in a
forest. A low brazier in the center held lit coals, sending off

comfortable warmth. The two guards took up positions at the doorway, leaving me by the fire, rubbing my hands and trying to decide if I was warm or cold or just plain numb.

A figure appeared in an opposite archway. Tall, solid, somehow embodying both calm and power. He wore a floor-length tunic of pale silken cloth, with a darker sleeveless tunic over it, leafy knotwork embroidered on the edges. His long, dark hair was draped behind his shoulders. He smiled kindly.

"Addie," Dominic said. "It's good to see you."

21

>>>———————>

The Last Homely House

For a moment I was afraid Dominic was going to come at me, arms spread for a hug, expecting to pick up where we'd left off before the breakup. But he kept his distance —probably aware of the striking, elegant picture he was making against this backdrop.

Then his eyes widened. "You cut your hair! I thought you had it pinned up!"

My hand went to my head. My hair was sticking up everywhere like some kind of deranged halo. Then Dom saw the stab wound on my hand. The bandage had finally fallen off some time during the trek here, revealing the puckered welt. It was actually looking a lot better—bruised, but the swelling was down. Lang Analytics was going to make a killing on those "healing herbs." But it probably didn't look good to someone who hadn't seen it yesterday.

Then Dom did come at me. "Oh my God, Addie, what happened? Who did this to you?"

I backed up a step, clutched the injured hand to my chest,

and said, "I think it's interesting that you assume someone did this to me and that it didn't just happen by accident."

That brought him up short. He pressed his lips together a moment, considering. Then started over. "What happened?"

This would be a perfect chance to throw Hapless Craig under the bus, but since I wasn't sure what Dom would do if I told him, I didn't. "It doesn't matter. Dom, you have to let me go back. Torres is going to think I ran away. He already doesn't trust me, and now he's going to assume I ran off to talk to you—"

"So? What does it matter what he thinks?" He said it matter-of-factly, the corners of his lips turned up with amusement.

"But he . . . I mean . . ." I stammered to silence. What was I afraid of, after all? That Torres wouldn't succeed and reclaim the island for Lang . . . or that he would? Or I just didn't want Torres to think badly of me . . . but I wasn't going to tell Dom that.

Then I noticed his ears. Strands of hair were braided at his temples, exposing the graceful arcs of his ears that swept up into perfect Elvish points.

I gasped. "Your ears!"

"You like them?" he said, tilting his head to show them off. That grin—that "look what I did" mischievous grin that he'd get whenever he finished some secret project, secret for no other reason than he loved a big reveal. My heart clenched. "Surgery," he added.

I blinked. Up to this point, everything had seemed extreme. The drones, the cybernetics, the nanotech, the remotes. Cutting edge, high tech, pushing boundaries. But this . . . seemed crude somehow.

"That's . . . committed," I said simply. I hadn't noticed if my captors had pointed ears. Was that a requirement for living here?

"Yes, it is," he said. To the guards, still lurking nearby, he spoke in Elvish. A dismissal, a formal thanks. The language was coming back to me.

The guards bowed at him and slipped back down the path. They actually bowed to him. This was off the rails.

This wasn't at all how I expected our first meeting to go. I wasn't really sure what I expected. More awkward. Less . . . epic. I went to a delicate carved bench near the brazier and sank onto it, holding my head in my hands. Dom hovered nearby, some of his elegant demeanor faltering as he hesitated to reach out.

I looked up at him. "Dom, what are you *doing?*"

The shield around the island was harder to see in daylight, but still visible if you knew what to look for: a kind of purplish shimmering, a faint haze that never really went away. It was still there now. Which meant Torres and the others hadn't yet been able to override the system with their improvised Ring. It had been hours; it should have worked by now. But it hadn't.

Dom looked up and around, following my gaze, then raised a questioning brow. I shook my head and didn't say a word about the shield, the hacked-together Ring of power, or anything else. Finally he sat on the bench next to me, but not too close.

He said, "As soon as I found out you were on the island, I just . . . I needed to know you were safe. Did one of those soldiers do that to you?"

"No!"

"I know how fragile you are—"

"I'm not fragile. I'm resilient."

That press of lips again. Recalibrating. "Of course. But I know Lang sent you here because of me, and the thought of you with those soldiers, so close to those guns after everything you've been through—I've never been so angry at the man, and that's saying something. If anything happened to you here, I'd never forgive myself—"

I glared. "Stop it. You're doing it again."

"Doing what?"

"Making it all about you."

"Oh. I suppose I am." For a moment he actually looked crestfallen. Elrond had never seemed so unsure of himself. But then the moment passed. "I put some water on to boil; it should be ready by now. You look like you could use some tea."

Oh God. Tea. How long had it been since I'd been near a teapot? Days? Years? Tears leaked down my face, and I scrubbed them away.

"Yes, please, that would be lovely," I managed to say evenly.

He disappeared through one of the arched doorways to an alcove and returned with a tray holding a simple ceramic teapot and a couple of small Japanese-style teacups, which he placed on a sideboard table. A wisp of steam rose up from the pot's spout, twisting like one of the carved branches on the wall. All perfect.

Methodically he poured two cups. "You still take yours black?" he asked, and I said yes. He offered me a cup, and I gratefully took it, nesting it in my cupped hands and breathing in its steam. It took all my will to wait for it to cool a bit before sipping, and not draining it in one scalding go. But even taking in the scent of it made my muscles unclench a notch.

Dom seemed to be clinging to his cup as a prop. "You've spoken with the other managers? How is everyone doing?" He remained standing, gazing over the railing to the glade below.

I sipped, and the hot tea lit up my whole brain.

"They're crazy," I said. "And paranoid, backstabbing. But what can you expect? This is an island full of Sarumans and Wormtongues trying to cover their own asses without losing any authority."

"Does that include me?" he said, throwing a grin over his shoulder. Oh, the wry grin with those cheekbones and those blue eyes . . .

Bishop to king seven . . .

"Why did you do it, Dom?" I asked. "You admired Lang so much, you were so excited to go work for him. And now, why . . . betray him?" *Betray* seemed like a strong word. I couldn't think of a better one, though.

He sipped. Bowed his head. Yes, we were both using our cups as props. Gave us something to do with our hands—something to do besides talk.

After a moment he said, "Because he betrayed us first. Do you know he's already marketing the stunner drone we developed to police forces for crowd control?"

I sipped. Still just a bit too hot. But the heat felt good. "We ran into one of those."

His eyes widened. "It didn't hurt you, did it?"

His concern was starting to seem oppressive. "Not me, no. But I saw it in action. I imagine the commercial applications that come out of this will make Lang very rich. Even more rich, I mean."

He gave a short laugh. "We thought it would be worth it, to get all this in return. But I thought . . . I thought he believed." His voice fell; he was tired and working hard to hide it.

"Lang suspected you would do something like this. Did he encourage you to? Is this all part of some plan of his? Accelerated R&D, I think Arthur called it. Three project managers enter, one manager leaves? The one most dedicated to the project?" I waited for an answer. He sipped enigmatically. "If he knew you'd go this far, why didn't Lang just fire you, kick you off the project?"

"Because I'm the best person for this job and he knew it." He gazed into his cup, frowned. "Because even if one of us staged a coup, he thought he could beat us. That he could win, no matter what. It's a game of chess to him."

I didn't tell him Lang's message. I wasn't going to be a pawn in whatever game they thought they were playing.

Dom went on, glaring out over his Elvish realm, not noticing my discomfort. "He let us get this far, then he gets to prove how much better he is when he beats us. No, the commercial applications really are just icing for him. What he really wanted was to prove he could win the game."

"But what's *your* goal?" I asked. "To beat Lang at his own game? There's no way you'll be able to hang on to all this. Is there?" Was there? What was Dom hiding?

He chuckled. "I've missed you."

I drank down the rest of the tea. I hadn't realized how cold I'd been, and now I wanted to melt. "Dom, let me go back to Torres and the others. I'll take a message back for you. I'll tell them anything you want me to. Let's just get this whole thing resolved so that nobody else gets killed—"

His brow furrowed. "No one's been killed."

He didn't know. He acted so assured, so omniscient. But he didn't know what had happened.

I laced my hands around the teacup. "Ten people on a Coast Guard crew died trying to get here when their boat crashed into the force field. So yes, people have been killed." And if he didn't win this, those deaths would be laid at his feet.

He swallowed, looked away. "I'm sorry to hear that."

Except he didn't sound all that sorry. I wasn't sure what remorse would look like on him; I wasn't sure I'd ever seen it.

"Dom—"

"I can't let you go back, Addie. I'm sorry. But, please—I know what I'm doing here. I have a plan."

"What plan? What are you doing?"

"Come, let me show you to your chamber. You can have a bath and get some rest."

Dom gestured through a different arched doorway, and I

walked ahead of him. This path overlooked the pond, trickling springs feeding into a pool ringed by moss-covered rocks
and a hanging mist, the scene made dream-like all by itself,
no technology required. I caught sight of a couple of other
figures moving on a path by another ivory cottage that looked
as if it had grown from the earth. Women wearing long, pale
tunics with silver belts, long hair flowing down their backs.
They looked up at us, and I wanted to hide. I'd never felt more
scruffy. What they must be thinking: *This* is Dom's mysterious
ex-girlfriend? His lost lady? This sad bedraggled waif?

And why did I even care again?

The path looped around the edge of the glade until it
reached a short set of stairs that led up to a gazebo, lacework
walls standing at the entrance of a room with hanging tapestries, ornate rugs on the floor, a lush pallet, a chair and washbasin, all in rich, warm burgundy and mahogany. The place
was a luxurious nest.

"There's a bath," he said, pushing back a curtain to reveal a
warm closet with what looked like a marble basin and fixtures.
"Clothes, if you want to change." He gestured to a wardrobe.
Silk gowns—silver-, dove-, rose-colored—hung within. Elvish
clothing. "Do you need anything else?" he asked earnestly. He
really wanted me to like it here.

I wanted to get a message to Torres. I wanted to make sure
that he, the squad, and everyone were all right. I wanted to find
out what Dom was planning.

"I think I'm all right for now. Thanks." And then I just stood
there, like an idiot, studying him. He was Dom, but alternate-
universe Dom, wearing the costume and this otherworldly calm
like he'd been born to it. I wondered, though, if the Dom I
knew with the geeky T-shirts and passionate late-night discus-
sions of tropes in Icelandic sagas had been the one in costume,
the make-believe Dom. He'd always said he never really fit in.

I couldn't tell what he was thinking.

"Despite everything," he said. "I'm glad you got to see this. I wish it were under better circumstances."

"I'm glad too," I said softly.

"Was . . . there something I could have done differently? To make you say yes, back then?"

"I don't know," I said softly, my voice catching. And I didn't. If he had built me a beautiful Elvish grotto, made me a perfect cup of tea . . . But I wasn't sure I remembered that moment we broke up so well anymore.

He took my hand. My left hand, the uninjured one. I was so surprised, I didn't even flinch. Then he just held it, like I was a butterfly he was afraid of crushing. I brushed his fingers; they were rough, calloused. He'd been working hard. He'd probably done more than design work—he'd probably literally helped build this.

When I didn't pull away, he grew more confident. He clasped my hand in both of his, drew it to his lips, kissed my knuckles, a dry press of lips, both polite and tender. My stomach knotted, my knees went weak—he used to do this in the old days. The first time he did was the first night I slept with him, except we had done it backward. We'd had sex, because we'd been drinking mead and watching movies and couldn't keep our hands off each other, and we'd had a great time. Then in the morning, still tangled up together in bed, he'd kissed my hand, the tenderest of gestures, as if to show respect, to tell me he would never take me for granted. He was *really good* at the hand-kissing thing. How could I not fall in love? It all came back.

Then he let go and slipped away, leaving me standing there, numb.

The bathing room had hot running water, which I was pretty sure wasn't authentic to any of the old epic stories, or Tolkien, or anything. But of course Lang's magical island had modern plumbing, because without hot showers who would want to stay here? On the other hand, I could imagine a few hard-core fans who would come here wanting a real—so to speak—taste of medieval fantasy questing and would forgo the hot bath. I did not.

The windows gave the impression of the room being open to the woods. Birdsong called through the trees. I felt exposed and wondered where the guards were. Strategically placed curtains allowed me to maximize privacy and still have a view. For just a little while, I had the feeling of resting in a mystical grotto, the hot water flowing from some secret spring into a basin of purest stone. Nothing bad could happen to me here. My hand even stopped hurting for a little while, the heat melting away the pain.

Stripped out of the fatigues, soaking in the hot water, I could forget about everything, for just a few minutes.

I woke with a start. Listened for screaming, for the sounds of battle. But nothing was wrong. I'd just dozed off.

Dusk had fallen; trees outside the window had turned into shadows, and the sky was nearly dark. The faint, distant shimmering of the force field flickered in the corner of my vision, like a half-hearted aurora. The team still hadn't managed to shut it down, which meant I had no leverage for dealing with Dominic.

I wondered if they were looking for me, or if Torres just assumed I'd switched sides. Fell under the island's spell. If I really was worried about what Torres thought, though, why didn't I try to escape? Why didn't I just leave my fatigues on and get the hell out of here? The island wasn't that big; I could find my way back to the Dwarf realm, or to Tor Camylot, or somewhere.

Was it because Riverhaven had tea?

I told myself I didn't matter. Torres didn't need me and didn't care if I had vanished.

Lanterns came on around me, flickering LEDs resembling candlelight. The soft light made the place seem even more otherworldly. Surely no place like this existed on Earth. Grabbing a towel helpfully placed on a nearby shelf, I bundled up and scurried to the bedchamber to change clothes and figure out what to do next.

Every detail of the room had been well-thought-out. The whispering silk of the daybed's coverlet, the gauzy curtains around the windows filtering the light just so, rustled by the slightest breeze. It would be easy to stay here, right in this room, and decide there was nothing else I could do. Let Dom take care of me, just like he wanted to.

A knock came at the door, and I flinched, wrapping the voluminous towel more securely around me. "Yes?" I said quickly, my voice cracking nervously.

I expected Dom to peek around the corner, even as I hoped he wouldn't. I still didn't know what to say to him. But it wasn't Dom. Instead a small woman with auburn hair and freckles—and, yes, pointed ears—stepped into view, but didn't cross the threshold. She had an eager smile and gave a quick little curtsy. She curtsied to *me*. I stared blankly.

"My lady, some of us are gathering in the main grotto to dine soon. Dominic asked me to invite you to join us, if you'd like. Or would you rather have food sent here, so you can dine in privacy?" She gazed hopefully—she wanted me to come to dinner with the others.

I immediately wondered what Dom's ulterior motive was.

What did he want from me? What did he think I could do for him? This dinner felt like an ambush. Scratch that, this whole situation *was* an ambush.

I was so quick to assume he had an ulterior motive.

I had an out. I could say no. Squirrel myself away in this room like the girl in the fairy tale who hides from the evil king she doesn't want to marry, demanding the most beautiful gowns of starlight, sunlight, and moonlight before she'll emerge.

Or I could just go to dinner. Do a little recon, Torres would say.

"Yes, I'll come. Give me half an hour," I said.

She beamed and dropped another quick curtsy.

"Wait a minute," I said, before she could scurry off. She turned back, curious. "What's your name?"

"Larelyn."

That couldn't possibly be her name. That had to be something she chose, something to go with the ears and the enchanted glade. On the other hand, given the names of some of my students in recent years, I couldn't be sure.

"Why are you here? I mean—what was your job, before? How did you end up here?"

"It's not really very interesting—"

"I think it's all interesting," I said. "A lot of my academic work is about modern interpretations of classic folklore. So all this—" I gestured, a wave to take in the world around me. "This is interesting. Why are you here?"

"I was a low-level graphic artist for Lang Analytics when the call went out about the new project. The more I learned about it, the more I wanted to be part of it. It kind of sucks you in, you know? Then I started working with Dominic, and we saw how much more this could be . . ." She turned pensive. "You know how you joke about what would happen if you found a wardrobe to Narnia, or got that letter from Hogwarts—and you think, yes, of course you'd go for it, of course that's what you want more than anything, for all of it to be real. When you know deep down you probably wouldn't be brave enough to step through. I mean—there are more Dursleys in the world than Hermione Grangers, aren't there? So it's easy to joke because you know it'll never happen. But then . . . but then suddenly the wardrobe opens. And I really wanted to be brave enough to step through."

She had a strained look on her face, like she didn't regret siding with Dominic against the company she worked for, but she was maybe not entirely sure she'd done the right thing. The story was still playing out, and it was different being in the middle of it, wasn't it? When you couldn't be sure of a happy ending.

Gently I said, "Met any White Witches yet? Been offered any Turkish delight? Sometimes I think it's not that people are afraid of stepping through the wardrobe—they're afraid they'll do the wrong thing once they get there." And they might not even be the villain—they'll be the misguided henchman who gets sacrificed for no reason at all.

She chuckled nervously. "Yeah, I suppose we all like to think we'll be Captain America, but most of us are just on the street trying to dodge falling buildings."

"Why not be Captain America?" I said, too tired to be angry but too annoyed to keep my mouth shut. "He was just a guy on the street, at the start."

Wringing her hands, she stared at me.

"Tell Dom I'll be there," I said finally.

Larelyn curtsied again and slipped out.

I vowed, then and there, that I wasn't going to curtsy to anyone while I was here.

22

Power Gamer

I considered putting those grubby fatigues back on, no matter how rank they'd gotten after slogging across the island. They were mine, they identified me, the way the foresters' tunics identified Arthur's people, the spiky armor identified the Dwarves, and the silken gowns the Elves. Did that mean I wanted to be identified as part of Torres's squad? I had to think about that.

In the end, I couldn't stand the thought of those reeking grubby clothes touching my skin after that nice hot bath I'd had, so I chose the most unassuming gown I could find. Gray silk with long sleeves, with thin silver necklaces and a moonstone pendant. The bodice was clinging but not skintight, and the skirt flowed in perfect folds. The light played off the fabric, rippling when I moved. It had been designed and made by people who knew what they were doing . . . and knew how to make someone who'd read *The Silmarillion* as a teenager feel graceful.

It was the simplest gown there, and it still felt too beautiful for me. All of this did. I'd barely managed to get my hair combed out, and no amount of Elvish magic would clear the puffy exhaustion from my eyes. I wrapped my injured hand in a fresh bandage so no one would have to look at the wound. Then again, if they saw it, it might remind them what the real stakes were out there.

On the ledge outside my alcove, I stopped and gasped. After nightfall, the glade turned even more mystical. Lanterns hung throughout the latticework buildings, creating pockets of soft gold, turning the arches and walkways into a painting of light and shadow. Light reflected off the pond, so the whole glade existed in a subtle glow, as if I moved through magic incarnate. Flute music drifted from somewhere across the water, just to make it even more ethereal. The scene couldn't have been more perfect if someone staged it. Ah, but someone had staged it. Designed, built, and arranged it for maximum impact. Picking my skirt up a few inches so I wouldn't trip on it, I made my way down the curving staircase to Riverhaven's main patio.

I was the last one to arrive, and two dozen people turned as I came through the archway. Dominic's design team. His followers. They came in a variety of skin tones, shapes, and sizes— they couldn't all be six feet tall, pale, and slender, thank goodness. But most of them had the ears, and they all wore Elvish gowns and tunics. Couldn't have mistaken them for anything else.

"Hi," I said, feeling a little stupid. Like I should have come up with something a little more flowery. "Greetings" or "Hail, ye fellow travelers."

"Addie, welcome," Dom said, approaching. Gracefully, elegantly, the fabric of his tunic shimmering as he moved. He reached to me, an Elf King inviting me to his realm. His smile was serene. Yes, leave it to him to handle a situation like this perfectly. "You look so lovely," he said, with a hint of longing. I fit the picture now. He had me right where he wanted me. "I'm honored that you've joined us."

I was pretty sure that was close to what Darth Vader said at the start of the dinner on Cloud City.

A feast lay spread out on a low table draped with brocade cloth. Olives, cheeses, fruit, smoked salmon, fluffy pastries. Delicate finger foods, exotic and interesting without being unfamiliar. Foods to nibble on while listening to witty conversation and poetry readings, displayed on silver platters, delicate ceramic bowls, slender utensils in art nouveau floral motifs. All 3D printed, but when I squinted, it was so very, very Elvish.

There were no chairs. Those gathered reclined on pillows and cushions. Dom set me to his right, and I perched as well as I could, too nervous to really enjoy this. Even as I kept thinking I so wanted to enjoy this.

Dom's staff studied me with stolen glances. They'd heard of me—apparently everyone on the island had heard of me. I couldn't help but think I didn't match what they'd imagined. Dominic's lost lady of song and story . . . and then me, waif-like and perpetually flinching at loud noises. But they smiled, talked of everyday things, the weather and inside jokes and small projects they'd been working on. Two of them had done much of the cooking for tonight, and everyone thanked them. All very polite.

Delicate crystal goblets had been filled with golden liquid. Dom's mead, probably. Proudly, he raised his cup. His followers did likewise.

"Please, everyone, join me in offering a toast to our most honored guest."

"Prisoner," I whispered, and he gave me a side-eye.

Answering murmurs ran around the table. I got some welcoming smiles—including from the men who'd kidnapped me, as if that would make up for what they'd done. A few turned raised eyebrows toward me, skeptical. The expression made them look more Vulcan than Elvish. To think, with the modification to their ears, they could cosplay in both worlds. How efficient.

I drank because it would have seemed rude not to. Then I drank some more because I needed it. The Elf to my right refilled my goblet from a silver pitcher. And then I drank again.

Dom wasn't finished. "And may I offer a second toast: to the strength of Riverhaven."

The answering cheers were much stronger this time. There was a fierceness to them, glaring with resolve across the table at me. A challenge, as if they saw me as an obstacle. A symbol of what they opposed.

I stared into the goblet instead of toasting and frowned. The strength of Riverhaven. What did that even mean? It was a battle cry.

"You know," I said into the following pause. "Until this moment I have never wondered who washes the dishes in Rivendell."

Everyone froze. I blinked back at them all. Well? It was a legitimate question.

"We take turns here," Larelyn said softly.

"Even Dominic?" I asked, and nobody said anything, not even Dom. Yeah, that was what I expected.

I glanced at him; he still had that amused curl on his lips, like I was behaving exactly how he expected and was pleased by it. I drank again, to hide whatever expression had crossed my face.

The Elves passed around dishes, marvelous-looking pastries, bowls of dates and figs, a plate of crumbly cheese, sliced apples, and fluffy bread with honey. Ordinary on its own, but made exotic by the setting, by being served up on silver plates and painted dishes. Delicate, lovely Elvish food.

I held up an olive and showed it to Dom. "What happens when you run out? I mean, I saw Arthur's village—you all have chickens and lettuce covered, but flour? Stuff like this? Or do you have an olive tree in a greenhouse somewhere? Your 3D printers are going to run out of material eventually, and you can't manufacture plastic here."

Dom said, "As soon as proprietorship of the island is established, we plan on starting trade negotiations—"

"Trade with *whom*? Do you think you have enough population here to form the basis of an actual economy? Means of production, Dom. You never did pay attention to Marxist theory in school."

"Addie, have some raspberries." He offered a wooden bowl filled with them, and I took several. I loved raspberries and he knew it. He refilled my goblet again.

"And what do you mean, establish proprietorship?" I said.

"Possession is nine-tenths of the law," he stated.

I squinted. "I don't think that works in real life."

"We have several lawyers on staff," he countered. "We've got this."

We used to have drunken arguments like this late at night, serious-but-not, about irrelevant topics that nonetheless felt weighty as mountains. As planets. He always said that the Galactic Empire's greater numbers and ruthlessness meant that they would defeat Starfleet. I argued that the narrative underpinnings of the two universes were so fundamentally different they could never coexist. He said I was ruining my imagination by reading too much theory and that I should let structuralism die.

I sighed. "I just don't see how you can win this fight—"

"All the more reason to try," said one of the Elves, who'd regarded me with skepticism, a stern-looking man with brown skin and piercing dark eyes. "Everyone loves an underdog."

"I'm in no position to argue with any of you." I stuffed my face with cheese and raspberries. Wondered what Torres was thinking about me just now. Glanced up at the sky, looking for flying monkeys. I only saw the purple shimmer of the force field, still intact. What had gone wrong?

Dom said, "I told you, Lang is already marketing the drone Tasers to police forces. The command ring patent alone will make him billions—"

"There's your basis of trade—intellectual property," I said, pointing. "Lang understands this. That's why you're pissed off at him."

Dom continued, undeterred. "Which means all of this is for what, to make rich shareholders richer? So that our technology—our magic—can be twisted to suit billionaires? Lang may have funded the island, but he doesn't understand it."

"All he has to do is take you to court—"

"And do what? Send another Coast Guard crew? Another mercenary squad? The island may belong to him on paper, but it's ours. Once we've taken control of Tor Camylot, we can change the passwords and biometric codes. Then it really will be ours."

"And then you can take over the world," I said.

Nobody said anything to that. They probably hadn't thought of it in quite those terms. "Saving the world" sounded better. But save from whom? For whom?

My head was swimming. So I drank more mead.

"You're not Elrond in this, you know," I burst. "You're not even Roy Batty in all his righteousness. You're *Saruman*. You think you're the master, but you don't see Sauron pulling the strings—"

"We're not evil," one of the others insisted angrily.

"Oh, no, no one's ever evil, everyone always has a good reason to do what they do, and if we could just understand it, everything would be okay, and no one would ever walk into a school with an assault rifle—"

Dom put his hand on my arm, and I took a shuddering breath. If they knew who I was, then they likely knew the whole story. Dom had probably told them, *She's fragile, we must treat her kindly* . . . The air felt like cracked glass, a breath would shatter it.

"We have dessert," Larelyn said brightly. "Chocolate-covered strawberries."

The tension broken, the others eagerly reached for the platter she passed around, the beautifully dipped and decorated fruit. And how long could they keep this up, this level of effort and work to make all this happen, this magical Elvish feast? Or was this all for me and they ate lembas waybread the rest of the time?

I took two.

The conversation progressed around me as if I didn't exist, and that was fine. I'd stuck my foot in it enough for one evening. Dom leaned back on his cushion, listening with a faint smile on his lips, a lord in his manor. Studying me when he thought I didn't notice.

The party broke up soon after. This wasn't a picture from a book or a painting; these people had lives and jobs and beds to sleep in. Some continued trying to be friendly to me. Some didn't. They all said good night to Dom, their voices filled with awe and respect. He knew all their names.

I tried to help Larelyn clear away dishes but was gently and sternly rebuffed. I was a guest; I was the princess. I should simply enjoy myself.

Dom finally rose from the table. "Addie, may I walk you back to your chambers?"

"Hmm? All right."

"This way."

He offered his hand and helped me to my feet. We walked side by side, my hand tucked in the crook of his elbow.

The walkway curved around a towering tree to a set of delicate stairs that led down to a path by the pond. We had just enough light to see by, to tell the difference between mossy earth and mirror-like water. The path drew us farther away from the archways, alcoves, and patios, to a spot where a set of glacier-smoothed boulders rested half in the water. Here, we paused.

"Watch," he said, and touched the ring on his right index finger.

Lights. Red, lavender, blue, slowly sparking to life and rising up from the foliage to drift along. Silent, gentle fireworks, sparking in the air, settling into steady glows that reflected on the water. There was some perfectly reasonable technological explanation. Wendell would say they were just LEDs powered by mini-drone engines. But I didn't care, because I knew what they were, what they *really* were. Fairy lights. Fairy magic scattered all over the pool, reflecting off the mist in the air, surrounding us with an otherworldly glow. I was in another world. I believed.

I wiped tears from my cheeks. It would be easy to let go, to not *worry*. If I could also believe that nothing existed outside this little pocket universe.

"It's so beautiful," I murmured. "It's all so beautiful." My sniffing kind of ruined the effect. I was a little bit drunk. "Why are you being so nice to me?"

"I'm trying to win you over," Dom said.

"I can see that."

Lord of his realm, he looked over the pond, his face and hair reflecting back the lighted colors. So satisfied. So happy. I'd never seen him this happy. The Elf King he'd always wanted to be. He'd never fit in, until now.

"I've missed you," he said softly. "This whole time, I've missed you. I didn't realize how much I would. I . . . don't suppose you missed me at all?"

I . . . honestly didn't know. I had convinced myself I didn't miss him at all. But now I remembered how easy being with him was. To just . . . tag along while he made his grand plans.

He went to one knee beside me. "Will you stay, Adrienne? What do I have to say to convince you to stay?"

"I don't know," I murmured. "I think . . . I think I need a drink of water. Two drinks of water."

"How much mead did you have?"

"A lot."

"Oh. Right."

He knew the routine. He put his arm around me and guided me out of the grotto, up an enchanted staircase, and across an impossible bridge to the alcove where I'd spent the afternoon. A pitcher of water was waiting, and he sat me down and got me to drink two glasses. And then I had to use the bathroom. Tolkien never discussed where the privies in Rivendell were, either.

When I reemerged, he'd lit several candles—real candles this time—and was seated on a delicately carved bench. Once again, he'd managed to make himself look like a painting. "Feeling better?"

"Yes, thank you." I sat next to him. I'd reclaimed enough focus to be able to return to the big lurking problem. "I have to ask, did you—"

But he started talking at the same time. "Did Lang specifically send you—"

We both stopped, ducked our gazes, amused.

"You first," I said.

"Lang sent you here because he assumed I would talk to you when I wouldn't talk to anyone else. Is that right?"

I pursed my lips, considering. "I was more like a last resort. The original plan was not to talk to anybody."

"That was never going to work."

"Well, yeah, we know that now." I smirked. "Arthur wanted to send me to talk to you right off. He's sure this is all a big misunderstanding."

"Misunderstanding, ha. Arthur was always clueless. This was always between me and Lang."

"You really hate him, don't you?"

"He's a monster," he said simply. "Exploitative, manipulative . . . He doesn't deserve Mirabilis."

"So the only people allowed on your island are true fans? Is there a test? They have to recite 'The Lay of Leithian' by heart? In Elvish?"

"That's not a terrible idea . . ."

I huffed, looked away.

"I'm joking."

"It's hard to tell sometimes."

"Addie. Marry me."

I stared at him, which was a mistake. Because he probably thought I was considering it. "You're joking again."

"Maybe just a little."

I touched his hand. He went very still, like he was afraid to move. Afraid to scare me off. Holding his hand, I played with the two rings. Spotted the buttons. The one with the gems had been the one to start the fairy lights. The other was a plain gold band. I couldn't see any kind of decoration on it. Maybe if I held it to a fire . . .

"Is there a One Ring?" I asked abruptly. "Tess says it never got made, but . . ." He smiled, and the gleam in his eyes was wicked. I looked at the plain ring on his finger again, rubbed it idly. Was this it? The One? "If this is it, why haven't you taken over?"

I only asked because I was drunk and was no longer self-editing. I was pretty sure he only answered because I was drunk and he thought he might talk me into siding with him.

"I'm just missing the passcode to get into the castle," he said.

I froze. Arthur had told it to all of us like it wasn't anything. And Tess was wrong, Dom didn't have spies in Arthur's camp, because they would have brought the code to Dom straight off. Dom had placed statues everywhere, but . . . we hadn't been near any of them when Arthur told us the code.

Oh my God, I had the code. He had the Ring.

"Addie? What's wrong? You've got this look on your face."

I was nearly choking on everything I couldn't say. Wouldn't say. Or . . . or . . . I could just tell him. The Ring might not work . . . or I could stay here forever and never have to think about anything ever again, or —

"Addie?" he urged again, holding my arms like he was afraid I might fall over.

"It's not real," I murmured. "I keep telling myself it isn't real, it's all just made up."

His touch was so familiar, and the setting so dream-like, warmly lit by candlelight, and we were already so close to the nest-like bed, all of it accompanied by the music of the splashing waterfall.

"It's real if we decide it is."

"But is a simulation real? This is a simulation. No, not even that — you've built a reproduction of a simulation, and errors have crept into the copy . . . I'm sure Baudrillard would have something pithy to say about this —"

He raised my hand to his lips, kissed it. And I leaned in to encourage him, and he kissed my lips. He tasted like honey and magic. I touched his cheek, let my fingers play with a strand of

his hair. Stretched like a cat when he put his arms around me.
I remembered the feel of him, all of him . . .

"You're still drunk."

"Yeah," I said.

"You might regret this in the morning."

"No, I won't," I murmured, and stood to pull him off the seat
and lead him to the bed myself.

I was warm, melted, and about to fall asleep when Dom nuzzled
my neck, and I flushed all over again. Made a happy sound and
wrapped my arm around his.

"Addie," he whispered. "You keep looking up. It's the shield,
isn't it?"

"Hmm?"

"Your mercenary. He's trying to shut down the shield."

"He's not my mercenary," I said.

"But did he find a way to shut down the shield?"

Outside, the sky over the glade shimmered with that purplish light.

"I told you, Torres doesn't trust me. I don't know what he
has planned." Especially now, when he probably assumed I'd
gone over to the enemy.

And had I?

"Never mind," Dom said, and kissed me again, and it was
very, very easy to believe I was in Middle-earth, in the Last
Homely House of the Elves, making love with the Elf prince of
my dreams. I could just stay here for a little while.

23

Precious

Turned out, the surgery to modify Dom's ears meant he didn't have much sensation left in them. Small price to pay, he'd said—everything else had plenty of sensation. But it did remind me that none of this was organic. All of it had been forced. This might be real, but it wasn't *true*.

I woke up with a smaller headache than I deserved. And I was alone. I could just about feel the space in the bed where'd he'd been, but he'd tucked the blankets back around me, leaving me warm and cozy. Snuggling into the soft sheets and luxurious pillows—no expense spared, really—I tried to enjoy the moment. The air was perfectly cool, morning light shrouded through a misty rain, the waterfall tumbling soothingly. I was inside a John Howe or Alan Lee illustration, and it was everything I'd hoped it would be. I could just stay here. Let Torres and the others come and rescue me. I'd tell them I'd been kidnapped—which was absolutely true. I didn't have to tell them how much I liked it.

Except . . . there was that question about who did the dishes in Rivendell. Where had Dom gone off to, and what was happening in the real world? The real world. What did that even mean anymore?

I rolled out of bed and quickly got myself put together. Left the silky gray gown draped over the back of a chair and found one that seemed a little more practical: brown, cotton, with a blue tunic over it. Just like what I wore in my early SCA days. It felt comfortable and awkward at the same time. Mostly it felt solid. I put on the boots I'd been wearing before. Somehow, the clash of styles—archaic and modern, gentle and rugged—worked. I had my feet in both worlds.

The fatigues were folded neatly at the bottom of the closet where I'd left them. Except . . . not exactly how I'd left them. They'd been moved since I put them there yesterday evening.

They'd been searched.

Kneeling, I held the trousers up, patted down all the pockets. The book with the bronze amulet, the ring from the spider maze, the glowing triangle—all gone. And so was my lucky d20.

"Dom," I murmured, and bit my lip. I was furious, but I wasn't surprised.

I turned, planning to storm out, and nearly ran straight into Larelyn in the doorway. Her eyes went wide, looking me up and down. I was gripping the grubby fatigues like they were a weapon.

"Um, hi, good morning," she said quickly.

"Where's Dom?" I demanded.

She straightened, squaring elegant shoulders and attempting a more serene expression. A more Elvish expression. "Dominic will be along shortly. Are you hungry? There's breakfast on the patio, if you'd like." She said this hopefully, like she just wanted me to be happy.

"I want to talk to Dom," I said.

"Would you feel better if you ate something?"

My jaw clenched. Of course Dom had searched my stuff. He'd acted like he was happy to see me, like he was really trying to keep me safe, when this whole time he just wanted to *use* me . . .

I couldn't figure out if I was hungry or not. "Tea," I muttered. "I'll have some tea."

I shoved the fatigues back in the closet and followed Larelyn out to the patio, where a beautiful breakfast spread had been laid out with all of my favorite foods. Scones, jam, strawberries, little wrapped bacon bite things. I looked at her a little desperately.

"All for you," she said, gesturing to the spindly chair at the leaf-like art nouveau table.

You aren't supposed to eat the food you're offered in fairyland.

All I'd ever wanted to do was escape. No, that wasn't true. All I wanted was for what happened to mean something. *Stories* meant something, and real life . . . didn't. *God has a plan, this is part of God's plan* — stupid people kept telling me that over and over again at Alex's and Dora's funerals, at the endless memorials.

There was no plan. Or if there was, it was cruel, and God was a terrible GM.

I went to the funerals and memorials because I wanted the whole stupid tragedy to *mean* something. And then it was over, and everyone else forgot, and it was just the other survivors and me standing there. My parents and older brothers watched me like I was going to explode, and I was in therapy twice a week for the first six months.

But the only meaning is . . . you just have to keep going.

That was a long time ago. This . . . was all going to come crashing down. Any minute now.

"Why are you doing all this?" I asked breathlessly.

"Because we can," she said, her smile sweet and guileless. "My lady, please sit, Dominic will be along in a moment—"

I clasped my hands, pleading almost. "You want this to look like magic, but I know how much work goes into it. Thank you."

Grimly, I went past the table to the next covered walkway, this one leading to a set of stairs that spiraled up to a part of Riverhaven I hadn't been to yet.

"My lady! Professor Cox, wait—"

I kept going, and Larelyn fluttered nervously but didn't follow.

The staircase led into the branches of trees, to a walkway that was curtained with shimmering leaves. This in turn led to a series of platforms that climbed even higher, to the edge of the rocks that marked the top of the waterfall. Past the trees, an ornate spire rose from a small cottage, a treehouse. The spire hid a set of antennae, the same kind of antennae we'd seen at every settlement on the island. The communications array that connected everything, that made the magic work.

I kept going up, moving too quickly, making myself lightheaded. Maybe I should have eaten breakfast after all. Soon, I couldn't climb any higher. The last walkway ended in a short set of stairs and a small, round structure. It had a solid door and no windows, unlike every other structure in Riverhaven, with its open arches and trellised walls. I pressed the latch, assuming it would be locked.

It wasn't. The door opened. The room inside was a dim office with two computer monitors, a keyboard, and a touch pad set up on an entirely ordinary desk. A couple of computer CPUs sat in the corner, green power lights glowing. A set of cables ran up through the ceiling.

I pressed one of the touch pads and the monitors came to

life, showing a dozen video screens, each with its own display in progress. On one monitor, the images were frozen, and I recognized a couple of the scenes they showed: Arthur's rustic village, and the path outside the Sphinx's tower. The Sphinx was still frozen by the path, right where we left it. It hadn't been reset yet. A couple of the other squares were blacked out, as if the cameras had malfunctioned. Or been destroyed.

These were images from the statues of Lang, scattered across the island. The blacked-out feeds showed the statues Tess had smashed. Dominic had been watching us the whole time we'd been on the island.

The second monitor contained another set of images, these showing dizzyingly fast motion, like an airplane sweeping over the canopy of trees. The images were outlined by fluttering black feathers.

Ravens. These were live feeds from the spy ravens.

Quickly, I sat in the chair and scrolled through the various feeds, looking for one that might tell me what Torres and the others were doing. Surely Dom was keeping a close eye on them. Three ravens appeared to be active. One seemed to be scanning the shoreline. Dom probably hadn't thought he needed to search the coast, until Torres's squad arrived and punched through the shield.

Some of the other video displays showed older footage, with time stamps from — I checked the time on the monitor — the previous evening, and also a couple of hours earlier. I played the most recent.

The scroll of trees filmed by the drone gave way to open space, a grassy field, and then a dirt road came into view. The image slowed, then tipped, as the drone swerved to change direction, which gave me a lurch of motion sickness and made my hangover headache worse. Then the drone hovered.

People came into view, part of a convoy of some kind: a

wagon pulled by a black-furred Warg and a troop surrounding it. I searched the tops of heads and hoods of the dozen people for someone I recognized, but this angle didn't show me much in the way of faces or features. Was the man in the black jacket Torres? Or was that a woolen coat instead of a jacket? I couldn't tell.

The next thing that happened, one of the figures in the caravan pointed up with a gloved hand. A flurry of motion followed, and a man in a green hat—*that* was Robin Hood, I was pretty sure—unslung a bow from his shoulder and drew back the string. The arrow that flew up was little more than a streak, I barely saw it, but the drone's image jerked, lurched, and went blurry as it tumbled out of the sky. The video playback froze.

Now, where on the island was this happening? At least some of them had left the Realm of Shield. Were Torres and the squad with them? Where were they going? I studied the images for some kind of label, coordinates that might tell me where on the island they were, and clicked on icons and apps. I could try to steer the raven, send some kind of signal. I was in so far over my head.

Abruptly, everything shut off, all the screens showing dead blue. I leaned back, hands away from the touch pad. I could have sworn I hadn't done anything to cause this. Biting my lip, I huffed a sigh and tried again, pushing the power button on the CPU, flipping the switch on the power bar. Then I wondered: even if I couldn't get any good information, I could unplug everything and . . . and break it somehow so that Dominic wouldn't have the information, either.

"Addie?"

I flinched back. Dom was standing in the doorway.

"Good morning," he said. Today he wore a gray-blue tunic and a silver coat, the colors of a winter ocean, and an ivory-looking circlet held back his dark hair. God, he was beautiful. I couldn't breathe.

A million excuses died on my lips. This was exactly like it looked. I suddenly decided there was absolutely no reason for me to make excuses for being here. If he didn't want me exploring, he should have locked the doors.

"I think I broke your surveillance system."

"The monitors have always been a little touchy. Larelyn says you didn't eat breakfast. You should probably eat before we leave."

"Leave to where?"

"You'll see." He nodded to the door. Obediently, I went with him. At his side, I could smell him, the warmth and spicy sweat of him that had filled me up last night. He offered his hand. I took it, and he guided me down the stairs and into the cool air of the forest.

"Maer aur. Ci maer?" he said.

"Fine, I'm fine," I murmured, answering before it even registered that I understood his Elvish.

"Regrets?" he asked.

"Oh, Dom. On what scale?" I shook my head. "Last night, no. No regrets."

He squeezed my hand and seemed pleased.

I took a breath and asked, "Dom, where's my stuff?"

He tilted his head, raised a brow. If I was a terrible liar, so was he. "What stuff?"

"The stuff you took out of my pockets."

"Describe it to me."

"My *loot*," I said.

"Let's talk about this over tea."

His smile was meant to be serene, soothing. But I couldn't shake the feeling he was getting ready to lie to me again.

The waterfall had begun to sound monotonous, and the air was just a little too chilly. Dom found me a wool cloak, and I wrapped it tight around myself. The tea did not taste nearly as good as what I'd had yesterday when I first arrived; I'd left it steeping too long when I went on my little exploratory trip. Dom sat next to me, tapping his fingers on the table. Leaning back like he was keeping himself from reaching out to me. I crumbled a scone to pieces on my plate.

"I had a ring, a plastic triangle, a book, and a d20." He should have recognized my lucky d20. I suddenly decided I didn't care about the rest of it, but I wanted my die back. But if he was interested in the other items . . . what did they mean to *him*?

"Addie," he started. "You've come into this so late, you can't understand everything that's happening here."

"And you think you do?" I said. "You're all telling different stories about it. You, Arthur, Tess, even Lang."

He looked away, letting out a sour chuckle. "You only know what Lang told you about this place. I'm assuming you read that book of his? His manifesto?"

"Yes, and Lang is *really* sketchy. But there's also everything I've learned myself over the last three days. What is reality but perception?" I finally ate a piece of demolished scone. Lemon and cranberry. It tasted marvelous.

"Too much theory," he muttered. "That's always been your problem."

"Dom. What have you done with my stuff?"

"Question first." He reached under his surcoat — somehow, the genius tailor had managed to work a pocket into it without ruining the lines — and produced a simple gold band. *My* ring, the one I'd found. His rings were all still on his fingers. "Where did you get this?" he asked, like the question was important.

I hated that I didn't trust him. I could feel the warmth coming off his body. I wanted to curl up next to him, let him wrap his arms around me. He smelled *so good*. But I didn't trust him.

"Where do you think I got it?" I replied. "You designed the island, put together the challenges. Where are all the places you hid rings of power?"

His lips pressed into a line, and the hard look in his eyes was supposed to hide his uncertainty. He didn't answer because he didn't know; he wasn't the only one making and hiding rings.

"How many rings did you make?" I asked.

"I only made one," he said, raising his hand, indicating the finger with the gold band.

I smiled. "You thought you were in charge, didn't you? That you were the game master? Well, so did everyone else. Bishop to king seven."

He furrowed his brow, narrowed his gaze. "What's that supposed to mean?"

I shouldn't have said anything. I shouldn't have pushed. "Lang said to tell you that, as a message from him." Dom's gaze turned inward, and he chuckled a little. The line might mean more to him. They had a whole history I knew nothing about.

"He knew it was you behind the mutiny all along," I said, testing. "You still think you're in charge here? You still think you can win?"

He straightened, tipped up his chin. Restoring the elegant Elvish persona, which had slipped a bit. "The others are gathering on the plain outside Tor Camylot. Tess, Arthur, the mercenaries. They might have found a way to reboot the castle without the Ring. I need to be there. You should come with me."

"Are you giving me a choice?"

"I'm betting you won't be able to stay away. Ready to take a trip?"

"I want my stuff back first," I said.

"You don't even know what any of it is for."

That wasn't the point. You didn't pick stuff up in a game because you knew what it was for, but because you might need it later. "I know what my lucky d20 is for," I said. "It's for luck."

He went to a sideboard table, opened a filigree silver chest there, and drew out the book, the triangle, and my d20. My relief was palpable, physical, and rushed out of me with a sigh. Neatly, politely, he set the three items on the table in front of me.

The ring, though, he slipped on his finger and gave me a little Goblin King smile, waiting for me to argue.

I glared. "One more thing: no blindfolds this time."

24

Leeroy Jenkins

Four of us traveled from Riverhaven to Tor Camylot: Dominic, two of his guards, and me. "I don't want to look like an army," he said wryly. Riding unicorns, we formed a striking company. The thing about robot unicorns, none of us had to know what we were doing in order to ride them. They were like carousel horses, freed from their endless circle. We didn't need skills; we didn't need to know anything. This was playacting.

Except they weren't playacting. Dom and his men were armed, with swords on their belts and bows and quivers over their shoulders. They must have felt righteous.

Dom's unicorn was caparisoned in beautiful silver tack and barding. They both sparkled. The unicorn had shining dark eyes, a lush thick mane dripping over its neck and around its ears. Enough mane to occupy a little girl with a brush and ribbons for hours. And that horn, that jewel-like spiral horn. The creature's nostrils flared as if it breathed, and it shook its head when Dom nudged it. But when it stopped, it stayed stopped;

not so much as a muscle twitched. I looked into the unicorn's eye and it was just glass. No personality, not like the Wargs. Either the programming on them hadn't gotten that far—or Dom wanted unicorns without personality. Which seemed kind of sad to me.

The sky no longer misted, but the clouds remained, a haunting fog pressing down on the treetops. The air smelled damp, and the unicorns' hooves squished on wet ground.

Our route took us through the forest north of Tor Camylot. Dom's people had trod out a good dirt path here, during the weeks they'd spent spying across the island and scouting around the castle. As we left Riverhaven's territory, the way grew less hilly, less rocky.

This might have been a lovely trip, if not for the stone in my gut, the feeling that something terrible was about to happen.

I glanced up once and saw a shadow, a tiny silhouette against the sky: it had wide wings, a long thin tail, and the squared-off shape of a little fez on its head. For all their Elvishness, Dom's company made enough noise to cover up the sound of its buzzing motors.

Dom and the others were focused on the path ahead and didn't see the spy watching us, and I didn't point it out. But I must have looked worried, because Dom reached over to squeeze my hand. "Everything will work out, you'll see."

For my part, I wasn't looking forward to seeing Torres and the squad again. Explaining to them. Because I knew what this looked like, me dressed in Elvish clothes, Dominic clucking over me with such possessive concern.

I wished I knew what Torres had planned. What we were riding into. I'd found a soft leather pouch with a strap and wore it over my shoulder, with my loot stashed inside. From the outside, I could feel the hard angles of my lucky d20. I didn't know what skills applied to this impending situation. Diplomacy? Bluff?

"Addie, I wish I knew what would make you feel better. What do you want? What would make you happy?"

"Right now? I want everyone to stay safe. I don't want anyone to die. Anyone else."

"Nobody is going to die—"

"Dom. You don't know that. You don't know anything about it."

"And you do?"

"Yes! Yes I do." I'd seen people die. Dominic never, ever had. "You all were so busy building these monsters and making these machines, you forgot it was going to be real people dealing with it all. You kept pretending it was still a game where everything was dice rolls, or you decided that your healing potions would be strong enough to fix anything. But the blood is real. People have already died, and I don't want to see any more blood."

"I'll protect you. I promise."

I stared at him, crazed laughter on the edge of my lips. I swallowed it back. "You can't." And he looked so confused in that moment, I felt sorry for him. "You're not in charge here."

The two guards rode a little behind, politely giving us space. I glanced back; their gazes were downcast. I wiped a stray, stressed-out tear off my cheek, and Dom's expression was so concerned, so pitying.

He really did want to protect me. That part I believed.

We continued on for a time. I straightened, trying to find some Elvish elegance of my own. Tried to act like I wasn't worried, if for no other reason than to keep Dom from hovering so much. We stopped for a quick lunch of bread, cheese, and cider, in a beautiful grassy meadow filled with buttercups that Dom must have created especially for the occasion.

The clouds broke. Our path went up a rise and gave us a view of Tor Camylot. The afternoon sun flashed over the plain before the castle, a gleaming tower in the distance. From this side, the lake spread out before it like a mirror, the gray walls reflected in the water, along with sky and clouds above. Willows dripped around the shore, and birdsong carried through the valley.

It was incredible.

In full daylight, the Elves in their regalia were blinding. That was probably the intention. As part of the design team, they knew how to put on a show.

"What makes you think you can take control of Tor Camylot when Arthur and Tess haven't been able to?" I asked, breaking the spell Dom was trying to cast.

"Because I deserve it."

The main tower still didn't have any banners flying. I might have been hoping that Torres and his crew had found a way inside the castle to hack into the control system. That it would all be taken care of, no further discussion needed.

No such luck. The island's shield was still active.

Our approach seemed to take forever. "What will you do when we meet the others?" I asked Dom.

"Talk," he said. "Just talk."

I had slept with this man last night. I had been determined not to regret it. But right now, it wasn't just that I didn't trust him—I felt like I didn't even know him.

The trail curved around and revealed a tableau spread out before us: tents, banners too damp to flutter, a couple of Wargs and their carts resting nearby, and people milling around it all.

Nothing modern was visible; this was like a scene from a story, with Dwarves and foresters and archers all gathered together for . . . for what?

A distant arm pointed toward us; people clustered and gathered to look.

"They've spotted us, my lord," the Elvish warrior riding at our flank pointed out, unnecessarily. We'd all seen it.

They should never have started calling Dom "lord"; it had gone straight to his head.

Dom came alongside him. "Good. Are you ready?"

"Yes, my lord," his two guards answered eagerly. Their gazes shone, their lips smiled, pleased to be part of the unfolding story.

"No," I said. I still didn't know where I fit into this adventure.

"Everything will be fine. You'll see," Dom said, and he came across as condescending rather than reassuring. *Now* I remembered why I left him.

We arrived on the wide grassy plain where the others had pitched camp. My stomach flipped over. This was fine, I reminded myself. We would talk, get this cleared up. Nothing to worry about.

Tor Camylot had a shadow now, and we stood near its edges. I had to crane my neck back to see the top of its towers. Across a short drawbridge, a wide, curved door, made of wood handed with iron, remained closed. A pair of gulls soared overhead. I was pretty sure they were real.

Dom touched a ring, and both his and my unicorns came to a stop. I had never been in control of my mount. I was sure there was a metaphor there. His guards fell into place on either side of us. Thirty yards ahead of us: everyone else.

On the right, the Dwarves, standing under their black and gold banner of the Realm of Shield. Tess and six of her people, fully armed with axes and spears, butts set on the ground. Most of her expression was hidden by the etched bronze noseguard of her helmet, but I could see her set jaw, her lips pressed together in anger.

On the left, under the red banner of the Realm of Sword, Arthur stood impassively, like the statue of a king. He wore a magnificent etched cuirass, leather gauntlets, high boots, a half cloak over one shoulder. A silver-hilted sword with a jeweled pommel hung on his belt, his hand resting on it, posing to present the ideal heroic picture. Around him, the foresters also wore their finest: grubby scouting clothes traded out for heraldic tabards of red and gold. Some of them wore the bowl-shaped helmets of the English yeomen of Agincourt. Robin Hood stood at Arthur's shoulder, and of all them he looked the most himself, still in his wool and leather, crisp red feather in his cap, his bow in hand.

Dom and his escorts didn't need the silver banner of the Realm of Arrow. They *were* their own banners.

And there, finally, was the hint of mundanity I'd been looking for: Torres and the squad, moving up front and center. Even they were showing the wear of the journey, with haggard eyes and matted hair. Almonte and Rucker flanked Torres, rifles in hand, at parade rest. Wendell was off to the side, a crate of gear at his feet. Torres had shaved since the last time I saw him; his smooth jaw seemed naked, unlikely. The other two men had scruffy beards started.

They could kill us all. Did they have secret orders from Lang to just kill everyone, if they couldn't get back custody of the island? Surely Lang wouldn't go that far. Surely Torres wouldn't. No, he wouldn't let things get out of hand. This would all turn out okay.

Wouldn't it?

Torres's gaze on me, *right* on me, was hard. Questioning.

Tess shook her head and pulled off her helmet. "Oh my God, Dominic. You are such an asshole."

"How are you, Tess? Surly as usual, I see."

I couldn't take this anymore, so I slid off the unicorn, awkwardly brushing out my dress to make sure it stayed in place, and moved off. Just to give myself some space. My legs wobbled but I managed to stay upright. My own team made up of just me.

"Addie—" Dom started. I threw him a glare.

"Professor, are you all right?" Torres asked calmly.

"They kidnapped me, Captain. Whatever else happens, I just want you to know that they kidnapped me. I didn't walk out on you."

"You look like one of them now."

"Not totally," I argued, sticking my foot out to show the sturdy, non-Elvish boot. I didn't have pointy ears, at least; I had that much going for me. But yes, I tried to look at this from his perspective. I'd come riding in exactly like the enemy. Dom had planned it that way. Brought me under his banner. "Also, they offered me a hot bath. I was weak." Torres ducked his head, hiding a smile. I didn't know if that was a good sign. An uncomfortable silence followed, each party waiting for one of the others to make the first move. Dom, Arthur, Tess, Torres. "Well, we've got four armies, anyway," I said under my breath. I glanced overhead but didn't see any sign of approaching eagles.

Dominic dismounted, leaving his weapons slung on the saddle, and came to my side. "Captain Torres," he said. "Nice to finally meet you in person."

"Can't say the same, Mr. Brand. Harris Lang wants to talk to you."

"I'm sure he does," Dom said.

Torres reached into the front of his jacket. The two Elvish guards twitched, hands moving to the quivers at their belts.

Dom waved them off with a gesture, and Torres eyed them warily. He raised both hands, revealing what he'd taken from his pocket: another of Lang's message devices. He came forward just far enough to be able to toss the device over. Dom came forward to catch it and offered the captain a mocking salute.

I wasn't sure this was a good idea.

"You know what this says?" Dom asked me, drawing me a little ways off, shielding both me and the message with a turn of his shoulders.

"Lang had one for each of the managers."

"Well, let's see what the Allfather has to say." He put his thumb to the sensor.

Lang's projected face appeared, faint in the sunlight. Reading his expression was difficult, but he seemed to be both smiling and glaring. The recorded voice was clear. "Dominic. If you're seeing this, things have progressed much further than I expected. This was supposed to be over by now, but you always did have a flair for the dramatic. I urge you to cooperate. If not . . . well. I'm coming for you." The message buzzed out in a burr of static.

The message had played softly enough that only Dom and I heard it. Torres waited patiently, like it didn't matter to him one way or another what Dom did.

Dom chuckled at the message, and the sinking feeling in the pit of my stomach grew claws.

"Dom, please. Let's talk," I said. "Let's all sit down and work this out."

"Oh, no," he said. "Not when I've got all the advantage."

"But what if you don't?"

He turned back to the gathering, to his enemy. "Captain Torres. You can't take command of the castle without my override key. I can't get into the castle without Beckett's passcode.

I intend to legally take possession of the island on behalf of my people. It's already ours in every way that matters. I have no other argument with any of you. Convince Beckett to give me that code, then we can talk. Come to terms. I'm willing to negotiate, but only after I have control of the castle."

Torres knew better than to react, but Arthur Beckett didn't. He looked at me sharply, gaze narrowed. Putting the pieces together. Realizing that I knew the code and wasn't helping Dominic.

And Dom saw the look. He studied me, frowning.

"You're not really in a position to negotiate, Mr. Brand," Torres said.

"Addie. What aren't you telling me?" Dom murmured.

"You can't listen to him!" Tess called angrily. "He's bluffing, he doesn't have an override key. I never made one!"

"And you were so sure I'd never be able to build anything without your help," Dominic said, laughing. "When I learned you were in talks with Garamon Tech, I stopped telling you about anything my team was developing."

"What?" Arthur said, turning on the chief engineer.

Tess sputtered. "That's a lie!" And even some of her own people looked at her, accusing. Unconsciously they moved away, putting space around her. They all believed it was at least possible.

"We found the encrypted emails," Torres said.

"Tess, what have you done!" Arthur put a hand to his head, like this was the greatest betrayal of all.

Dom chuckled, clearly enjoying this. "I told Lang I'd contact him when I flushed out the spy. But I changed my mind." He gazed on them all, so smug, so sure he was in control.

Almonte stepped up then and spoke to Dom. "So is that why you activated the shield, to keep Selvachan from selling secrets to the competition?"

"That's part of it," Dom said. "It confirmed for me that Mirabilis shouldn't serve corporate interests." He held out a beseeching hand. "Arthur, Tess, it's not too late, you can still join me—"

"Mr. Brand," Almonte said. Urgent and focused, she moved into the space between the groups, supplanting Torres. The captain blinked after her, seemingly startled for the first time this whole trip. "Can you confirm that you activated the shield that has prevented anyone approaching the island?"

"I think I just did."

"Leah?" Torres asked. "What's this about?"

Almonte reached into her front jacket pocket and drew out a small plastic packet. Flipped it open to reveal a government ID and leveled her gaze at Dominic. "I'm Special Agent Leah Almonte with the CGIS, and I have the authority to arrest you for the murder of the crew of the USCGC *Point McKinley.*"

Well, I didn't see that coming.

25

Doom and Great Deeds

Torres gave Almonte a sidelong look and spoke a nonplussed "Huh."

"Sorry, sir," she said. "Couldn't let on."

Befuddled, Arthur tilted his head. "CGIS, like NCIS but Coast Guard? Is that even a thing?"

Glaring, Dom set his jaw. He was trying to get out of checkmate. He'd flip the board if he had to. "Agent Almonte, it's just you, one person not working for Lang, against all the rest of us who are," he said. "You can't win here."

"Actually, I'm with her," Torres said.

"Yeah, I think I am, too," Tess added.

Arthur sighed. "Harris Lang is a visionary; I'd follow him anywhere. But this . . . this is a federal murder charge, Dominic."

"I don't acknowledge your authority," Dom declared, accompanied by a sharp swipe of his hand. "Any of you." He turned to his guards, ready to give some kind of command.

Almonte—she'd been a secret agent this whole time?—

started forward to confront Dom. As if he would just go along with letting her handcuff him. I turned to him, to try to talk him into backing down—

But then Arthur Beckett called out, "Now!"

Robin Hood made a gesture, and a half-dozen drones roared up from behind a canvas tent and fanned out over the gathering. They were small, agile, similar to the stunner drones that had come after us earlier. Designed to swoop in and stun us all. Trying to get the jump on us.

"Stand down!" Torres hollered. "Stand those things *down!*"

Dom's Elvish guards nocked arrows to bows and let fly. One missed, and the second clipped a drone, which wobbled then resumed flying—and it shot out its wires to its assailant, striking. The man twitched and fell, stunned.

Rucker and Wendell both tackled Robin Hood. The Dwarves seemed to be running, except one who was jumping and swinging a battle-axe at a drone.

Then Dom was at my side, arm across my chest—and he pressed something hard and pointed against my neck. "It's not a gun, Addie. Stay calm, just play along, everything'll be fine."

If it wasn't a gun, then what was it? My knees gave out and I almost vomited. He braced me against him and held me upright. Gasping, I grabbed his arm, but his weight tipped me just off-balance. He held me immobile.

"Beckett! Call off your drones!" Dom called. "Everybody stop where you are!" His grip across my chest was confining, strong. Protective in the way of a straitjacket.

But everyone stopped. Almonte stood with her hands raised in a conciliatory gesture. The drones powered down, their mechanical whines falling silent. In the stillness, everyone was looking at us, which was exactly how Dom liked it.

"Jesus, Brand, you really are an asshole," Torres said. "You know what she's been through and you still pull this shit?"

"You're not in charge here, Torres." Dom laughed.

"What is that?" Torres demanded. "What's he holding?"

Wasn't a gun, Dom said. I wasn't sure I believed him.

"It's a fucking wand," Tess muttered, disgusted.

I didn't dare struggle. I couldn't see anything but my nose and Dom's arm locking me against him. Breathe, breathe . . .

"Dom, we never tested those," Arthur said. His voice was taut, shaking almost. "You can't use that on her."

I was going to pass out. I wouldn't be able to stop it. I could feel my brain misfiring. I needed to sit down, to get hold of my breathing—

"You understand, don't you, Addie?" Dom demanded. "Now we're in a real standoff. Your mercenaries still have the most firepower. They can mow us all down and clean up the mess after."

"They won't," I gasped, my tongue sticking to my teeth because my mouth had gone so dry. "They wouldn't . . ."

"With federal authorities involved, they can sweep all this under the carpet. This will all just vanish. Tell me, Addie, do you trust your Captain Torres? Can he really look after you the way I will?"

"I know the passcode," I choked out. "Arthur told us the passcode. I can get us into the castle."

"Really?"

"I . . . I think so. Just . . . please don't let anyone get hurt. Please."

"That was never my intention," he murmured. "Come, walk with me."

Stumbling, I let him guide me backward, toward the drawbridge and its gate. His remaining guard was kneeling by his fallen comrade, who started to sit up, shaking his head.

"Cover us," Dom said, and the guard nodded, placing another arrow against his bow.

"I don't think you'll really hurt her," Torres called out.

"You also think I'm crazy, don't you?" Dom said. "It doesn't matter what you think. One way or another, Addie understands what's happening here."

"No, I don't!" I gasped. "Dom, please—"

"Hush. It's going to be all right."

"And now I've got him on kidnapping and assault," Almonte said, with an air of disgust.

"Jesus Christ, Dominic!" Tess called. "Stop this!"

I should have been brave. I should have tried to fight him. Tried to wrench out of his grasp using one of those nifty moves they always did in the movies. Except I could guess how well that would—or wouldn't—work in reality.

I was just a prop for him, I'd always only ever been a prop—

"All of you back off," Dom said. "Once I get control of the castle, we can talk. I promise."

"Your override isn't going to work!" Tess shouted.

"Quiet," Torres said calmly. "It's going to be fine."

Dom flinched. A small hesitation.

"Dom," I murmured.

Our footsteps sounded hollowly on the wooden bridge, and then we were at the gate. The castle wall loomed next to us. It looked pitted, aged, spotted with lichens, but it was all fake, set dressing. I could see behind the curtain everywhere now. Dom wasn't an Elf King and the whole illusion fell apart.

He managed to keep the wand at my throat, that arm bracing me against his body, while reaching to touch a spot on the wall: a small bronze box set into the stone. It was a cover that opened to reveal a keypad that lit up when exposed to the light.

"Why would Beckett give you the passcode?" Dom asked.

"Because he was cooperating with Torres. He just *told* us."

"Do you think it's the right one?"

That gave me a moment's pause. If it was the wrong one,

well . . . "I'm pretty sure," I said. "He doesn't seem like much of a schemer."

"Tell me, Addie."

"It's 'One Ring to Rule Them All' but with the last letter of each word capitalized instead of the first. No spaces."

"My God, that man has no imagination. Tess was always trying to get him to use random password generators and he just wouldn't. That's probably the password on his bank account. Will you type it in, please?" He shifted, hauling me around to face the keypad.

"What if I say no?"

"Don't," he said.

I typed in the password. Messed up a couple of times and had to backspace. Tried again. Dom was tapping his finger on my shoulder.

"Hurry," he said.

"I'm trying. This is actually a pretty good password—"

"Addie—"

Then I got it. The light over the keypad turned green. A couple of metallic clunks sounded behind the wood. And the gate popped outward a crack.

"Finally," Dom said, grinning.

"Last chance, Brand," Torres said, calling from the other side of the bridge. "Give up now, I'll put in a good word for you."

Dominic ignored him. The gate swung open and he hustled me inside.

"You're in the castle. Now let me go, Dom. Please," I begged.

But the gate slammed shut behind us. Now we were alone, locked together in a stone passageway, dark and dank like a cave, leading through the castle's thick outer wall. It felt like a trap. Finally, the scream that had been gathering in my lungs broke out and echoed against the stone archway. I tore out of his grasp and hit him. Pounded fists into his chest, slapped his face. Slapped it again, like some stupid ineffectual pawn. And he just stood there, taking it.

Pulling away, I slumped against the wall, covered my tear-streaked face with my hands. I was dizzy. I hadn't taken a good breath in what felt like hours, and my whole body was shaking. I could smell the firing range, and no one had even fired a gun. Breathe, breathe, breathe.

Dom waited. At least he remembered enough about being with me that he waited until I could look back at him without crying. I hugged myself and let a tired breath shudder out of me.

A second bronze plate, another control panel, was set into the wall on this side of the gate. Dom worked at it, punching in commands. Changing the passcode so no one would be able to follow us.

"We've won," he said finally, grinning wide. "You'll see. We've won."

"There's no 'we' here," I said, my voice creaking. "Let me go, Dom."

He put his hands on my shoulders. "Addie, don't you want to see the castle? Please. I can tell how much you love it here. Please stay with me, you'll be happy, I promise—"

"'Just let me rule you . . . and I will be your slave'? Is that the line?"

His brow furrowed. "What is that from?"

"'You have no power over me,'" I finished the quote, and he still didn't figure it out. "I know refusing to memorize *Labyrinth* isn't the exact reason I left you, but it sure didn't help."

Beyond the passage lay a grassy sward, the castle's bailey, an open stretch between outer wall and the inner structure. The keep rose up at least six stories, a wall of stone with occasional windows and murder holes. It all seemed dead. I wondered if it was haunted.

"There," he murmured, pointing across the bailey to yet another bronze box, at the keep's wooden door. "Now we see where the real power is."

Grinning madly, he grabbed my hand and hauled me with him across the lawn. He slid back a panel, revealing another keypad, into which he punched a series of commands. Prongs popped out of a slot. He pulled one of the gold bands off his finger and fitted it between them. His gold band, the One Ring.

"Goddammit," a male voice muttered softly behind me. But when I turned to look, no one was there. Dom and I were the only ones here—

Oh.

I very, very carefully did not look behind me again.

We waited, as if there'd be fireworks or a golden banner unfurling from the flagpole on the tower, along with trumpets blaring. Letters scrolling across the doorway, *You're a winner!* Dom stared at the door like he expected something to happen, and nothing did.

His hand curled into a fist, which he pressed against the door. With a frustrated sigh, he yanked the ring out of the prongs and put it back on his finger.

Then he chose the other gold band, the one I'd found, and tried that instead.

A small, happy chime played, but in the context it sounded mocking, a Disneyland ride gone wrong. Dom didn't look happy.

"Addie, this is very important. You have to tell me. Where did you find this?"

"At the gate of the spider maze," I said. "South of Arthur's village."

"Shit," he muttered, dispensing with the Elf King persona entirely.

"What's wrong?"

"I don't know what software this just triggered."

"And this is why we look for traps before opening the door," I said, scowling. "This is why we don't go around activating strange rings, because they might have been made by the Dark Lord to enslave you. You know this, Dominic!"

"But it's mine, this island is mine, *I* designed it, I know what's possible—"

A familiar, whining hum rose up then, growing louder, filling the bailey. Drone engines, whirring around the corner of the keep. A half dozen of them hovered into view, sounding monstrous in this closed, stony space.

"Dom!" I pulled on his tunic and searched for an escape route.

The drones had wings. Gray bat wings stretched on metallic fingers, gliding. Chunky bodies, leering faces in pockmarked gray.

Gargoyles. They were drone-sized gargoyles, a foot across. And they had guns.

26

Dungeon Crawl

However grotesque their faces were, with horns and tusks and leering eyes, they weren't really gargoyles. Frozen, they were mobile statues rather than stone come to life. Not like the Sphinx or the Wargs, which had some kind of personality. Their guns were long barrels protruding out of their chests. A swarm of them came around the keep, straight for us, firing a continuous stream of *cracks*, accompanied by a cloud of gray smoke.

The person in the invisible cloak tackled me from behind. "Get down!"

Rucker. In a flurry of motion, the invisible cloak's hood fell back and the edges rippled around him, bringing him in and out of reality. He shoved me hard toward the alcove and the keep's door.

"Hey!" Dom said angrily, glaring at the soldier.

"Get *down*, asshole!" Rucker reiterated.

Six gargoyles raced over us and looped around for a second

run. The weapons welded underneath them let out ear-numbing blasts. Bullets pinged against nearby stone and threw off sparks.

"They're firing real bullets," Dom said in a daze. "How are they firing bullets?" He didn't seem so much shocked as confused. "That wasn't part of the design specs. Everything's supposed to be safe. Mostly."

Determined, he pointed his wand—just like in all the movies—and pressed a button on the grip. A lightning blast of static, like something from a Van de Graaff generator, burst out the tip. The force of it threw his arm wide, and the blast sparked against the stone wall. The gargoyles zoomed past, unharmed.

He stared at the wand in his hand in amazement.

I shouted, "And you had that thing pointed at me!"

"I—"

The gargoyles made a wide arc and came around yet again.

"Shut those things down, Dom!" I said.

Panicking, he went back to the keypad, but his hands were shaking.

"Fix this," Rucker ordered him.

Dom glared back. "How did you get in—"

"Magic," Rucker said, leering. "There's no one inside the castle could be steering those things, right? This is automated?" He had left his rifle behind but held his handgun. He fired twice, and two drones exploded and fell in pieces. The remaining group of them swooped on.

My heart raced so fast my chest hurt and my throat felt like it might burst. "You have to open the door."

"It's not working—"

"Dominic!"

The gargoyles changed tactics. The destruction of some of their number must have triggered some kind of algorithm, and now instead of dive-bombing us, they circled around to face the alcove where we were hiding. Rucker fired a couple more shots, but the drones were dancing, circling, charging directly back and forth in an unpredictable rush. He was in front of me, shielding me.

The others outside the walls could probably hear the gunfire. I wondered what they were doing. I slammed my body against the door, but it didn't budge. I wasn't even sure it had hinges. I couldn't see a way to force it open.

With a sudden hiss of static, a portentous voice in a proper BBC English accent emanated from the keypad. "To open, say the magic word."

Dom seemed taken aback, staring at the device for a moment, then said, *"Mellon!"* The Elvish word for "friend," from the riddle.

Nothing happened. The door did not open. "Dom, you built all this. What is it? What opens this?"

He shook his head, eyes wide with panic. "I . . . I don't know. Uh, let me think a minute . . . 'the magic word'!"

As in *Say "the magic word."* It was almost clever—if you were a thirteen-year-old boy.

Still, the door did not open. Magic word . . . so it wanted an actual magic word. We didn't have time for this. Rucker was still shielding us, holding off the gargoyle drones.

"Abracadabra!" I shouted. "Open sesame! Shazam!"

Dom tried a whole string of words as well. A bunch of Elvish I didn't understand. Then, in desperation, "By the power of Greyskull!"

Nothing.

The magic word. I closed my eyes. Took a breath. And said, "Please?"

The door slid open, whirring on a motor. The drones hovered in closer, closer, still firing, a rattle of nerve-shattering gunfire. I shoved Dom ahead and hauled Rucker's arm to pull him in behind me. Operating on some kind of optical sensor, the door slipped shut behind us. A few more shots fired, bullets pounding into the wood. Then nothing. We sat in darkness. The room, corridor, wherever we were, wasn't lit.

Dom ranted. "Please? *Please?* That is the *stupidest* goddamn riddle. When I get my hands on whoever programmed that . . . that *idiotic*—"

Rucker groaned and slid to the floor. I couldn't support him and fell to my knees beside him.

"Professor. My belt. Light . . . on my belt. Here." Rucker's voice was thick with pain. I found his shoulder, arm. His hands were wet, but I followed them to where he gestured on his belt, unhooked a Maglite from its holster, and turned it on.

Rucker was covered in blood. He must have been shot a dozen times.

"No no no no no." I clung to his shirt.

"Professor," he said, choking. "S'okay."

"I'm sorry, I'm sorry . . ." I cried it over and over again.

He kept trying to pat my arm. "Don't . . . don't freak. Don't. It's not the same . . . it's not."

But it was, that feel of blood on my hands, soaking into my clothes, a wet that smeared thickly, sticky and sour. The way his eyes wouldn't focus on me, it was exactly the same. Dora had died instantly. Alex . . . hadn't.

I remembered.

He worked to speak clearly. "Shut it down. Get . . . get Torres. S'okay." He made each breath with effort. Reaching out, he caught my hand after a couple of misses. Blood made his grip slippery. In the flashlight's white glow, his face was pale, his eyes gleaming.

"I'm sorry . . ." I cried, squeezing him as if it would anchor him.

"No," he said. "Professor. Addie. Not your fault. Get Torres. Go. Go."

The words shuddered, his voice growing weak, falling to a whisper. His desperate wheezing breaths stopped. His hand went limp, his eyes went blank.

I thought I would never have to go through this again. I bent over him and sobbed gasping breaths. The dark closed in, the light grew small, and if I never moved again that would be all right.

"Addie —" Dom touched my shoulder.

I shook him off and screamed, "Don't touch me! You don't get to touch me!"

He took a step back. He actually looked scared. Good.

"Addie. Stop, please. Crying won't help."

I bared my teeth at him. "Yes, it will! This is what grief looks like! I'm allowed to cry as much as I want, so fuck off!"

He didn't like it because he couldn't fix it.

"Addie," he said softly. "Hold the light up here a minute."

I could barely see, I'd been crying so hard.

"Addie, please."

I scrubbed my face and held the light in the direction of the voice. A now-familiar bronze plaque was mounted in the stone by the door. He pushed a button on the keypad, and torches flared, one by one, down the length of the corridor. The flames danced. The smell of burning fuel was strong and cloying in the closed-off room. Rucker lay slumped up against the wall like a prop in a haunted house. Except that his hand was still warm. And I did stop crying, because I could only scream for so long before my voice gave out. The echoing noise hurt my ears. I wanted to go home, but I was stuck in this room, this castle, this island.

"Alex and Dora," I said, trying to catch my breath. My mantra, my memory.

Dom looked at me and said, "Who?"

I stared. Because he knew. At least, he used to know, but he had forgotten because the names didn't mean anything to him. My stark reaction jogged his memory, and he said, "Oh, wait. Yeah. Sorry."

Rucker's last words told me to go, call for help, get Torres. So that was what I had to do.

"Dom, where's the control room? That's where we need to go to reboot the system, right?"

Uncertain, he looked down the passageway. "It's up. In the tower. It should be this way."

"*Should be?*"

"The whole castle's probably been trapped to keep me out. But I mean apart from that . . ."

"Fuck," I murmured.

He pulled the nearest torch out of its sconce, studied the walls, looked one way, then another. Pursed his lips. "We can do this, you and me. We've done this kind of thing a million times."

"In *games*," I said. "Lang booby-trapped the castle because he knew what you were going to do. He *knew,* and he set a trap, and you walked right into it and got Rucker killed!"

"But I had the Ring . . ."

"The Ring is a trap, it always was. Your ring was never going to work. Probably something in the software, I don't know enough to figure out how he did it. But you couldn't resist trying the other ring."

"If we can just get to the control room, we can still win!"

We'd already lost. "I'm going to get Torres," I said, and went to the door.

"But those gargoyles—"

"I'll run."

"Addie—"

The door was locked, and no voice gave us instructions. A different locking mechanism had snapped into place, probably when Dom activated the torches. The trap would let us in but not back out.

Well, then. "Only way out is through," I murmured. We were in a long stone corridor, ending in a T intersection. "Which way?"

"Left, I think."

"You think?"

"Yes. I'm pretty sure."

"I don't suppose you have any paper to make a map. Or chalk to mark the way?"

"Um . . ."

Next, I did the unthinkable, but only because I was pretty sure Rucker would approve: I searched his body. All his pockets, and whatever else was clipped to his belt. In addition to the flashlight, I found a compass, a utility knife, a power bar. And a grease pencil. He'd dropped his gun at his side. I left it there.

Dom nodded at the weapon. "Maybe we should bring—"

"No."

When I opened my pouch to stash my new loot, something inside it gave off an unnatural blue-green light. I drew out Arthur's plastic triangle, which wasn't just glowing. It pulsed, with the steady rate of a heartbeat. I breathed a sigh.

"What's it doing?" Dom asked.

"Not sure." I turned it one way and another, held it up to the torchlight. Interesting—when I held it down one side of the corridor, it glowed brighter. Down the other—the light dimmed. "Is it . . . is this telling us where to go?" I tried it again, and the pattern repeated. "Dom, how is this working?"

"I don't know," he murmured. "That's not one of mine."

This must have had some of the same tech as whatever transponder guided the spiders in the maze. It was all so wonderful, a few engineering and software principles could build all of this—and Arthur knew. He'd tried to say the triangle wasn't important, but he must have known it could guide us through the castle. He wasn't any better than the rest of them.

It's dangerous to go alone . . .

We should get started. "Do you know what other defenses might be installed? What else Arthur and Lang could have cooked up?"

"I . . . I don't know. We had so many designs in preproduction. None of this is like I thought it would be."

Somehow, I wasn't scared anymore. I wasn't nervous. I had a job: get to the control room and shut it all down. I'd either be able to do it or I wouldn't.

"But really . . . ." Dom gazed ahead like there was actually something to look at. "How hard can it be?"

"Oh my God," I muttered, and marched past him.

The torches on the wall didn't continue past the first corridor. All we had then were the flashlight, Dom's sputtering torch, and a glowing triangle that pulsed more strongly when pointing in certain directions. I moved slowly, listening for clicking gears, for the hum of electricity that meant drones or mechanical monsters. I checked for markings on the floor or walls that might mean trapdoors or hidden panels. At each turn I marked the wall with the grease pencil, then backtracked to make sure the marks stayed in place.

It was exhausting, paying this much attention. But I had to do it; I didn't trust Dom's help. Right now, he was the classic definition of high INT, low WIS.

We came to another intersection. This one continued straight and branched left.

"Left," he said, but not as confidently as I would have liked. This was Dom pretending to be confident. But the triangle agreed with him, this time. The left-hand branch ended in a set of stairs leading up. I marked the turn and our progress.

Dom frowned. "You don't need to do that—the place isn't that big."

"I'm not taking any chances," I said.

We reached the stairs, and I tested every stone on every step before putting weight on it, and got to the top landing without incident. This was weird. A trapdoor should have opened under us by now. Screaming death ants should have poured from the ceiling. Something. Dom followed without a word. At the top, the passage curved and gave us three choices: straight, right, or left.

"Is this castle bigger on the inside than the outside?" I asked.

"It's an architectural technique of stacking corridors that makes it harder to keep a sense of direction. This *was* part of the specs I designed."

"Then you know which way to go?"

"Straight," he said. "I think."

Our glowing guide agreed. I marked the route.

After the next turn, we came to a room. We could continue through the passage on the other side, but the room also featured a set of ornate double doors. They seemed incongruous; instead of medieval stone, these were painted, with gold leaf rococo flourishes.

Would the designers have put something important like the control center behind a fancy set of doors like this? Or was this a trap? The triangle faded when I pointed it at the doors and glowed at the corridor beyond. I started to move on, but Dom stopped at the doors.

"These are mine." A smile touched his voice. "I know what this is."

"I think we should keep going. The triangle—"

"Let's look in for just a moment. You'll like it, I promise."

Oh, all the fairy-tale wonders that could be lurking behind those doors. An invisible orchestra playing a perfect song to dance to, a table of pastries and liqueurs labeled *eat me, drink me* . . .

"Dom—" He reached for the handle, and I went to his side. "Just a minute, let me at least look for traps."

I held the flashlight close to the door handles and searched for needles, secret buttons, triggers, sensors, anything. Did the same with the hinges.

"I didn't put any traps here."

"So?"

"Addie, please—"

"Stop. Saying. That." The doors weren't locked and didn't seem to have anything that would jump out at us. "Well, here goes."

I turned the handle and pulled.

We stepped into a ballroom, like something in an English manor house. Way out of period if you were talking medieval. The floor was a beautiful parquet in a zigzag pattern. Patterned paper and mirrors covered the walls. Lights came up, LEDs in crystal chandeliers casting a butter-warm glow over everything.

"And this is for the dancing princesses," I murmured, walking in a slow circle.

Dom stood a little ways off, looking exhausted but smiling. The torch cast orange highlights on his face. "Remember? Time was you'd have given anything to dance in a room like this." He held his hand out, turned his foot just so, as if he expected to bow at the opening measures of a delightful piece of music.

"Dom. I'm covered in blood." My dress had Rucker's bloody handprints across the sleeves.

Music started, the strains of an orchestra echoing from an unseen sound system. Probably triggered by opening the door, which had also activated the chandeliers. I recognized the song —the waltz from Khachaturian's *Masquerade*. Classical, cinematic, and more than slightly demonic.

"Dom?" I murmured. By the stark expression on his face, I guessed he hadn't programmed this particular music, either.

"I think we should leave now," he said.

Behind Dom, the ornate double doors slammed shut, and electric bolts whirred into place, because of course they did. From each corner of the ballroom, hidden doors slid open. Figures came through. Demons, fairies, men with wolf faces, women with eagle heads. Dancing.

Dominic was right. I used to dream of elegant evenings wearing fantastical costumes and dancing in a grand hall like this. I'd watch historical movies and play the ballroom scenes over and over again, to learn the dances. That scene in *Labyrinth* rewired my brain. But this . . .

It was strange, creepy, and also somehow beautiful, and that was the point.

"Maybe they won't hurt us," I murmured, but their AI-driven glass eyes looked at us, and somehow the spiral twirls of their dances brought them closer. One raised a hand, another curled its fingers, which flashed metal.

They had steel claws.

Dom and I backed into each other, shoulder to shoulder, and the inhuman dancers drew closer.

My voice shook. "Do you think the door on the other side of the room is unlocked?"

"I hope so," he said, grabbing my hand.

Dominic turned me aside, whirling, just as a cat-faced man in a frock coat swiped at me, putting a gash in my dress. We crossed the room arm in arm, dodging past one couple and another, zigging when any of them got too close, zagging into an open space of ballroom that was never open for long. We had to keep moving, in our own crazed version of a waltz.

Dom hissed—a claw slashed him on the shoulder. More dancers seemed to fill the space. Pretty soon we wouldn't have any chance of a clear path.

"Run," he said, his voice tight, and we charged to the simple door at the other end of the hall. If it was locked . . .

Dom put his shoulder down and crashed into it. The door popped open and we fell through it. Quickly, he whirled and slammed it shut again. The music continued throbbing through the wood.

I sank to the floor, gasping for breath. He leaned above me, also gasping. He looked back at the door with something like fear.

I reached. "Your arm—"

A tear in the sleeve revealed a line of dripping blood. He shook it off. "Just a scratch. God, I always hated Jane Austen," he said.

Shaking, I pulled myself to my feet. "You spent three years going to English Country Dancing with me and you hate Jane Austen?"

He shrugged. "I liked the clothes. And it made you happy."

I couldn't anymore. I couldn't. I laughed.

"Addie—"

"I'm stuck in a castle with an ex-boyfriend who had unlimited funds to invent tortures for me . . . this is hell. I'm in hell."

"I promise, when I'm in charge I'll get all the fail-safes back on—"

"It's out of your hands."

We were in yet another stone corridor. At the end of this one, a short set of stairs led up, and this took us to a chamber with three doorways. Each of the wooden doors had a rune carved on it. Now if I could only remember which rune meant what. My mind, my memory, all my academic knowledge were failing me just then. They might as well have been a toddler's scribbling. I was so tired.

I held the triangle flat in my hands and moved to each door, holding it up. And it glowed exactly the same in front of each one, a kind of lackluster blue, as if we had worn it out. We'd gone off track; the transponder didn't work anymore. Dammit.

"Which one of these leads to the control room?" I asked.

Dom stood next to me, his shoulders slumped. "I . . . I don't know. I'm sorry."

"I guess we try them all." I started on the left. It opened into a long, dark corridor. The center door also opened into a long, dark corridor. So did the one on the right.

Three long, dark corridors branched off in three directions. I almost started crying.

"Simple," Dom said. "Keep it simple, like the Sphinx riddle. This wasn't designed for PhDs."

We took a step back and looked at the runes again. The center door had an X, with marks on the left and right, like a sideways, stylized figure eight.

"X marks the spot?" I asked, uncertain.

"That." Dom pointed, suddenly excited. "That's the symbol that marked the entrance to the Lonely Mountain, isn't it? In *The Hobbit*?"

I couldn't remember. "But that doesn't mean it's the control center. The Lonely Mountain—"

"Had the treasure. The prize. Let's try it."

We took the center corridor, and I couldn't help but think we'd missed something.

Ahead, something roared. It was a stereotypical, uncreative roar, echoing down the stone passage. A single monstrous sound, a few seconds long, and then silence fell hard. It should have been laughable, except I had blood on my hands, and I didn't trust the man at my back. In that context, the roar reached into my primal brain, some ancestral memory of terror. The vibrations of it continued echoing in my skull.

The Lonely Mountain had treasure . . . and a dragon.

27

>>>———→

No Living Man Am I

I s that a dragon?" I asked.

"Um. It might be."

"And not a soft, cuddly Reluctant Dragon or Toothless or something like that, I'm assuming?" He shook his head. "Why would you have a dragon guarding your control room?"

"Boss-level challenge for dungeon crawlers," he said. "It was supposed to be fun."

I wanted to punch him.

Ahead, the tunnel ended in a bright room. High windows let in natural light. The roar echoed again, a sound that seemed to rumble through the stone. We both hesitated, our bodies resisting moving forward. We came to the end of the tunnel and crouched by the corner. A breeze ruffled my hair, pulsing in time with the monstrous breathing.

The room, predictably, was filled with piles of gold. Or rather, collections of 3D-printed items designed to look like gold. Coins, goblets, plates, chains, crowns, jewelry. Chests with gold spilling out of them in mountainous slopes. A satisfyingly standard dragon's hoard, ripe for stealing, enough to set any adventuring party drooling.

And atop it all, the dragon.

Its sinuous body coiled, filling the room, tail pressed to the wall, tip tickling the snout at the end of a narrow head, itself at the end of a reaching neck. Hind and forelegs tucked in, sharp black claws dug into the gold as if anchoring itself. Red scales shading into black, the great mound of its body shimmered in the afternoon light angling in from high clerestory windows. The room was the size of a high school gymnasium, and the dragon filled it.

Thankfully, it was asleep. The periodic roars were its snoring. Its sides pulsed regularly, breathing in and out. Every now and then its great round chest heaved wide, its mouth parted, and the huge noise rattled out. I pressed my hands over my ears and still my head ached with it. Each of its several dozen teeth were as large as my arm, and the points of them shone brightly.

I hoped this dragon's riddle would be as simple as the Sphinx's had been. All we had to do was not steal from its hoard, and we'd be safe.

"Oh my God," Dom whispered.

I was having trouble breathing. Primitive wiring in my brain wanted me to flee and never look back. The air was hot and smelled like brimstone and gasoline. "Does that thing breathe fire?" I asked. "Is that part of the specs?"

His eyes had grown wide and panicky. "I don't know. I just don't know anymore."

"How're we supposed to stop it? Is it riddles? An arrow in a weak spot on its scales? Serve it tea? What?"

"I don't know!"

"Shh!" I hissed, after the dragon's breath hitched a moment. We froze, watching. The steady breathing resumed, another roar snoring out. "We go back. We go back and try the other passageways."

"No, look," he said, pointing. "*That's* the way to the control room."

On the other side of the chamber, directly behind the dragon, was a double door with Celtic knotwork carved into wood and big iron rings for handles. There didn't even seem to be a locking mechanism on it.

"Are you sure?" I whispered. "I mean really, really sure?"

"I told you this was the right way."

This was so not the right way.

The thickest part of the dragon's tail blocked the doors. The sleeping beast had left the narrowest of gaps along the wall. If we were very quiet, very careful, we might be able to sneak along the wall, via that gap, without disturbing the dragon. If we could move without shifting that great carpet of loose treasure.

I was going to throw up.

Dom stared, glassy-eyed. "We should be able to get past it if we're really quiet."

Those piles of gold were going to shift and make noise the minute we stepped on them.

"So it's designed to respond to noise?"

"Other monsters were designed to respond to sight and sound, so maybe not? But if we could get the conversation algorithm to work, it was going to look you straight in the eyes. It would have been *amazing*." He was fidgeting with one of the rings on his hand. "None of this was supposed to happen like this," he muttered. "If I'd just had more time . . ."

He was definitely Saruman in this whole scenario.

But I had an idea. "Wait here a minute," I said.

"Wait!" he called, then looked back over his shoulder in a panic. But the dragon remained asleep.

"I have an idea," I said, adjusting my grip on the flashlight. I started back down the corridor the way we'd come.

"Addie—"

"Wait for me. Just wait."

I moved quickly, but cautiously—some traps might have been designed to be triggered from the opposite direction. All those hours of Dungeons and Dragons, embedded in my brain like a nervous tic. The ballroom was a problem, but without Dom's misplaced confidence urging me forward, I found the corridor we *should* have taken, bypassing the demonic dance.

I had a bad moment of thinking I was lost. I couldn't find any of my marks, I had three different options and had lost my sense of direction. But then I saw torchlight—the row of torches in that first passage drew me on.

Rucker's body lay in a wide pool of blood. My bloody footprints led away from him. All of it drying and sticky, smelling both sharp and sour. I swallowed hard, locking it all away. I could freak out later.

Once again, I looted his corpse, unhooking the invisible cloak from around his neck. I should have taken it right from the start . . . but, well, I cut myself a little slack. No amount of D&D would have prepared me for this. It took a little doing, shifting him, letting his bulk fall to the side while I pulled the fabric out from under him. I swallowed back bile. *He'd want me to do this,* I repeated, over and over. More than that, he'd be proud of me. Yes, that felt right.

Finally, I freed it. Holding it up with one hand, I ran the flashlight over it. It had a couple of holes from bullets but seemed mostly intact. But how did I turn it on? I studied the edges, the collar—there, the clasp on the collar had a button. I pushed it, making sure to keep my finger near it so I could find it again.

The fabric shimmered, spat a static hiss for a second. Then vanished, right in my hand.

"I solemnly swear I am up to no good," I whispered. Then I ran back to the dragon chamber.

I arrived just in time to see Dom step into the room. He'd left the torch lying in the passage; it had sputtered out. Now, pressed to the wall, he attempted the trek around to the control room doors.

"Dom!" I whispered, as loud as I dared. He held up a hand —wait, just wait. He seemed determined. I held my breath.

Dom was only to the first corner when I realized the dragon was holding its breath, too. The great flanks had stopped pulsing, and the roaring snore hadn't sounded in the last half minute. Still at the entrance, I didn't dare call a warning to Dom. He glanced back at me with a hopeful smile, as if to say it was all going to be fine—

Scales rippled, muscles under skin contracting, the body lifting from its coils, limbs flexing to hold the weight. It didn't matter anymore how Lang's team had accomplished this. The dragon was real, alive, and terrifying.

"Dom!"

The monster lifted its head and looked directly at him. An arrow-shaped face curved back to horns, and its wide mouth seemed to smile. Scaled brows blinked over shining onyx eyes.

A riddle. It would ask us a riddle now, and we would answer and be allowed to pass. My knees trembled; I felt faint. This was the beast of nightmares, going back thousands of years. Small humans weren't meant to encounter creatures like this in real life.

Dom stood his ground, feet braced on gold and gazing up at the creature. Like some kind of hero. The dragon drew back its head, revealing the length of its neck, reaching all the way to the vaulted ceiling. Its breast swelled as it inhaled, and its lips parted to show off fangs.

I ran, not caring now about making noise or drawing attention. Way too late for all that. Dom was frozen; he had to get out of there. I grabbed his arm, pulled him back. At last he seemed to wake up—arm in arm we charged back to the entrance. The dragon couldn't follow us into the passageway.

Before we could get there, though, we slipped on gold coins. Flubbed our DEX checks. We both fell hard, and the dragon made a hollow, hissing noise, like that of a blowtorch lighting up.

Clinging to each other, we scrambled, sliding on cascading coins. We were close, so close.

Then the fire came.

Flames roared from the dragon's mouth in a focused stream. We dived into the passage. I wondered if instead of sheltering us, the enclosed stone space would act like an oven, baking us. I flattened onto the stone, curled up, hands instinctively over my head. Dom collapsed next to me.

The air around us seared, like we were sitting too close to a bonfire. The fiery breath lasted only a couple of seconds. Then I was suddenly cool, simply by contrast. Except for the choking scent of burning fabric and hair.

I remained hunched, waiting for the torch-like blast to come again. The flames hadn't come directly into the passage; the blast was aimed at the wall inside the room; we'd only gotten a glancing edge of it. My heart was racing, I was holding my breath—but the fire didn't come again.

Dom's weight pressed against me, but he wasn't moving. "Dom, come on. Dom."

Groaning, he shifted, half rolling over, revealing the blackened burns across his shoulder and face. His hair still smoldered, ends curling up in white ash near his scalp. That fantastical pointed ear was blistered. His tunic and cloak were burned, disintegrating, falling off him. Edges of it still smoldered, smoke rippling from the edges of destroyed cloth.

"Dom!" My voice pitched high and cracked. Patting him down, I smothered the last glowing bits. He grunted, flinching away from my touch. The skin on his shoulders and face seemed to be getting redder, welts starting to pucker. And his beautiful long hair—half of it was just gone.

A growl like the rumbling of a distant storm echoed. Scratching footsteps sounded as the dragon lurched. It swung its neck, lowering its head to the mouth of the passage.

"Dom, we have to go. If it flames down this corridor, we're dead."

He nodded, his eyes shut tight, his face taut with pain. I started to pull his arm over my shoulder, but he cried out and jerked away, cradling the arm to his chest.

"I think I broke it when I fell." His breathing came faster and faster. He was hyperventilating.

If we didn't get out of here, that wouldn't matter. "Come on."

I clutched an intact corner of his tunic and pulled. Gritting his teeth, he whimpered. With him leaning on my shoulder, we managed to limp to the end of the passage.

Another roar of flames sounded, and heat washed through the passage, waves of it roasting the air. We lurched away, and the fire didn't reach us. Dom collapsed, curled against the wall, breathing hard and shaking.

That could have been me, if he hadn't shielded me. I knelt beside him, afraid to touch him. I didn't want to hurt him, but I had to help. "Dom, you're going into shock. Slow down, breathe slow, please."

"I'm sorry," he murmured around shallow breaths, his eyes half lidded. "I screwed everything up . . ."

I glanced back to the treasure room. The dragon didn't blow fire at us again, but it didn't go back to sleep, either. Instead, it appeared to be pacing a circle around the room. Its great red bulk would appear in the doorway, then slip away, the tail flicking in its wake. The sound of ringing gold chimed under its steps. Then, a minute later, it appeared again. Like it was keeping guard.

Trapped. We couldn't go forward now. We couldn't go back. Dom wasn't in any shape to go anywhere at all. I huddled next to him on the floor.

"Addie. Love. Here." He pulled the rings off his fingers. All of them. I couldn't tell which was his and which was the one from the spider maze, the true and the fake. Depending on your point of view. "Shut it down. Shut everything down."

"I can't . . . I can't."

He moaned, pulling his arms close, shivering.

I couldn't. But I was the only one here, and I was afraid Dom was dying. I might have hated him right now, but I didn't want that. *Promise me no one will get hurt . . .*

Somehow, my lucky die ended up in my hand. I had reached into my bag to deposit Dom's rings, and the d20 was there, and now it was in my hand.

This was stupid. Rolling dice had no relevance in the real world. I had no useful stats to speak of. I was hurt, I was weak, my life was full of trauma . . .

I rolled the die, which bounced and clattered on the hard floor in front of me.

Natural 20.

I retrieved the die, shook out Rucker's invisible cloak, and draped it over my shoulders. "Dom, I'm going to get help."

He didn't respond.

28

➤

Critical Hit

When I touched the button on the clasp, the cloak gave a static hiss and went invisible. Slowly, I crept along the stone wall, moving away from the rattling sound of Dom's breathing and toward the huffs and clatter of the dragon.

I knew of lots of ways to stop a dragon. Or at least evade one, depending on which one you were dealing with. (1) Slay it, which took effort, bloodshed, and a skill set I didn't have. (2) Make friends with it, if it was the right kind of dragon. A tea-drinking dragon, for example. I wasn't sure the design team had even considered tea-drinking dragons, but they should have. As a traveler to Questland, I for one would pay extra for the "drink tea with a dragon" excursion.

This did not look like a tea-drinking dragon. Or (3) I could trick it.

That one, I might manage.

I pulled the hood of the buzzing cloak over my head. On me,

the hem brushed the ground. I looked down at my own arm—
and saw the stone-like floor under it instead.

It wasn't perfect. The crackling of static continued, telling
me the cloak wasn't fully intact. If I looked in a mirror, I imagined there'd be gaps in the illusion. Holes, where Rucker had
been shot. But maybe the dragon wouldn't notice. Its visual in-
terface might not be that sophisticated. Breathing shallowly,
clasping the front of the cloak firmly closed, I slipped around
the corner and into the dragon's chamber.

It continued marching a slow circle around the room, its
head scanning this way and that, searching. It didn't move
quickly—it lifted each leg and carefully set it down before
lifting the next. But it was just so *big*. Its tail swished back
and forth, scraping piles of gold with it. The membranes of its
wings covered huge stretches of floor, and its neck was like a
tower. I would get knocked over by a swish of tail or a breeze
from its wing without it even noticing.

For too long, I stayed frozen, just watching it. How could I
not? I was a mouse confronted with a cat. A big, scaly, evil cat.
The opposite door seemed as far away as the other side of the
island.

Patterns in the dragon's movements emerged. When it got
to the far wall, one claw braced against the corner to launch
it into the next turn. The head swayed in a regular rhythm,
looking one way, then the other, then back. Tick, tock, like a
metronome. Too steady to be natural. And every circle it made
around the room took the same amount of time.

This was just like playing Dragon's Lair. In the end, the
dragon was a machine.

The next time it came to the doorway, I pressed myself flat to
the wall, held my breath, and let it pass. As soon as the whip-
ping tail went by, I followed, stepping as carefully and lightly
as I could. I kept a hand on a wall to help my balance—every

time I put my foot down, coins slipped underneath me. The floor was uneven, treacherous. I was sure every scrape, every clink, echoed and that any second the dragon would swing that head toward me and roast me in flames. In my effort to stay quiet and steady, I was moving even slower than the enormous monster. If I took too long to reach the door, it would loop back around and then those huge black eyes would be looking straight at me. I had to remember to breathe.

The hood of the invisible cloak acted like blinders. If I wanted to see the room, I had to turn my head and scan. Maybe it was better if I couldn't see the beast moving up behind me. So I focused straight ahead at the door and moved. Past the next corner and on, step by step. I had a bad moment when I stumbled, dislodging a gold plate that sent the coins beneath it sliding with the chiming of bells. I froze, shored up against the wall so I wouldn't fall on my ass. Turned to look at the dragon, sure that I would see it staring right back at me.

It hesitated, just a moment. The relentless steps paused, and the head swung around on its immense neck. I ducked so the hood fell over my face, hunched so that what was left of the cloak faced out, making me look like a stretch of pocked gray stone. Or so I hoped.

A moment passed, and another. The dragon snorted; it almost sounded frustrated. The air smelled of soot and embers. The door was only a dozen yards away.

I could do this.

The chimes of shifting coins resumed as the dragon continued its trek. I moved as well, hurrying now because I wanted to close the distance and be done with this.

The door had a carved arch around it. I reached for it like a swimmer struggling for a dock. The dragon's steps drew closer. Grabbing the edge, I swung into the recessed doorway and collapsed, huddling. The dragon's head reached forward, a dark eye blinking—and it passed me by, swinging its bulk past the door, where I sat curled up and shivering. It didn't see me.

Gods be praised.

It continued its circuit.

The doors didn't appear to have a lock. Pulling or pushing at the big iron rings did nothing. They didn't even shudder on their hinges. I searched for the familiar bronze plate, a ring-shaped slot. Nothing. I couldn't find anything and swallowed back a sob of panic. The dragon was on the far side of the room and coming back around.

Flattening my hands, I ran them over the wood, feeling every inch, searching for some detail I'd missed. There was always some button hidden in the carving, some discolored wood indicating the secret latch—

And there it was.

The central carving was a Green Man, split down the middle where the two doors opened. The eyes were odd, offset a little, rising out of the wood more than they should. I pushed . . . and the door popped open.

A monstrous breath snorted behind me as the dragon whipped around at the noise. It gave a snort, and in a panic I shoved against the doors and fell out of the treasure chamber—

And tumbled onto a tile floor. Modern tile in what looked like a perfectly mundane office. It might have been my building back at the university. The sense of displacement was dizzying, and the plain smell of floor cleaner seemed alien.

The dragon's footsteps rattled through coins and shook the air around me. Quickly, I turned and slammed the doors shut, closing off the danger. I sat hard on the floor and gasped for breath. But no flames billowed, no fiery inferno engulfed me.

The doors on this side were painted industrial beige and

had no visible wood grain. Ahead of me stretched a plain hallway. Fluorescent light panels in the ceiling were dark. A reverse wardrobe, spitting me out into normality.

Doorways stood on each side of the hallway, four total. At the end of the hall, light came from an open room. This was where I headed, when I finally collected myself.

The control room.

The clean open space had a couple of windows and skylights filling the place with natural light. Somehow, despite all that had happened, it was still daylight outside.

A horseshoe of desks occupied the center of the room. On them were dozens of computers and monitors. Neatly secured wires and cables were tucked out of the way. On one wall, a whiteboard had a list of tasks written on it in blue, as if the people who worked here expected to come in at any moment, just like any normal day.

Baby dragon petting zoo floor plan, read one item. *Tea with fairies,* read another.

On another wall, a giant flat-screen TV was dark. Here and there, pictures and posters were hung: concept art, drawings, funny cartoons, a birthday card, a poster for the 1981 film *Excalibur* in all its disco-fantastic glory.

Computers hummed with undisturbed serenity. The screens were all in sleep mode. The central desk in the horseshoe, the one closest to the giant TV, had the biggest monitors, the most hardware. I tapped the touch pad resting here.

The large central monitor came to life with an animated graphic of the burning Eye of Sauron. Vague ambient roaring hissed gently from a speaker. And whose idea was this, Arthur's or Dom's?

Giant red text emerged from the Eye's burning flames, letters made to look like Elvish script but written in English.

PASSWORD

I pulled over a keyboard, blew some of the dust off it, and typed:

onErinGtOrulEtheMalL

The image on the screen swiped away, revealing a normal desktop and a shortcut icon helpfully labeled "Park Override." With a relieved sigh, I clicked on it.

The screen went black. In the middle, a series of glowing green letters appeared.

PARK OVERRIDE: INSERT KEY.

Beside the keyboard, what I had thought was another touch pad now glowed a green to match the text. The override key. The One Ring.

Well, fuck.

I dumped my bag out on the desk and sorted through my loot. Of them all, the one I was most sure what it did was the d20, which I was going to keep in my pocket forever from now on. I put it away, since it was most definitely not the override key.

The two gold bands: one genuine, one treacherous, and I couldn't tell which was which. I didn't know if this system was set up to lock out bad tries. How many attempts did I get before activating the override became impossible?

I picked one of the gold bands and set it on the touch pad.

A short, angry buzz blasted from speakers around the room, and I jumped, letting out a scream. My heart raced and I held my throat.

The words on the screen changed:

BAD KEY. REMAINING ATTEMPTS: 2

I sank into a seat, dizzy, scared, stomach clenching. What could I do but place the second gold band on the pad?

The buzz this time wasn't any less aggravating. My hands were shaking. I couldn't calm down.

BAD KEY. REMAINING ATTEMPTS: 1

"Okay, let's think about this," I murmured. First off, there was no guarantee that anything in my bag was the right key. Not any of the rings. Beckett's piece of Triforce had gone dim, as if overwhelmed by the sheer number of computers around it. That left . . .

The Origin of Mirabilis. The book was right there, the twisted amulet seeming muted and dull in the room's diffuse light.

Who was the game master here, anyway?

Carefully, I explored the cover, feeling around the edges of the amulet, searching for how it had been put together. And there, just at the edge of the spine, a latch. A tiny wire that clicked when I pressed it, and the snake and ivy knotwork popped out of the cover.

One chance to shut the whole thing down or make it a hundred times more difficult. I lay the amulet on the touch pad. Waited, my whole body braced, for the buzz.

Instead: a soft chime.

The sound of an operating system powering down.

On the large monitor a new graphic replaced the plain black, a couple of graphs showing power levels that sank to zero.

I sat in the nearest chair and covered my face with my hands.

A door across the room led to the castle's ramparts, a walkway around the outside of the keep. I went out just in time to see a squad of helicopters arrive. Four of them swooped past the castle and hovered for a moment before moving off to a field on the far side of the walls, where I could no longer see them. They must have been waiting all week for the shield to drop. The sky was a clear, bright afternoon blue. Not a hint of purple in sight.

I couldn't see the front gate from where I stood, so I didn't know what Torres and the others were doing. All the doors would be unlocked now, all the drones and defenses shut down. All the magic rings would stop functioning.

But the knives and arrows and guns would all still work.

I should get down there. I should check on Dom. I should tell Torres about Rucker—but he'd find the body before I could reach him.

Back inside, I tried to find a radio, a cell phone, something —the squad carried a satellite phone to use to contact Lang once the shield was down, but I didn't know how to call it. We hadn't expected to get separated, not like this. Back on the computer, I tried to find a way to access security cameras or some kind of loudspeaker that I could use to announce I was okay and in the control room. But the computers all appeared to be dead now.

Or I could just let them find me. It was out of my hands now.

The control room had a kitchenette attached, with coffee-makers, an electric kettle, and lots of tea. But inside the fridge I found a couple of bottles of mead. This time, I bypassed the tea and grabbed the mead. With it, I went back outside to wait, slumped against the stone wall. The view was toward the north, across the slate-gray lake and up to the forested hills.

The westering sun painted a golden haze over the trees, and gulls sailed over the water.

I was halfway through the mead when Torres found me. That wasn't an indication of how much time had passed but of how decisively I'd upended the bottle. Really, Torres didn't take long to find me at all. The door opened, I glanced to see who it was. Turned back to the sun, the fresh air, and my exhaustion.

"I didn't know what to do, so I started drinking. Captain, have you ever had mead?" I held up the bottle.

He came over and slid down next to me on the stone walk.

"You look terrible, Professor."

I took stock. My dress was slashed in multiple places, covered with blood, and singed around the edges. Blood had dried in the cracks on the skin of my hands. The way my face itched, I had probably smeared blood there, too. My stabbed and bandaged hand was the least of it, now. I looked like I'd been through a war.

"Did you find Rucker?" I asked.

"Yes."

"I'm sorry."

"It's not your fault."

"You know, that's practically the last thing he said. 'Not your fault.' And I just sat there crying all over him." I sniffed, but I was all cried out.

The door opened again. A man in fatigues I didn't know leaned out. "Sir? Control room is secured. We've got a comm line to Lang Analytics set up. Almonte's called the Coast Guard; they're sending a chopper, too."

Torres answered, "I'll be there in a minute."

"Mission accomplished," I murmured.

"Yeah. Thanks to you."

I waved him off, shook my head. "Not really."

"You didn't ask about Brand."

"Is he going to be okay?"

"Medics have stabilized him. He's being airlifted out. We'll know more later."

"I still kind of want to punch him."

"Not worth hurting your hand over."

"Did anyone else get hurt?"

"Some scrapes and bruised egos. Everyone else will walk out of here."

"Did you know about Almonte being undercover?"

"No, I didn't."

I offered the bottle again. "You really look like you could use some of this."

He accepted and tipped the bottle to his lips. Winced at the taste and handed the bottle back. "Too sweet."

"Well, I like it." Drank more. I could keep drinking; there was a second bottle in the fridge.

"Addie. Are you going to be okay?"

"I'm sending my therapy bills for the next ten years to Harris Lang," I said, and he chuckled. "What's going to happen?"

He shrugged. "Get the rest of the island secured. Pick up the rest of the staff at the various settlements, take a head count. Let Lang's people sort out who's who. I guess Almonte will be the one filing criminal charges."

"Yes, sure. But what's going to happen to all this?" I gestured with the bottle, out and around to everything. "I know it's been an awful week and too many people died. But this . . . it really is wonderful. I know you don't understand, but—"

"You threw the Ring into the volcano and the world ended anyway?"

Maybe he did understand. "That's just it, in *Lord of the Rings*, they saved the world from Sauron—but it was a new world. It was the end of the age, the Elves left Middle-earth forever, and nothing was ever the same. They saved a new world but destroyed the old. I suppose it was inevitable that someone was going to fuck it all up to begin with." I sniffed, started to wipe my nose on my sleeve, and gave up, sighing despondently. "I'm not sure any of them really understand—it's not the stuff. It's not the magic, the unicorns, the rings. All that's just *things*. Fantasy is about what you *can't* patent. Honor and heroism and . . . and . . . hope."

"Come on, Professor. Let's get washed up." He stood, offered his hand, and I let him pull me to my feet. I wobbled. He kept hold of me, and I leaned into him. He never let go.

"I think I'm a little drunk," I said.

"That's all right, you deserve it. I won't tell anyone."

"Sure you don't want to join me?" I lifted the bottle.

After a moment, and with a wry smile, he took the bottle and drank.

29

Fellowship

A nd if you'll just sign right there, Professor Cox, Captain
Torres. And you, Dr. Wendell." Special Agent Leah
Almonte was wearing a precise charcoal-gray suit
and looking scarily polished. She showed us the lines on the
documents in front of us. Torres still glared at her like she
had personally betrayed him. Which she sort of had. When the
Coast Guard wanted someone on the island to investigate the
deaths of the cutter crew, well . . . She was right there. She
hadn't told him because she couldn't risk blowing her cover—
someone on the island might hurt a federal investigator when
they wouldn't hurt someone working for Lang. They were more
scared of the billionaire than they were of the government.

We all signed.

My right hand was healed enough that I could hold the pen.
Took me a little longer than usual, and the signature was slop-
pier than I liked, but I did it. True to her word, Almonte got me
in to see a specialist as soon as we returned to the mainland.
After a thorough exam, including X-rays, the doctor declared

my hand was in much better shape than it should have been. "It's like magic," she declared, then looked confused when I laughed. She gave me a round of antibiotics, a tetanus booster, and a strong suggestion to get some additional PT. I would always have a scar, a vertical, puckered line between the bones of my ring and middle fingers. I heard guys dig scars.

Almonte collected the papers. And the pen, alas. It was a nice pen—I'd planned on stealing it.

The three of us sat at one end of a conference table in a nondescript room done up in gray, with soul-sucking fluorescent lights, in a federal office building in downtown Seattle. The chairs might have been padded once, but were now compressed beyond reason. The table was plastic laminate. No windows. A vent in the ceiling let in a thin hiss of air.

Expressionless, Almonte returned to the other end of the table, joining her two companions, a pair of men in perfect government suits. She added the documents to a stack of manila folders in front of her.

A week had passed since our adventures on Insula Mirabilis, and this was supposed to be our final debriefing. I had asked to have a lawyer present and had been politely and firmly assured I wouldn't need one. So I had to make do with Torres and Wendell. The captain glared at the Feds sitting across from us like he could slit their throats without touching them. He was back in the suit jacket and T-shirt, like when we first met. Wendell had on a suit, no tie. I wore a skirt and blazer, the kind of thing I wore to my dissertation defense back in the day. The clothes felt strange. As much a costume on me as the fatigues and the silk Elf gown.

I thought I might at least get a paper or a book deal out of the experience, analyzing what happens when a bunch of tech geeks inadvertently re-create a catalog of fantasy tropes during their unscripted high-tech LARP. But Lang Analytics' lawyers locked us down under a raft of NDAs faster than I could break a pencil.

And then the FCC and FTC and the Coast Guard and Pentagon and a couple of other government agencies besides got involved, and *everything* got locked down. Almonte's friends here were NSA.

At first, we weren't sure what sort of criminal charges would result from everything that happened on the island. At the very least, a whole chunk of the staff might be charged with theft. Or Lang might want to sweep everything under the rug to avoid publicity. But the Coast Guard wanted the deaths of its crew answered for. And there was Rucker.

I learned that his first name was Andrew. He had a younger sister and his parents lived in Eugene, Oregon. I got permission to write them a letter, as long as I didn't tell any details about what had happened. I was able to tell them that he had saved my life, and I hoped that knowing that would give them some comfort.

For what happened to the Coast Guard crew, Dom agreed to a deal in which he would plead guilty to charges of negligent homicide. Part of the deal was no one else on his staff would face murder charges. He threw himself under the bus to spare the rest of his team. It would have been heroic — except that none of it should have happened in the first place. He was still in the hospital, recovering from extensive burns. I hadn't seen him since I left him behind in Tor Camylot. I wasn't sure I wanted to.

Then suddenly Harris Lang was also under investigation and reportedly in the process of having a nervous breakdown. Another charge of negligent homicide against him was potentially on the table as well, Almonte revealed. His software had triggered the traps at Tor Camylot; that was what had killed Rucker, so he might be on the hook for it.

But Lang had vanished into a private medical facility, and everyone we were dealing with now were underlings. Somehow, I'd gotten paid. We all did, but it was on condition of not talking to anyone about what had happened and never contacting Lang. The treasure felt cursed.

"You understand," said one of the other men, the nondescript NSA heavy. "This absolves you of any further implication in the case. You are on record as independent contractors, you fulfilled your contract requirements as described by Lang Analytics, and were properly compensated—"

Torres started to say something, but the man held up a hand. "Generous benefits have been distributed to the survivors of the fatality on your team. You waive your right to any further involvement, and in return you will not be called upon to testify in any resulting litigation or criminal proceeding. That's clear?"

"Yes, it's all been explained," Torres said.

The man smiled a dead smile. "Then you understand. Good."

"What's happening to Mirabilis?" I asked, figuring this might be my last chance to do so. "All that work, all that technology—"

"It's being confiscated," Torres said. "For the sake of national security, I imagine."

The dead smile widened a millimeter. "The evidence in this case is being thoroughly investigated."

"By whom?" I asked. "How?"

He looked hard at me. "Thoroughly. Investigated."

"Top. Men," I murmured.

"I'm guessing we don't really have a choice in all this," the captain said, and seemed amused. Like this wasn't his first rodeo.

"That would be a good assessment, Captain Torres. This must be why you're in charge."

Almonte walked us out of the office herself, all the way to the front doors. "For what it's worth, I couldn't have done the job without you."

Torres said, "I'd have rather worked for the Coast Guard than Harris Lang."

"But you wouldn't have gotten Lang's paycheck from the Coast Guard. Be grateful, sir."

"I'm never hiring you for a gig again."

She looked away, smiled. "Yeah, I know. Professor Cox, it really was nice working with you."

"Yeah. Likewise." I actually meant it, but it ended up sounding sarcastic.

She gently booted us out of the building and turned to walk back through the lobby, heels clicking.

"Man, she's good," Wendell muttered.

Out on the sidewalk, we were all a little dazed but at least not under guard. I blinked up at the sky, the sun reflecting off the skyscrapers around me. Wrinkled my nose at the smell of car exhaust. I'd only been on Mirabilis for a few days, but I still wasn't quite used to being back in the noise and glare of modernity.

Torres sighed. Looked at me. "How're you doing?"

"You keep asking me that."

"Well?"

"Therapy is kind of tough when you're under a dozen layers of NDA. Lang Analytics offered its own in-house counselors. But. Well."

"Yeah."

"Is that it?" Wendell asked. "We just go home now?"

"Everybody wants a sequel, hmm?" I said. Maybe this was

why. No one could imagine the characters *just going home. The Iliad* had *so many* sequels.

"No. Absolutely not," Torres said. "This is a one-off."

Wendell frowned. "I'm a little sad I didn't get to see River-haven."

"You know what we do?" I looked around. No taverns in sight, but there was a Starbucks on the next block. "We go to the Green Mermaid. Can I buy you guys a cup of coffee? I've got Harris Lang's money burning a hole in my pocket."

"I thought you'd be happy to get away from us," Torres said.

"I'm going to need someone to talk to, and you guys are it. Sorry." I shrugged. I wasn't really sorry.

"Coffee it is," Torres said.

And we set off.

"So," Wendell started, hands stuck in his pocket, a fake-innocent look in his eyes. "Is this a bad time to mention I might have forgotten to take some of that Mirabilis tech out of my pocket before we left?" He lifted his hand, opened his fist. And there was a ring. A simple gold band.

"I did not just see that," Torres said. Grinning, Wendell slipped it back in his pocket. "Shit, Wendell, what the hell?"

I wasn't surprised. This was how the stories always go.

Acknowledgments

The very first edition of Dungeons and Dragons by Gary Gygax and Dave Arneson was published in January 1974, which makes it exactly one year younger than I am. The way I see it, I had the great good fortune to grow up in an Age of Wonders, part of the first generation to live in a world with fantasy gaming, one of the first kids to get to play with *Star Wars* action figures, to experience the joy of 8-bit dragons on the Atari 2600 and then lose our freaking minds over the leap in technology to the 16-bit Nintendo. I watched Bakshi's *Lord of the Rings* before Jackson's, I was near the same age as Sarah when *Labyrinth* first came out, and if David Bowie's Jareth and Tim Curry's Darkness ever teamed up . . . well. Formative doesn't begin to cover what was going on here. There is a generation that was the first to read Tolkien, and I am the grateful beneficiary of all the magnificent fantasy they produced in their turn.

All of this is to say that any thanks I can express will be inadequate. All the stories I've absorbed, all the games I've played and gamers I've known, every musician at every Ren Faire I've ever tipped, every piece of fantasy art I've admired, all the creators who've inspired me—it's all here. It's not about any one thing, it doesn't draw on any one source. It's about the community and the culture that has grown up around these worlds.

I've been working on this story in one form or another for a long time, and it feels like reality has just about caught up to the premise—that a super-immersive technology-driven fantasy resort would be marketable. It's not just about the sufficiently advanced technology that appears to make magic possible. It's about a culture hungry for worlds and stories filled with magic. That embraces a sense of wonder instead of being suspicious of it.

The world is a much friendlier place for geeks and gamers than it was when I was in high school and the only way to get geeky T-shirts and crew badges and obscure movie posters and the like was at convention dealer rooms in hotel basements and mail order. (I about fell over the first time I saw Target selling *Star Wars* T-shirts.) From big pop culture conventions to ultra-immersive theme parks, this has all become mainstream. I've been privileged to live through that evolution. Even as it all becomes so much more commercial, the fans and readers and gamers and cosplayers and all the rest are still the beating heart. To the community that makes all this possible: thank you for existing.

As I said, any individual thanks I can express will be inadequate because so much has influenced this story. But I want to be sure to mention the particular gaming communities who've welcomed me over the years: the Science Fiction Society at the University of York (aka Freaksoc) when I was there in 1993–94, the Science Fiction Club at Occidental College in 1994–95, and the Boulder AD&D campaign in which my compatriots graciously tolerated Meg the Bard taking over the world (always watch for the things that fly . . .). Thank you to every GM

who ever put up with my aggressively noncombatant characters.

On the practical side of things, a big thank-you to those who
helped release *Questland* into the wild: my agent, Seth Fish-
man, for all his support and the Come to Crom talks; my edi-
tor, John Joseph Adams, who had his work cut out for him this
go-round (no, I haven't played fifth edition, I'm sorry!!!), and
the team at HMH; my Monday-night dinner party, Max and Yaz
and Anne and Wendy. And thank you to my family: Mom and
Dad and Rob and Deb, and to my niece Emery for dancing to
"Magic Dance" with me.